BROKEN MELODY

NIKKI HAASE

Dedicated to Casey Clayton
I miss you more than words can say.
Until we meet again, Puss.
With love,
Boots

PROLOGUE

The house is quiet and dark. Alone once again, the only real sounds are my staggered breaths. Cautious and slow as they might be, they are still audible. My own shadow makes me paranoid, as if it is cast from someone else entirely.

No one is home except for me, my parents' pride and joy, the straight-A student who is guaranteed a promising future from her teachers. Thankfully school has finally ended. I have my diploma in hand and no longer need to worry about keeping up with my classes.

The flames lick greedily around the wick as I watch the wax melt slowly away. No one will barge through the front doors of this humble abode to disrupt anything. It's almost like a self-induced solitary confinement. Only better. On the table lies a metaphorical mountain of all sorts of drugs. They sparkle in the candlelight, taunting and teasing.

I can't just let them sit there, now can I? I can't let them go to waste.

Any sensible person would disagree with me. Any sensible person would just get rid of any evidence of drug possession to avoid a possible run-in with law enforcement.

Well, I'm not a very sensible person, and I tend to ignore the voice in my head that is a bit more reasonable. I know what I am doing will destroy a part of me and shatter everything—everyone—in my life. I have long since realized that this hideous beast that disguises itself as temporary bliss will slowly devour me, but I hardly care. All losers and no winners here, but I still have hope that I can kill the monster inside me.

My body begins to ache. The need to inhale what is in front of me grows stronger alongside my paranoia. I don't bother turning my stereo on to drown out the sounds of my body doing what bodies do: breathe, pump blood, and tremble with anxiety. My mind shuts down, and the instinct from the demon in me takes over the bleak common sense that I had once possessed. With shaky hands, I slowly cut a few lines of cocaine and lean over the table. It burns my nostrils with a familiar pain that I lust for and after just a few seconds, it slams into me. It works through my nasal cavity and hits my brain in a wave of euphoria and concrete. My head shoots forward and I sniffle before making three more lines and repeating the process until I nearly forget who I am. The drip from the drugs makes my throat and tongue tingle with numbness. I bag up just enough for a handful of lines later and shove it into my pocket.

I am in complete bliss.

Standing up straight, I clean everything in a frenzy, making sure I get every nook and cranny. Even the tiny specks of dirt in the cracks of the table don't get past me—I take a credit card from my pocket and carefully pick them out. Once that is done, I head into the small, dirty bathroom and fix my makeup. There is no need to do my hair, as I shaved it off a few nights ago when my impulse control had left me. I'd been sober that night, but I hadn't felt like I was.

I hide the drugs in a loose floorboard of the house before heading outside.

How is everyone so oblivious to what is going on?

Maybe they're too worried to speak up and do something about it. Perhaps they know that if they confront me about my addiction, I'll just use more to forget the conversation ever occurred.

It's okay though. I am far past help. I *am* the monster I'm trying to kill.

CHAPTER ONE

Hands practically swinging at my sides, skipping down the street with my head in the clouds, I make my way through town. I'm supposed to wait for someone in order to re-up my supplies—I've made an arrangement with a guy. Not that I need to—I have enough to last me a lifetime. A lifetime might end tomorrow though, and what if I suddenly run out?

I can't have that. I need to prepare.

Taking a small piece of cardboard from behind a dumpster, I carry it until I find Skylar waiting for me. He leans against the wall of a brick building with a cigarette dangling from his lips. His blond hair hides a bruise, making his soft blue eyes appear black. I don't mention it and sit on the sidewalk next to him with my cardboard. With a sharpie from my back pocket, I scribble on the piece of scrap, letting my hand weave intricate designs and mazes in order to appease the anxious energy that soars through me. My muscles are trembling, and the baggie in my pocket weighs a ton. Over my shoulder, Skylar watches me draw.

"Are you serious, Alana?" he asks. "It's too early."

I look up at him from the corner of my eye and grin. He's right. The sun has just poked its head from atop the tall buildings around us, and I am flying. "I'm not high."

"Yeah, okay," he scoffs. "What will Casey think?"

I shrug. "She'll get over it."

The moment the words escape my lips, I curse myself. Yeah, the drugs are speaking over me, but I should have more control. Shouldn't I? I practically worship the ground my girlfriend walks upon, yet I keep disappointing her.

I am trash.

I snap back into reality as Skylar is mumbling a sentence, but I am unable to decipher what he's saying.

Ignoring him, I continue to draw while moving my body and head around to the sounds of my own rhythms. We grow silent, and I begin to fall into boredom. The high is quickly wearing off, and I don't want to dip away just yet to take more. People slowly begin to emerge from their apartments and head out into the sunlight, shuffling to their jobs or classes. I throw my marker at an innocent passerby and laugh as he yells at me.

Skylar chuckles with me, but shakes his head as if he's disappointed or ashamed of my actions. I watch as he slowly retreats into his mind again. The man continues to yell at me before he storms off, fuming.

Skylar's mental distractions are the perfect advantage to take a hit without him noticing. I pull my baggie from my pocket, stick a manicured fingernail into the bag, and scoop out a small bump. I quickly tuck the drugs back into my pocket before he comes to. Unable to sit any longer, I jump up and bounce on the balls of my feet. My eyes are continuously searching for my dealer. I need to curb the beast in my head with another much louder monster, and he has the tools I require.

With that silent mental cue, the man emerges from a small group of people. I take a wad of cash from my bra and tuck it into my hand. As if I am floating, I hop across the street. The concrete is still there below me, but it feels like clouds.

"Hey, Sunshine," he greets me. "You look lovely."

"Yeah, yeah." I wave him off. "What's good today, Creature?"

He doesn't use his real name in fear that it'll make it easier for the cops to pick him up or the competition to pick him off. Or he's just as paranoid as I am.

And I refuse to let him use my real name. He has told me he doesn't care what it is.

"Oh, you're going to love this stuff," he exclaims.

He has long messy hair and dark eyes. His face is slender and matches his grimy demeanor. Creature tries to stand tall and tough, but the only thing that keeps him above the game is his excellent stock of drugs and his gun.

I have no illusions—he is excited for the profit he is receiving, not my benefit of getting a good high.

"Cool, cool," I state while rocking back and forth, needing to speed up the process.

I stick my hand out and shake his firmly. He takes the cash I have tucked in my palm and swaps it with the drugs. He smiles wide. It's fake and not really meant for me—it's meant for the money. Creature isn't my friend, or anyone important for that matter. I probably won't give it a second thought if Creature is killed. I will just have to find a new dealer, and there are plenty in this city.

My bra now heavy with the drugs, I head back across the street. Skylar has finally snapped out of his daze and is watching me with his arms crossed over his chest. The blank expression has disappeared from his eyes, but the deep, dark sense of loneliness has returned. Skylar comes from severe abuse.

I should rephrase that.

Skylar still lives with the bastard that beats him and his brothers. They can't seem to escape, and it terrifies me. Well, it does when I'm sober.

Hands on his shoulders, I stare into his eyes. Skylar glares at me as if I am a child that needs to be told I've done wrong. He, however, cannot find the words to reprimand me. What could he brand into me that I haven't already heard?

"Are you okay?" I ask.

"Fine." He pushes my hands off and shakes his head.

The energy from the most recent hit is making me spin in circles around him, laughing in small bursts at the mere thought of our existence and how meaningless it really is. We don't matter. Not really. Our deaths, our lives, all mean nothing to strangers.

And that's okay.

The death of stars means nothing to strangers.

We are stars.

I twirl around Skylar while he watches me, rolling his eyes. I am so engrossed in my own world that I don't see Casey approaching. She grabs me by my belt loops and pulls me in her direction. Her blonde hair cascades down to her shoulders like waves of gold. Her green eyes light up as her cheeks blush with her bright smile. She is my angel. My heart swells when I see her and I can't stop grinning. I point to the mess of drawings I have created on the piece of garbage cardboard.

"It's my brain," I inform her.

She kisses me. "It looks like a map to a mystical land."

Her lips are soft, and she nuzzles into my neck. All I ever

want to do is make her happy. Still, I keep failing at that. There is no way she's satisfied with me. She'll leave the second another woman—one with real potential to build a family—walks into her life. Casey grabs my hand and holds it tight. She interlocks our fingers and gives a sharp jerk of her head toward Skylar, urging him to follow. He does without argument, lighting a cigarette as he falls behind us. She guides us along the streets to an unforeseen destination, but I will take on almost any task to kill time and to calm my drug-induced mania. I keep my eyes glued to Casey in front of me. She is a beautiful person that somehow mistakes me for the one she loves.

CHAPTER TWO

We find ourselves at a park. It has a new pavilion and a small playground made of wood and metal. I don't remember playing on it. Perhaps I did long ago. The memories of my past are fuzzy and mostly out of reach. Nothing tragic happened to me, I've just filled my body and soul with copious amounts of deadly, intoxicating substances that prevent pieces of my past from returning to my memory. We sit down at the picnic table as night falls and blankets us. Citizens with any sense in them are inside their homes, awaiting dinner or dessert. The traffic in the small city is slowly dying down as fewer people venture out. We are alone in the silence. I wrap my arms around Casey, and my staggered breaths begin to calm down as my heart races faster, begging for another hit. She leans her head back into my chest, and I play with her hair, gently untangling the knots with the tips of my fingers.

"Hey, Skylar, did your brothers say when they were going to pick us up?" Casey asks.

So our destination is not unknown, and we were meant

to end up here all along. I should pay more attention to my surroundings and what is being discussed more often.

"Around midnight." Skylar's voice is distant.

I don't bother trying to spark up my own conversation with them. Skylar is lost inside his prison of a mind, and my own brain is too scattered to find anything to discuss. To ease my overactive thoughts, I sing quietly to Casey. It is off-key and nearly a hum, but it somehow coaxes her to sleep. Skylar stands and stares off at the playground. I stop singing and look up at him curiously, eyes drilling into him.

He sighs. "I don't think I'm going to stick around."

Why doesn't he want to stay with us and away from the house he lives in? Or he isn't going home. I don't really want to press the issue.

"Want me to pick up anything for you?" I ask.

"What else can you get?" He runs a hand through his messy hair.

"LSD and E maybe," I say under my breath.

"I'm good." He shrugs and begins to walk away before turning back to face me. "I'll let Xavier know not to meet here. We weren't going to do anything anyway." His hands dig themselves deep into his pockets, and he leaves with his head down.

I watch him closely, wondering where he is going.

About an hour passes where neither Casey nor I move so much as an inch. A dark blue car with heavily tinted windows pulls up into the parking lot. The loud bass that pounds from it stirs Casey awake. A tall man in a business casual suit with greased-back hair steps out of the car and looks around before heading towards us. I push Casey off me, stand up, and position myself in front of her defensively. My chest is pounding. Did I rip someone off? Am I going to die?

"Sunshine and...?" The man's deep voice asks. His skin is so pale it nearly glows in the moonlight. He wears a fedora, which he keeps adjusting with his bony fingers.

"Rain," I add quickly before Casey can speak.

"Ah. Sunshine and Rain then," he repeats. "Follow me."

I grab Casey's hand and have her walk closely behind me. I'm not sure why I follow the guy; I don't even know how he knows me. Maybe an instinctual part of me can smell the drugs on him.

If only my instincts weren't so stupid.

"Creature's in the car," he tells us as we walk quickly to the vehicle.

I feel Casey grip my hand a little tighter like a warning or silent cry of fear. It doesn't keep me from following the stranger like a child after its father. He holds the door open for us, and we slide into the back—billows of smoke exit before we step in. Creature is in the driver's seat, and the mystery man rides shotgun.

"Hey, Sunshine!" Creature voices enthusiastically.

"Creature." His fake friendship annoys me.

"And your friend?" He guns the engine.

"Rain." I keep my voice bland and my emotions flat.

Silence awkwardly falls over us. The tan leather seats are hot, sticky, and torn up. Me and Casey's fingers are intertwined and I see Creature and the mystery guy watching us carefully through the rearview mirror as if we are insects under a human's magnifying glass. The nameless man turns the knob on the radio and the bass of hip-hop music fills the dark silence. We don't speak to one another for the drive. I don't even know why I got into the car, and I viciously curse myself for not just telling Casey to go home or find Xavier and the others and hang out with them awhile.

We stop by a white, run-down house in the middle of

nowhere. The grass in the yard is surrounded by a short chain link fence and burnt brown from the sun. A broken gate stays open as an invitation for malignant spirits and drug addicts. Most of the windows are boarded up, and the paint and siding are peeling. Unsafe stairs to get onto the wrap-around porch has long since rotted away. Creature cuts the engine once he parks on the curb.

"What are we doing here?" I question.

"Dropping off Rabbit and picking up Tiger."

I raise an eyebrow. "What?"

Tiger is a businessman in the drug world. One who knows a dead addict doesn't make him any money. He's taken plenty of us to the ER or the rehab center, depending on what the situation calls for. He'll still sell you a bag the day you get out though.

Creature points at the nameless man with milky skin. "That's Rabbit."

He looks up at us when his name is spoken and adjusts his hat again with shaking fingers. His eyes dart away from us.

"Does he live here?" Casey asks, eyes fixated on Rabbit.

"Nah, he just does ice here. The house is empty, so it's safe for tweakers. Tiger is just getting the stuff ready for him and two other guys and then we'll leave," Creature rambles on.

Rabbit paces back and forth beside the car, chewing at his fingertips. He watches the house with wide, nervous eyes. Creature leans against the fence, one leg bent back to prop himself up. He smokes a cigarette and looks at the cracks in the concrete, waiting patiently. I keep my hand wrapped in Casey's as we sit on the trunk of the car. Finally, someone walks out of the house and satisfies our anticipation. His stride is confident, head held high and shoulders rolled back. He goes over to Rabbit and ignores the rest of us to hand him a small bag of crystalline pebbles, taking the wad of cash from his palm. Rabbit smiles wide, showing a few missing teeth, and darts for the house.

The moment the sketchy pale man disappears behind the slammed door, Creature throws his cigarette onto the ground and jumps back into the car. The rest of us pile in silently, and we drive off.

"Hey, Sunshine!" Tiger calls out with excitement.

"Hey!" I pound his extended fist.

He reaches back and rubs my head. "It looks good, kid."

"I know." I smirk, and Casey kisses my blushing cheeks.

Tiger tends to wear black pants and button-up shirts. His hair is cut short, and his face is clean shaven. His green eyes are bright, and his very essence pulls everyone he meets in closer to him. Tiger looks like a clean-cut businessman set out to change the corporate world. It's the perfect deadly concoction a drug dealer needs to be successful. No one will ever suspect a man so well dressed to be involved in something so low.

"This lovely lady must be Rain?" His tone raises in question.

"Yes." I let go of her and she rests her head on the cool window.

I don't know why, but I trust Tiger.

I shouldn't trust anyone—most certainly not my drug dealers.

"Creature said you're looking to pick up?"

I shoot Creature a disapproving glance, but don't address him. He'll probably get a percentage if I do buy anything.

"Yeah, sure."

I am always ready to pick up more if it's in front of me. He gives me about five ecstasy pills and four tabs of acid.

How convenient.

I'll be set for a few days, or the week if I play my cards right—especially with the stash of cocaine I have hidden in the floorboards and the loot in my bra. I wish I paid attention to how much money I had shoved into his palm. My own hands shake nervously as the monster inside eagerly makes the blind trade. It doesn't care—it just wants to be fed.

We talk aimlessly about nothing until Casey and I are dropped off a few blocks from my house. Casey doesn't say a word, and she barely looks my way. I don't blame her. She has no reason to give me any sort of attention right now. She has been forced to meet the creepiest person I know: Rabbit. My mind races at my carelessness as we walk.

Could she become a target if I fuck up?

CHAPTER THREE

I walk Casey home to make sure nothing happens to her due to my stupidity. Perhaps I am being a bit too paranoid, but I figure you can never be too safe. She lives with her mom in a ranch home. Their driveway is short and fat and leads up to a one-car garage. The lawn is trimmed nicely, and two cone-shaped bushes frame the front door.

"I love you, Alana." She kisses my fingers before leaving.

With my hands in my pockets, I walk to my house as the guilt tears at me. I have to shove this black cloud of an emotion deep into a dark corner of my mind. I don't want to feel this. I don't want to feel *anything* except the escape of being high.

When I get home to my small Cape Cod house made of bricks, I hide my newly purchased drugs in a flowerpot on the front porch before stepping inside. The television sounds distant in the living room as I hear my parents laugh at something on the screen. I waltz past them silently into the kitchen, plug mp3 speakers into the wall, and turn the volume up just loud enough to drown out the TV. Picking up a knife, I chop vegetables on the butcher's block that rests on the counter, focused on making the perfect salad. I'm not left in my comfort zone for long though; my dad has broken himself away from the television and enters the kitchen.

"You're home late." It isn't really an observation. It is a demand for an answer.

"Yeah." I set the knife down on the counter. "Sorry about that. I took Casey out on a date and it ran later than expected."

"Oh. Just don't let it happen again, okay?"

"Not a problem." I smile politely.

Did he really just buy that?

When he turns his back and walks out, a dark wave of inexplicable angry emotions makes my blood boil. I stab the blade into the cutting board, lodging it tightly into the wood.

"Crap," I mutter under my breath as I pry the knife out with a forceful tug.

I do my best to redirect my focus back to the salad and ignore the screaming within me. My head swells, and my eyes begin to fill with saltwater. I finally give up on the salad and slouch onto the floor with my back against one of the green cabinets. Emptiness invades my brain as guilt for letting my parents down hits me like punches to the stomach.

They are good people. Yeah, they vacation a lot, leaving me behind to watch the house. And my mom will go off on tangents about her ex-husband being an evil bastard, but I can't tell which of these stories are lies or facts. I hardly notice it anymore. Being high all the time helps with that.

They can't see the monster. They are completely blind to it. I force myself to tame the beast when they're present and only let them see the shining, excellent young woman with a 4.0 GPA.

I can't let them know I am falling apart despite the love they give me.

I want to dissociate myself from the broken Alana and become Sunshine, a creature of the night who doesn't know who they are. I will become another statistic, lying on the floor and choking on my own vomit.

I am okay with that—an end to the misery.

The monster is okay with that.

CHAPTER FOUR

It must be about four in the morning when the cravings slam into my body, jolting me into an unwanted, awakened stupor. The want—the *need*—is far stronger than any other emotion I possess. I stumble around the house in a daze. I can only do this when I am alone, when it's silent and the sun is barely poking its head above the horizon.

Am I too paranoid?

I shut the curtains, take a few candles, and scatter them around the living room. One by one, I light them with a box of matches, and I admire the eerie shadows they cast against the walls. I push the blue sofa back about a foot from the shoddy wooden coffee table I made in the eighth grade for a required shop course. The hardwood floors echo as I drop to my knees and pry the loose floorboard back. Pulling two small bags from the hiding spot, I set the board back into place. Kneeling at the table, I dump the contents from their pouches.

I make two skinny joints with some sticky buds, put them aside, and then begin to cut lines of cocaine. My heart jumps and my stomach lurches when the bells above the door sing to indicate that someone has entered the house.

Why don't my parents lock the stupid door?

I stare at the drugs as my mind races into a million different directions.

I can't hide them fast enough without being obvious.

Where would I put them anyway?

I can just snort the cocaine right away; the charges on weed must be less.

No, weed is a schedule one. Cocaine is a schedule two.

Does that mean it's safer?

I continue to argue with myself, staring at the drugs but not moving.

"You okay, Alana?" Skylar sits down on the couch.

My heart finds its proper spot, but the racing takes longer to calm. My attention back on what I'm doing, I roll up a dollar bill and snort the lines. The drugs burn their way through my nasal cavities, numbing the back of my throat. I shudder and feel a smile creep its way across my cheeks.

"I made a joint for you." I take one of the little rolled beauties and hand it to him.

I watch Skylar get up from the couch and light it on a dying candle flame. He takes a sharp inhale and exhales a cloud of smoke and a chorus of coughs. I head to the kitchen to grab some booze. My father keeps a bottle of whiskey and dark rum in the top cabinet, and there is soda in the fridge. I mix the three ingredients in an empty water bottle and grab two shot glasses before heading back to my stoned friend.

"What's in this?" he asks, examining it as if close inspection will give him the answer.

"Uh, weed?" I pour the shots as I talk. "Smoke it. Good, isn't it?"

"Yeah, great."

I plop down next to him and tilt my head back to slam down the shot; a 'woo' noise escapes me as the disgusting taste lingers on my tongue. I hand the second one to Skylar, and he swallows the shot without a reaction. He inhales the rest of his small joint in two huge puffs and uses the dying butt to light the second one. After exhaling a cloud, he hands it to me. I take a small puff, but don't fill my lungs. I don't want it to mess with my cocaine high. Mornings aren't for things that make you hungry or sleepy. He takes a large drag and coughs again. Skylar pours two more shots, takes both, and then refills one of them and gives it to me. I want to tell him to slow down, but I can't. It would be too hypocritical of me to call him out on starting his day high and buzzed.

My body vibrates with energy and I have bees living in my bones. I shoot up from the couch and run around the house, gathering the candles and cleaning up the evidence of my twisted rituals. With the curtains thrown back by a dramatic sweep of my arm, bright, yellow sunlight illuminates the house with her devouring, eager rays. I push the couch back to its original spot while Skylar lies on top. Cocaine gives me muscles of steel apparently, and I can take on the world with this drug.

I am Super Woman.

I yank Skylar to his feet and roll my eyes when he groans.

"What are we doing today?" I ask, jumping on my toes.

"I don't know," he answers dully. "Get me a bag of Chex Mix?"

I slide across the floor into the kitchen and tear the

cabinet doors open, but I can't find any sign of snacks. I look around the room for something that's close, and all I can focus on are the bananas on the counter. I pull one from the bunch and shrug; I can't be bothered to look any harder. My mind has already decided to abandon this task. It needs a new one. I run back into the room and throw him the banana.

"This isn't at all what I asked for." He looks at the fruit and then back at me. "At all. This isn't even close, Alana."

I don't care. I need to get out this house with its small space and enclosing four walls. "Now what?"

"I don't know. Let's start a riot and burn something down," he says casually.

"What?" I feel my face beam with enthusiasm. "Really?"

"No." He shakes his head and laughs. "I'm not letting you do that again."

I had taken *way* too much one night and tried to convince a group of people to burn down a new corporate office building. The taxes had skyrocketed when it went up in our city. That could have just been coincidence, but I blamed it on the building—and I made others think the same thing. It wasn't until I was arrested that I shut up about it. Skylar had waved to me, nearly cackling, when I was put into the back of the police car.

I felt like a goddess that day—a deity that is easily hand-cuffed by a man in a blue uniform.

Skylar slides his phone from his pocket. "Xavier texted me." He looks up from the screen. "He wants to go out with everyone today. You in?"

"Not doing anything else," I agree. "Do I need to text Casey?"

"He already did," Skylar says.

I take off for the bathroom and look at my reflection in

the mirror. The girl staring back has a small nose, green eyes with the lights flickering out, a slightly angled chin, and cheekbones that are vaguely sunken in. With black liner, I sculpt my eyes with wings in an attempt to look like a person that isn't strung out—although nothing can hide my telltale pupils. I cake on a coat of red-tinted matte lipstick and stick in a pair of earrings. Skylar is waiting patiently for me with my heeled boots dangling from his fingers. I take them and give him a rushed thank you as I shove them onto my feet.

"Are we doing something fun tonight?" I ask as we leave the house. "You've been dead lately, so you could use it." I want my best friend to stop looking like he's viewing the world through a shard of dirty glass.

We can't do that in public at a restaurant full of people.

"Yeah." His head hangs. "Sorry."

"Oh, shut up, Sky," I growl. "Will your house be empty?"

"Yup." His lips curl and I watch his face brighten just a little. "They'll actually be gone for the week."

"Let's hotbox your house!" I jump in front of him, eyes darting around.

"No," he states firmly and walks around me. "We're not exposing Michelle to that."

Michelle is his younger sister. He—along with his two older brothers—are extremely protective of her. She looks a lot like Skylar with blonde hair and blue eyes. I can't remember how old she is though; maybe three.

"Can I at least crash at your place?" I beg. "I wanna get wrecked. My parents will be back tonight."

"You always wanna be wrecked, Alana."

I don't want to be wrecked all the time.

I want to be *numb* all the time.

There are too many times that intense waves of energy

tend to make my skin crawl, buzzing under the surface like a swarm of bees, before throwing me under a black wave of emptiness. I will do anything to hide myself from that feeling—of toxic nothingness.

"Fair enough." I clasp my hands together and follow him with small steps. "Puh-lease? Just one night."

"Ugh," he groans. "Fine, but only if your parents will watch Michelle for a bit."

"Deal." I lock my arm with his and skip with him down the street, singing Disney songs at the top of our lungs.

We keep this up until we find ourselves at the restaurant where Xavier told Skylar to meet him. He slumps down against the building and waits. My eyes scan with caution and I pull a small bag containing one bump from my bra. I roll up the dollar bill and stick it into the powder, inhaling the contents. With the dollar back in my bra, I throw the baggie under my shoe. My eyes brighten with the drugs just as Skylar's eyes are extinguished of their light. He looks far too gone for even the devil to grab hold of him.

I'm not sure if I'm envious or scared.

While we wait, I text my mom to ask if she won't mind watching Michelle for the night—I never need to explain myself to them. She quickly responds that she's more than happy to watch the ball of energy and joy.

Casey is the first to arrive. She slithers her way between Skylar and me and interlocks our hands. She kisses Skylar's cheek. He nods politely and keeps silent.

"Party at my house tonight," he finally says.

"Yeah? Can you give me weed?" she asks.

"I can," I interject, pulling a joint from my boot.

"Perfect."

Two middle-aged couples are watching us. Our fingers are interwoven and our noses are touching when I slip the joint into her bra. They stare at us in shock, shaking their heads.

"The fuck you looking at?" I shout.

They jump, and Casey squeezes my hand. Fury enters my blood. I want to curse more. I need to release the energy that surges through me. Skylar pulls himself away from the wall and holds the door open for the startled couples, who are smiling nervously as they shake their heads and curse me under their breath.

"Oh, look. Skylar's being nice," I taunt, unsure why it bothers me. All I know is I can feel it in my veins.

"Good." Xavier's deep voice makes my muscles jump from my bones as he seems to appear from nowhere. Michelle is seated on his shoulders, her long blonde hair pulled into a ponytail and her nails painted pink.

He chuckles at my reaction and fist-bumps his youngest brother once he returns. Xavier has a shaved head and dark stubble around his jawline. He's in relaxed jeans and a faded graphic tee. His body is large from years of weight training, and his aura is like a protective light that surrounds those he cares about. He just wants us to be safe and happy. He wants us to make smart decisions and keep focused on goals that will make us rise to the top.

The problem is, I completely ignore every effort he displays to save me from my own sins.

"Hey Michelle, wanna have a sleepover at my house with my parents?" I ask, smiling.

"Yes!" Her rosy red cheeks light up, and she leans forward, grasping Xavier's face, pursing his lips together. "Can I? Please?"

"Of course, monster."

The soft roar of an engine—that is in dire need of some work—pulls up to the curb next to us. The passenger door of the white car opens, and three more of our group step out. Casey greets the girls with hugs and walks them closer to us. Sarah, with long brunette hair and curves that can slay an army stands next to Xavier, arm tucked into the crook of his. She pulls her hair around so it rests on one shoulder, and her shirt is made of silk and drapes below the curves of her hips. Kellie—a petite young woman with jet black hair and chestnut-colored eyes behind large-framed glasses and freckles on her nose—rests her head on Skylar's shoulder. Lily, her hair dyed a bright blue, stands by herself. She's wearing heeled boots and skinny jeans. She's petite like Kellie, but will punch your lights out if you so much as look at Kellie or Sarah in a bad way. Part of me had fallen in love with Lily before I met Casey. That was a lifetime ago.

The white car drives off to park, and the last of the brothers walk up. Dante, a relatively scrawny man who's just beginning to fill in with some muscle, runs a hand through his messy black hair and nods to Skylar and myself. He's almost as tall as Xavier, but can't quite reach his brother's mass.

"Ladies." He gives us a half-cocked grin. Smoke falls from the rolled-up tobacco.

Skylar makes a face and gives him a middle finger greeting. Xavier steps next to Dante and stares him down.

"Put it out," he demands.

"Why?" Dante laughs and blows smoke into his older brother's face.

Xavier glares at him and rips the cigarette from Dante's lips. He stomps it out under his boot while maintaining eye contact with his brother. "Can you not act like an asshole for just a few hours?" Xavier nearly pleads. "All of you. Behave. Understood?" He looks around at each of us.

"I'm never a bad influence," Dante retorts with a grin.

"I don't wanna be good!" Michelle crosses her arms at her chest before fist-bumping Dante.

Dante takes her from Xavier and hoists her onto his own shoulders. She beams and wraps both arms around his head.

I place a delicate hand to my chest and gasp. "I am nothing but a delight, Xavier. I'm shocked you'd think I'd ever cause a scene." I smirk, and he rolls his eyes.

I wrap my arms around Casey and hang onto her as we walk into the building. It's one of those big chain restaurants that look the same no matter which one you walk into. Tourists and passersby flock to them because despite bragging about wanting to go on adventures, they need something that reminds them of their own stupid towns. There are random items plastered along the wall like a museum set up by a drunk toddler: a few old newspaper articles, a boat oar, scattered masquerade masks, an axe, and a broken guitar are just a few of the things I notice. The floors are tiled, and the tables are made of thick wood with laminated slab tops.

Sarah and Xavier take the lead and let the hostess know how many people are in our group. She ushers us to our table in the back of the restaurant. Xavier pulls Sarah's chair out for her before sitting down himself. Skylar does the same for Kellie, and the smile that splits across her face could melt worlds. Skylar's eyes light up for a moment, and he wraps his hand in hers. Dante places his sister in a booster seat before pulling Lily's seat out, and then sits down. I pull Casey's chair out and motion for her to sit down with a wave of my hand.

"Only the finest of thrones for a queen." I push her in.

Her cheeks grow red, and she giggles when I sit down beside her. A waitress with suspenders weighed down with cheap and disgustingly optimistic buttons comes to our table. Her fake smile is wide and doesn't fade as she talks.

Xavier hands his fake ID over and orders a beer. Skylar and Dante both take soda. Kellie, Lily, and Casey ask for iced tea. I only want water with lemon, and Michelle gets apple juice. The waitress returns quickly with a tray of our drinks. The place is packed, and the chattering noise sounds like a swarm of locusts.

How is she so fast?

Are we her only table?

"Are you ready to order yet, or would like more time?" She keeps smiling.

Is she human?

No one is that happy.

She deserves all the tips just for pretending to be that damn pleasant.

"Yeah, we're ready." Dante speaks first. "I'll take the salmon steak and a side salad."

"Me too!" Michelle chimes.

"No. You don't like fish." Xavier looks at her sternly and she glances at Dante, pouting.

"How about you get chicken nuggets and we'll split it. Deal?" Dante holds his fist out.

"Deal." She bumps it and sticks her tongue out at Xavier.

One by one, we order our food. I just take the house salad. I can't eat while hyped up on cocaine. My body doesn't need food. It needs stimulants.

We eat in silence, our silverware greedily scraping against the plates. I mindlessly push the food around, forcing myself to eat it leaf by leaf. The only time anyone speaks is when Xavier has to tell Michelle to finish what she has. I watch Dante take two more of her nuggets. She grins at him and slides the salmon he placed on her plate back onto his.

"I don't like fish," she states.

"Good, because I do." Dante gobbles it up dramatically, sure to show his sister the chewed-up food while Xavier pretends to bang his head on the table.

We look up at each other with full and satisfied smiles. Xavier calls the waitress over and asks for the check. When he gets it, I watch his face drop. He shuffles through his wallet and stares back down at the check.

His eyes are wide. "I can't afford this. I need help, guys. I miscalculated."

I look around the room. I have an idea! We *won't* pay.

"Lily, you're small enough to get out the window in the bathroom, right?" I whisper.

"Yes, so are Kellie and Sarah." She smiles and takes Kellie's hand. "We'll pry open the window to the men's room then."

Xavier has his head on the table. I know he doesn't agree with this, but we don't have the money. A few minutes after they leave, Skylar and Dante go to the bathroom. When they head into the restroom, Casey and Xavier step outside as if to smoke cigarettes. I sit at the table with Michelle in silence. No one is paying attention to me. I can just walk out the front door.

"Let's go, monster." I help her off the seat, holding her hand as we make our way to the door.

No one says a word. No one tries to stop me. I meet up with the others a few paces from the restaurant.

"We ate for free." Dante laughs. "Alana, you are the best person I know!" He ruffles my shaved head and kisses the top of it.

CHAPTER FIVE

After we drop off Michelle, I fall behind the group as we walk to the brothers' empty house. I search my body for a pick me up and my heart races when I can't find one. My fingers shake as I nearly tear at my skin, and I want nothing more than to find drugs I've forgotten in a pocket.

Good thing I keep stashes at every house I step into. Whether they know it or not, they have just as many drugs in their place as I do in mine.

I feel no shame, just anticipation and excitement.

When we arrive at the shack of a house, Xavier undoes the bolt locks and lets us inside. The paint is peeling from the porch and the concrete steps are cracked, the corners completely smashed off. Their house smells like cigarettes and booze. The floor is stained, and the walls have lost their white color. Dishes are piled in the sink and the countertop and the television are splintered through the center. There is no food in the fridge, but there is a case of beer, and two bottles of whiskey sit in the freezer. Dante lights up a cigarette when we enter the living room and offers one to Xavier. He takes it and uses Dante's to light his. They sit on the old, worn-in tan couch and exhale together. Xavier props his feet up on the water stained glass coffee table. A few cigars are resting on the top, waiting to be enjoyed.

Or taken apart and enjoyed with something much more heavenly.

"Twenty bucks says Alana has fun things for us to do." Dante looks at me.

"Does anyone even *have* twenty bucks?" I ask as I walk off to find one of my many stashes.

There is a bit of weed under their parent's box spring, two bags of cocaine in their bathroom, a handful of Adderall, and two ecstasy pills in their kitchen. I return with the loot, and everyone has made themselves comfortable in the room that reminds me of Rabbit's meth house. Sarah is lying on top of Xavier as he plays with her hair. Dante is nibbling on Lily's ear, and Kellie is trying to get the attention of Skylar, who has retreated into himself. This house is a warzone, and he is a soldier doing what he has to in order to keep his sanity intact. I throw the weed into Dante's lap, and he awakes from his Lily-induced stupor. He straightens, grabs a cigar from the coffee table, and begins to remove the guts. I watch for a few moments in awe as he rolls the blunt while barely paying attention to his own movements.

"Hey, guys," Dante says, still working on his masterpiece. "What's brown and sticky?"

We look at each other in silence. Lily lifts an eyebrow.

"A stick." Dante chuckles to himself. "What's red and looks like a bucket?"

"A red bucket?" Lily chimes in.

"Good. Now what's blue and looks like a bucket?"

"A blue bucket!" She beams up at him, eyes shining.

"No!" Dante licks the blunt to close it. "A red bucket in disguise!"

"You're such a dork." I laugh, and Dante smiles at himself, pleased with his jokes.

I dump a small amount of coke onto the table and ignore Xavier as he scolds us to clean it up. He is perfectly okay with marijuana because it isn't harmful. However, the things I want are. I make up three lines and take two. Seeing the hunger in Lily's eyes, I give her the dollar and point at the last one.

"You're with friends."

Before Dante can protest, she jumps down and snorts the thick line of white powder. Her body trembles, and she looks at me with a wide grin. I return it happily.

"Two more lines," Dante demands when his handiwork is completed.

I oblige and hand him the straw. He inhales both in one fluid movement, shaking his head when the drugs take hold. It makes me wonder how often he has done this. Is there a stash hidden somewhere in his room? Does he snort lines after a beating to become numb?

With shaking fingers, he lights up the blunt and passes it to Xavier. He takes in a deep inhale to fill his massive lungs, and a plume of thick smoke surrounds us. He doesn't cough as he passes it to Sarah, who politely declines and gives it to Lily. Sarah stands up from the couch and turns the stereo on, letting waves of hip-hop encase us with heavy bass and lyrics we can hardly understand. In our haze of smoke and powder, we don't notice that Skylar and Kellie have left the room. Kellie is storming out when we finally snap out of our drugged stupors.

"I'm done. I'm done," she keeps repeating before slamming the front door behind her.

"Well, damn," Dante breathes out.

Skylar is sitting at the kitchen table just behind us. His

hands are flat on the surface, and he's staring straight ahead as if locked into place. His eyes are wide, and his lips are no more than a thin line. There is fear in every part of him. Xavier, Dante, and I get up and rush to his aid. I grab a bottle from the table he's sitting on, pour out a small shot, and try to offer it to him.

"Alana, move," Xavier commands, and I back off, taking the shot myself.

He sits in front of Skylar and slaps his hands, but he just keeps staring into space. Dante kneels next to Xavier and keeps his eyes on Skylar.

"Come on, buddy, wake up." Dante snaps his fingers in front of his younger brother's face. "Come on. I know what's going on in your head, but they're not here. You don't need to do this." He holds Skylar's face in his hands. "Even if he was here, we would protect you. I could take the hits. We need you back, bro. Come on."

They look at each other and shake their heads, unable to bring their brother back to earth. Casey and Lily have run off after Kellie while we continue trying to pull Skylar back.

I have promised Skylar that I will help him in any way possible when this happens, even if I don't know how.

CHAPTER SIX

I lean over Skylar with my hands on his shoulders, lips lingering a bit too close to his ear. "Skylar! Skylar! Sky!" I shout. "Wake up! Where you at?"

He looks up at me with confused eyes and I pull him to his feet. I hug his limp body tightly and kiss his forehead. "Welcome back."

"I did it again, didn't I?" He glances around at the faces staring at him.

"What happened?" Sarah gives him a hug and holds him out at arm's length.

Xavier pulls her away and softly tells her to give him space. He takes her aside and tries to explain what we know. Skylar has built an impenetrable wall around him that sometimes takes over. We don't know what it is, only that it scares us. They can't afford to see a doctor to get him the help he needs, so we just do our best to keep him with us.

All I know is I need to save him, because if I can save him, then I can save myself. Right? That's how it works?

"Where's Kellie?" Skylar scans the room, frantically searching.

Dante pats his brother's shoulders. "You're better off."

As if on cue, Lily and Casey return without Kellie. Skylar just shrugs, uncaring.

"See?" Dante hands Skylar the smoking blunt. "Better off."

Silence overtakes us, and we just stare at each other. Lily and I are still bouncing on our feet, but the energy of the others doesn't match ours.

"Can we get to the roof?" I look at Xavier, who shrugs. "Good! To the roof!" I raise a fist and lead the way.

"To the roof!" Lily repeats after me with enthusiasm. Dante locks his arm with hers, and they skip together down the hall.

I fall behind a few paces and watch them, wishing they could see themselves as well as I can. I wish Skylar could become more aware of the ghost that he is becoming. I can see the strong bond between Lily and Dante as if they are linked together by iron chains. There is something in Dante that I can't quite pinpoint, but he keeps that smirk on his face—cracking stupid jokes and making his sister as happy as can be—regardless of whatever it is that swims in his head. I see how Sarah looks at Xavier with so much love that he is scared by it. He is careful with her, fearful of repeating his abusive father's behavior. They pretend there is nothing wrong with Skylar. They pretend there is nothing wrong with me.

Do the drugs make me see more, or do they make me blind, forcing me to see only what I want?

Before I make it up to the roof, I pull Skylar back by his arm. "Hey, help me gather your instruments. I wanna bring 'em up."

"Okay," he agrees. "We only have a few things though."

We trudge around the bedrooms and grab what we can

find. A bass guitar is in Dante's room. It's the only clean thing in there. Dante can play anything he holds. It rests carefully on a stand, shining like a star. Two acoustic guitars sit on Skylar's bed, and he grabs them both.

Night falls quickly as the brothers play endlessly on their rooftop. They don't need to speak to one another to stay in sync and let the melody flow around us. Eventually, one by one, we pass out up there. My gaze shoots from person to person, I don't quite take them into my mind. They are wisps of silhouettes, unable to find a place in my psyche. Dante and Lily, Xavier and Sarah; they are such perfect pairs. Like puzzle pieces, they fit together flawlessly. And here I am, desperately trying to be perfect for Casey.

I can't be though. Not with this monster that has made a home in me.

Casey is asleep, curled up with her knees to her chest.

I turn my attention to Skylar as he watches the cars in their early rush hour below us. I sit on the ledge beside him. The silence between us is peaceful and brings serenity. Skylar eventually drifts off to sleep at my feet. He looks like a corpse; he doesn't even flinch.

I stay on the overhang with my feet dangling over, watching people walk by below. I get up when I hear Xavier groan awake. Sarah wakes with him, and they nudge Dante and Lily into consciousness. Dante is the one who shakes Skylar awake. They are gentle with one another and leave Casey asleep for me.

I hop down from the edge of the building and make my way to her. I bend down, lips lingering by her ear, "Wake up, beautiful!" I shout.

"Oh, good morning," she says in a small voice.

"I didn't see you there." I stand up and look at her with a grin.

She just kisses my head and walks back into the house with the others. Dante helps me bring everything back inside so the instruments don't have to sit out for days. My stomach lurches when I realize I took everything I had hidden in their house the night before.

Now I have to face the screaming in my head completely sober.

I can only hope that a magical drug nymph will appear at the doorstep like a fairytale mailman with a bag of free cocaine.

Inside, Xavier and Skylar are both drawing on pieces of scrap paper. Xavier sings a tune under his breath that I can't place. Casey, Lily, and Sarah nibble on food at the kitchen table while I sit with them, pulling apart a piece of bread but not placing it into my mouth. Dante emerges back into the room with his hair still wet from a shower. He's only wearing a pair of black jeans; his head is tucked down as he lights up a cigarette in cupped hands. He must have forgotten that we are still gathered there, because he rarely lets anyone see him without a shirt on. And for good reason too. He has purple bruises around his right bicep and a few more on his forearms. There's a large brown and green one on his ribs and red marks on his chest. Some in the shape of fingers cradle his shoulders, dangerously close to his neck. He looks up at us and exhales smoke.

"What?" he challenges.

"Are you still thinking about getting tattoos?" Casey asks, stumbling over the words as she grasps them from the air, piecing together old conversations.

"Yeah." He looks at his bruises as if examining them will replace the grotesque colors with works of art.

"You should see whoever Alana and Casey saw." Xavier pokes his head up.

Casey has a vine tattooed around her leg, and I have a bunch of black and white sketched flowers on my right bicep to cover up old self-harm scars. My dad paid for it on my eighteenth birthday. I can't remember the guy's name though. Judging by Casey's shrug and confused look, neither does she. Casey's fingers trace the petals and I shudder.

My head is pounding, and I can no longer listen to them talk, or breathe, or exist. I lay my head on the couch and curl up into a ball. Perhaps I am just sick. I have caught some weird stomach bug and I need the extra rest.

CHAPTER SEVEN

My mind is clouded, and the internal screams are louder now. It takes me a moment to realize I haven't slipped into a sudden coma. Casey placed my head on her lap and is rubbing the stubble on my head. I'm not sure why, but I am more startled awake by that than the fight between Dante and Xavier. The oldest brother has Dante pinned against a wall with his forearm to his neck. Yeah, Xavier can probably take down anyone who tries to challenge him, but Dante's psychological jabs can do much more damage than a tackle or punch. He's capable of speaking the kind of words that chew away at you for weeks, making your insides raw.

I watch Dante's lips move as he murmurs something for only Xavier to hear.

"What are they fighting about?" I whisper to Casey.

"Something about Andy and their dad." She peers down at me. "I'm honestly not sure."

Andy was one of their brothers; he killed himself a few years ago. He was older than Dante, but younger than Xavier.

Xavier lets his brother go and hugs him tightly—Dante

returns it. The altercation, whatever it was about, is over. It's resolved quickly, and no hard feelings will linger between the two men. The girls leave one by one, each needing to return home so their parents or roommates don't think they've been kidnapped or something. Knowing I should do the same, I force myself up from the couch, and ask Xavier for a ride.

"Yeah, I need to pick up Michelle anyway."

When I arrive, Michelle runs to her older brother and shouts bye before heading out. My parents are waiting for me with their arms crossed. They try to block the path to my bedroom—and my drugs—with stares that drill holes into my skin. Cautiously, I make my way past them. I can sense them behind me, like shadows stalking mine. On the coffee table of the living room sits a half empty bottle of alcohol mixed with soda. *My* half empty bottle of alcohol mixed with soda. The one I had made for Skylar a couple nights ago.

Shit.

My parents step in front of me once more before dramatically sitting down on the couch. Their faces stone and their eyes are filled with disappointment. A pit of guilt forms in my stomach as they watch me, waiting for a response. I look at each of them. My mom has adoring and loving features. Her soft, deep brown eyes against her long, curly honey hair makes her pink cheeks shine. My dad has a shaved head, a dark beard, and green eyes. His posture is straight and stern. He's struggling to look threatening and serious. He's definitely more concerned, incapable of wrapping his head around what they have discovered. The last thing they want is to find an empty liquor bottle stolen from their cabinet. Although I have been taking liquor from them since I was about thirteen, I stare back at them, not willing to speak first.

"Is this yours, Alana?" My mom finally asks. Her voice shakes, and she pushes the bottle towards me.

"Yes," I whisper.

"It's half full," my father states, staring me down. "It wasn't even opened yet."

"Half empty," I correct him.

He ignores the defiance.

"You drank half of that bottle already! We just bought it three days ago!" My mother says in shock.

I nod nervously, looking down at my feet. There isn't an ounce of shame in me for drinking or stealing their booze. Any guilt I feel comes from being caught. I should have been more careful. I barely hear my father's punishment for me as I begin to think of the string of lies I am getting ready to produce.

"Do you understand me, Alana?" His sudden booming voice causes me to look up.

"Yes." I nod.

"Why did you do this?" My mother's voice is soft. "You're such an intelligent young woman. Why would you do this?"

I want to laugh. I want to fall to the ground with tears of insanity streaming down my face. An intelligent young woman doesn't fill her nose with powdered poison. An intelligent young woman doesn't crave a high the way normal people crave sleep after a long day. I am not who they think I am.

"I was curious," I finally say. "I kept hearing how great and hilarious things are when alcohol is involved, so I gave it a shot." I chuckle for good measure. "Hangovers suck though." I raise my hand. "I won't do it again."

They seem to buy it. The lies and the face filled with

41

false regret are getting much easier to mimic and recite as the days pass. They believe that this shell of a body I put in front of them is really me. I feel like the only part of myself that is truly real is the one on drugs.

I had my first sip of alcohol when I was twelve at Skylar's house. I discovered my love for stimulants when I was only fifteen. I was temporarily prescribed Adderall and abused it significantly. My parents figured it wasn't working and stopped it altogether. Needing the fix, I found Creature, and my relationship with cocaine was established. Xavier and Dante introduced me to weed, hoping it would quench my thirst for a higher plane of existence, but it doesn't hold a candle to what I want. What I *need*.

My parents mention something about a three-day trip to the city, and I wish them luck. They leave by the afternoon, and I am alone once again. The moment I know they aren't going to turn around and come back for forgotten items, I let the monster fully take over. I no longer have to keep the mask glued to my face.

I am unsteady on my feet as I stagger to my bedroom. I'm not thinking anymore—only acting. I rip the handmade hem on my quilt open and take out a small bag of cocaine that I hid there one night while high.

Which could have been any night, considering I am usually high.

I tear the top off and dump the contents onto the floor. I make a crude line and snort it. Maybe these urges are all in my head. Maybe the pain is a figment that my subconscious has created to justify this horrible habit.

I place a bit of the powder on my fingers and rub it against my gums, sighing as the twitching begins to cease. When the drugs hit, I jump to my feet as if a new life has risen into me.

The stereo cranks out punk rock music, pounding throughout the empty rooms. The music isn't loud enough to drown the screaming in my head though. The now locked liquor cabinet taunts and teases me. Like a snake's tongue, it hisses its sweet nothings at me. I search the house until I find the key taped underneath my parent's bed frame. Slamming open the doors, I sip from the bottle. The coke keeps my throat numb, so the liquor goes down like water. I put the bottle on the floor and dump some more drugs onto the coffee table. They are laid out before me like a Christmas gift. I snort the coke and let it burn my nostrils as my heart pounds until it's trying its best to worm its way to the outside of my chest. I can hear it in my ears, and it's found small homes in my fingers. I lie on the floor while my mind beats me up.

It tells me I am worthless.

It tells me that I am a waste of space and that I need to do something more with my life—something fulfilling.

It tells me to get higher.

The bells above the door jingle, and I hear Dante and Skylar announce their presence. I jump to my feet, begin rolling a joint, and set up three more lines after turning down the stereo. My chest has settled to merely a flutter, and part of me hopes that Dante will partake.

Drugs are better with friends.

I hand the joint to Skylar without looking up. I feel him take it from my fingers and spark it. He inhales, coughs, and hands it to Dante. Dante then passes it back to me, and I inhale a healthy lungful of smoke. Despite the cocaine, it burns my throat and I cough up a cloud like an asthmatic dragon. My head spins and grows fuzzy as a grin creeps across my face. Dante pats me on the shoulder and kneels beside me at the table. I hand him a cut straw and watch in awe as he takes in all three lines. He motions for me to give him the bag. I hand him the last of it, and like an artist, he cuts up three beefy, beautiful crystalline hits before handing me the straw.

"Get on my level," he encourages.

"Honey, I *live* on your level." I laugh and breathe in the nose candy.

Dante says he doesn't do hard drugs often. It's a rare occasion. When he does though, I take advantage of it. I absorb the rays like I'm on a beach vacation. We talk erratically with one another about the spiritual purpose of animals, the hoax or reality of psychics, and how we're going to create a solution to save the world.

If only we could figure out what it is.

Meanwhile, Skylar flicks through the channels on the television, settling on a comedy before changing his mind and scrolling once more. Dante stands up from the floor, goes to the kitchen, and returns with a bottle—another one of my parents' bottles. I'm already in the grave, so why not make it comfy? He downs a swig and passes it to me. I repeat his motions, still hardly tasting the liquor. We pass the booze until Dante returns to the floor. His eyes flutter, and he leans his back against the couch.

"I tap out," he breathes.

I wonder if something happened at home. Had he been punished for something? Is he hiding new bruises? I don't want to interrogate him, so I'll just let him find a peaceful numbness in my home.

I am the last person who will tell someone that doing drugs and drinking won't solve the problems that tear your soul to shreds. On the contrary, it is the only therapy I know that works.

"Hey, guys," he murmurs. "What's red and bad for your teeth?"

"Hm?" I ask.

"A brick." He chuckles to himself as Skylar and I giggle.

I sit beside Skylar and hand him the bottle. He shakes his head and gives me the joint. We hang out quietly as the TV plays to bring in noise. The smoke we exhale makes thin layers of clouds swirl around us. We dare not reach for them for fear that they might dissipate and leave us naked to the poisoned atmosphere. My mind, still fully awake and alert, fights with my body as it begins to shut down. The cocaine is slowly being defeated by the alcohol and marijuana as I struggle to keep my eyes open. I don't want to sleep, but the weight is crushing me. My chest feels tight, and I can see colors dancing behind my eyelids. Shivers travel down my spine like snakes, and I let the darkness wash over me.

CHAPTER EIGHT

It is as if my eyes are permanently fixed to look through lenses that haven't been properly cleaned in ages. The TV plays an old re-run episode of something I watched when I was about fourteen—maybe fifteen. I can't pinpoint it. I tear my eyes away from the screen and stare at the door. I am alone. Dante and Skylar are nowhere to be found.

Three hollow knocks sound from the door. Their vibrations travel through the floorboards and into my toes. I make my way towards it with forced footsteps. My brain is piecing it together:

I know this place.

I know this time.

But I am asleep.

I open the entryway and two men, a year or so older than myself, stand at the threshold.

Perhaps they are even older? I don't know. I am bad at guessing ages.

The one with long hair grabs me by the forearm and pulls me outside. His grip is rough as he and the other yank me away from the light of the porch. I gulp hard and look at them in wonder. Part of me is terrified and knows I should run. The other part of me though—the part that needs drugs to survive in this painful world—is unhealthily attached to these men. They are lifelines. The younger of the two is clearly in charge, and he demands my release. He shakes his hair from his face before he smiles warmly at me. As if that's supposed to make me feel better. I hand the older one forty dollars before one them finally says anything.

"You can call me Tiger, and this guy here is Creature." He gestures to himself and then to his friend.

I nod and open my mouth, but Creature quickly stops me. "Don't tell us your name, kid. We don't care. Give us something to call you later, cool?"

"Yeah," I say casually. "Sure."

"First time?" Tiger looks at me.

I nod nervously.

This isn't at all like the anti-drug programs the schools shove down our throats. Tiger and Creature offer to stay with me, and I accept. They teach me how to cut lines and roll the perfect dollar bill. They teach me which fast food restaurants have the perfect straws and how to catch my breath between big lines. Tiger pats my back as both encouragement and a sign of safety. These guys aren't going to let any harm come to me.

Except addiction.

Except possible overdose and the end of my life as I had previously known it.

The word "euphoria" isn't strong enough to describe what I experience when I take in my first line. My skin feels new, my brain is sharp, and happiness seeps through my pores like an overflowing water fountain. My world is made of clouds, and I am on top of a throne made of jewels and gold. I can't be touched up there. Worries cannot find a space inside of my brain.

Time speeds up, and I can sense the urge, the craving, scratching away at my chest and stomach like a hellhound begging to be freed from its chains. I meet up with Creature again, and he hands me a large bag. I bound to my room. I scream at myself to stop, but I can only hopelessly watch my dream-self smash the chunks of the white powder into a fine dust to make the lines heavier and to make the intake a bit less painful.

I *need* this.

I carefully set up and roll a dollar bill. Drawing in a few deep breaths, I lean in and inhale the drugs though my nostrils. The effects wash over me like warm ocean waves. The feeling is undeniably pleasant and uplifting. I am floating on clouds again and my mind is bent around happiness and inner peace. I smirk as the drugs work through the layers of my skin. It's like I've learned what sunshine tastes like.

It is unbridled joy.

The dream goes dark again, and my chest begins to ache. My stomach churns, and an acidic liquid is making its way up my throat, jolting me awake. I hold the vomit in my mouth as I rush to the bathroom and expel the burning acid into the toilet. Reality is only slightly worse than the dream. I rinse my mouth out before heading back into the living room. Skylar is curled up under a blanket and snoring. Dante is passed out on the floor.

It is two hours past noon.

I shut the lights off and let the sun seep into the house through the windows. I sit back down on the couch, light up a joint, and smoke until my mind shuts off for just a moment.

CHAPTER NINE

Energy courses through me as I jump around Dante and Skylar. As always, they just stare and watch. My feet dare not jump off the sidewalk's curb as I bound around like a kangaroo on springs. I don't care about the stares I receive from people who are also outside. We don't have any plans; we just want to keep the brothers and Michelle away from their house as long as possible—and the walls at mine were caving in on me. My muscles twitch and my teeth chatter. My chest feels like it's going to explode.

I shouldn't have taken those extra lines.

It's worth it.

Casey tries to hold my hand, but I have to let go and flex my fingers periodically. The world is spinning and it's hard to breathe. I have to get my lungs in order again. Xavier grabs my shoulders, forcing me to turn and look at him.

"How high are you right now?" he asks slowly.

"Five foot two." My words tumble over each other and meld together.

"Alana." He frowns. I can see the bruise on his arm and

49

one on his collarbone. I stiffen. He's hurt, but he won't show it. Not here.

"Pretty far out, but I'm okay," I try to convince him.

"No, you're not," he says matter-of-factly. "Give me names—or at least one name."

Odd thing is, I understand this language. I speak it fluently.

Okay, maybe it's not so odd. Not for me.

"Rabbit," I tell him quickly.

"Is he cheap?"

I shrug. "Don't know. Not one of his customers. He looks like he'd be pretty easy to con though."

"Good."

And with that, he walks off, leaving us at the park alone. It becomes dark fast and even though I ask to keep going and keep walking aimlessly until we stumble upon a new adventure, we still end up back at my house. Well, not all of us. Dante and Lily have gone off somewhere else.

Where? I'm not sure. I don't care.

Xavier's destination is easy to figure out at least.

I stare mindlessly at the TV as it spews out cartoons that I can't focus on with both eyes open. Casey is asleep on my lap, and I wouldn't dream of moving from my spot. I will just have to watch cartoons forever.

I suppose there are worse ways to go out.

Cartoons can't kill you. Can they?

"Does anyone know where Xavier is?" I ask, trying to get stupid animated murder thoughts out of my head. I know where he is; I more so want to know if anyone is aware when he'll return.

I'm growing curious of our previous conversation where I spoke of Rabbit and his potentially cheap drugs.

"He said he'd be home soon." Sarah sounds troubled. "I'm sure he's fine."

Who is she trying to convince? Us? Her?

Worry begins to seep through me like sludge. I hide the feeling—no need to alarm anyone. Hopefully Rabbit won't sell anything too weak and Xavier is flying.

Casey stirs awake, but stays put. Skylar and Sarah relax on the floor in front of the couch with their legs stretched out before them. The bells above the door jingle and none of us flinch. It isn't until a bag of marijuana is thrown onto my lap that I look up. Xavier towers behind us, struggling to keep his eyes open, a grin on his face.

"A-thank you." He nods once.

I fist bump him and open the bag. The thick aroma fills my nose as I breathe in a lungful of the scent. Nothing can beat this intoxicating smell. It is begging me to let it caress my lungs and soothe my soul.

But it will *never* be strong enough to make the urges stop.

Xavier pulls Sarah to her feet and starts to seduce her. We ignore them as they make out in the dining room. Eventually, they find a bedroom and kick the door shut behind them.

I hand Casey the bag and a pipe, and she packs it quickly.

We pass the piece between the three of us that remain and shout at the couple fucking in my house. Skylar and I imitate their moans and shouts while Casey laughs at our perverted antics. Moments pass, and the noise stops. The cartoons from the TV are eerie against the sudden backdrop of still silence. Sarah and Xavier don't emerge.

We smoke more, and the infamous munchies crash into us. We devour tubes of Pringles, ice cream bars, and grilled peanut butter and jelly sandwiches. After chugging enough water to save a town from drought, we pass out in the living room, Casey nestled in my arms with her head on my chest. Skylar has stolen a pillow and blanket from my parents' room and curls up, falling asleep under the coffee table.

In the back of my head, like a bomb in my dreams, I hear a door click open. The sound shoots me awake and I immediately curse my alerted sleep. Xavier is standing, naked, a mere four feet from me.

"Dude! No!" I shout and throw a pillow at him. "You need to have pants on in the living room."

He looks embarrassed and heads back to the room he came from.

"Sarah is naked, too," Xavier says, returning with a pair of jeans on.

"Yes," I say slowly. "How do we know that and you don't?"

His eyes widen and he leans back. "Shit. What was it that Rabbit gave me?"

"Drugs," I tell him with an amused grin. "Probably drugs."

"How high were you last night?" Skylar goes up to his older brother with concern.

"I don't remember coming here. I barely remember having sex with my girlfriend. I mean, my mind is starting to piece things together. It's blurry though. I completely blacked out. I don't know what I took," he rambles.

And I thought I was reckless.

"You'd better remember something," Skylar warns him.

Xavier rolls his eyes and takes Sarah in his arms when she joins us. Casey kisses my neck and pulls me with her towards the kitchen. She turns the stove on and asks for a pan and eggs. I stand beside her and help her cook breakfast for the group. I only have eggs, lunchmeat, and cheese in the fridge, so we make a scramble. When we sit around the table, I force the food down my throat. I am completely disgusted by it, only wanting to let the devil I've named Sunshine to have her way.

CHAPTER TEN

After a few days, I tell my real friends that I will be out of town for a bit. It's a simple lie so I can be alone with the addiction. My muscles twitch beneath my skin as I set up my lines. I can't get them together fast enough, and my mind refuses to focus fully. Once I inhale the drugs into my bloodstream, I lie on my back and stare at the ceiling. My heart tries to escape my chest as I clench and unclench one fist. My breathing quickens, and I feel annoyed.

This isn't strong enough anymore.

This is boring.

I need something more.

Pushing myself up from the floor, I make another beefy line. This also isn't enough.

I groan—distraught and irritated—grab my phone, and click on Creature's name to dial his number. I'd text, but there's more of a guarantee of an answer if I call.

"What?" he asks, pissed off.

"It's Sunshine," I say flatly.

"Yeah, and?"

"I'm bored. I need something." My voice is cautious as it

trails along the last word.

"Stronger or faster or different?" he questions, still frustrated.

What's crawled up his ass to make him so peeved?

"Different." I'm hesitant. "What are you doing right now?"

"Just come over and find out." He chuckles. "Oh, no. Wait. You don't know where I live, do you? I'll have Tiger pick you up in thirty minutes. Be ready."

He hangs up, and it takes me awhile to travel back to earth. My mind is too scrambled to tie my own shoes, let alone get ready to leave the house. So, I just pace back and forth in my room. Sunshine is winning, killing every bit of me, and I am doing nothing to stop her.

"Sunshine!" There are three loud knocks. "Open your door!" Tiger shouts.

"It's unlocked!" I call out.

I pull a baggy shirt over my torso and shove on a pair of slip-on boots. The jeans—faded and ripped—hug my legs like tights. By the time I come out, he's talking to my father. I'm not sure what they're discussing, but my dad is smiling and soon shakes his hand. Tiger gives a sharp head tilt towards the door, walking back towards it after bidding my father a farewell. His fitted jeans crease at his knees as he moves.

"You should lock up your house," he informs me.

I brush it off.

"What would I owe you?" I ask, changing the subject.

"Nothing."

My heart skips a beat, and I smirk despite myself.

The air is cold, but his car is taken over by heat. We ride in silence, not making an effort to hold conversation. We aren't in the vehicle for long—only three songs play on the stereo. Tiger pulls into a parking lot that belongs to a beat-up apartment complex. The red brick is faded and dirty, and the light above the main outdoor staircase flickers like the introduction to a horror movie. We climb up three flights of stairs and walk to the end of the hall. The place smells like piss and beer, and it makes my eyes sting. The floor has carpeting that's so worn out it might as well be old wood with oriental designs imprinted into it. He opens the door, which reads 8B.

"Sunshine!" Creature yells when we step inside.

The house is poorly lit and thick with smoke. Creature leans over a small pot of something made of strong, nose-burning chemicals. Rabbit and some girl are lying down on the couch half-naked. They have the appearance of corpses in each other's arms as their eyes dart around the room. Their minds are awake and alert, but their bodies are locked in a near comatose state.

Tiger walks up next to Creature and watches whatever it is he's doing. I just stand there, looking around. An old wooden table is in front of the shabby couch. The carpet underneath it is mouse-eaten and musty. I balance on the heels of my boots, pretending to control my impatience. The TV plays some useless news show. I wonder why it's even on. There's no way Creature gives a shit.

"Yo, Sunshine, give us the bag that's on the table," Creature instructs after a few long minutes.

I do as told without question. They're giving me free stuff for the night; I will become their personal twelve-hour servant if I have to. Tiger takes the bag from my hands and pulls out three syringes and pulls some of the liquid from the pot into each one. I don't pay much attention to what he's doing; my brain goes blank as my breathing hitches. Before I know it, he hands me a syringe.

CHAPTER ELEVEN

"Sunshine," Creature flicks my shoulder, "take the thing. You doing this or not?"

I open my mouth to say something, but words fail me. So, I just remain dumbfounded.

"You don't have to if you don't want to." Tiger is gentle. "We have other things."

"Will it be worth it?" I ask nervously.

Creature grins. "That's for you to judge."

I want to punch him in the throat.

"I'm in." I let the words out with a sharp exhale.

We walk back into the living room, and to my pleasant surprise, Rabbit and the girl are gone. We plop down on the stained couch. I try not to think about what this seat has gone through during its life. I observe Creature carefully as he ties his arm off with the belt that was around his waist, taps the inside of his arm, and injects the drugs into his veins. I go to do the same, but quickly stop, looking at Tiger for guidance. Creature calls me an idiot under his breath.

Tiger grabs my arm and forces it towards him. He slaps the inside of my elbow until the area stings a little and brightens to a soft shade of red. My veins pop up as he pushes just above my elbow. He again asks if I'm okay with this, and I again confirm that I am. Tiger pierces the needle under my skin and injects the drugs into my blood.

I smile and sigh happily as they work through me faster than I thought possible. It's only seconds before I let my body fall back with the high; the euphoria finds a home in each one of my muscles, bathing every part of me. Tiger injects himself quickly with finesse and ease, and we sit in silence, nothing but our breathing and the stupid TV for noise.

"So, what did I just take?" I ask, rolling off the couch and landing on the floor. I already know the answer, but I suppose I just need clarification.

Tiger pats me on the back. "Heroin."

"Hey, Sunshine, how old are you?" Creature asks mindlessly, picking apart the already worn couch.

"Eighteen," I respond dully, letting the cool floor encase me with the high. I find a knot on the underside of the coffee table and begin to dig at it.

"Damn," he exhales with guilt.

"You guys?" I don't know why I keep the conversation going. It's not like I care.

"Tiger's about twenty-two and I'm twenty-five."

We talk amongst ourselves, but all I really focus on is how the tips of my fingers are now bleeding because of the knot in the wood. When the conversation starts to become forced and dotted with too much awkward silence, we snort a couple lines and throw around a bottle between us. Next thing I know, I'm waking up on Creature's kitchen floor, cheek pressed against the dirty tile. My fingertips throb, and my arm has a small bruise from the needle's mark. A boot nudges at my ribs and I groan in protest.

"Come on, Sunshine. Time to get up." Tiger yawns.

I pull myself to my feet and crack my back.

"Taking any home?" he asks, pointing to a few of the rigs.

"Yeah, sure." I rub my head. "Just, uh…show me how to do this."

Step by step, he walks me through the process. Anxiety builds in my chest and stomach. I pay him, and he drives me home. My mind is calm despite the cold, empty negativity running rampant in my mind. The high last night was better than I could have imagined. It kept the monster at bay. I can't wait to try more, but I decide I have to be patient. Besides, I have cocaine I can snort.

After calling throughout the house to make sure I'm alone, I cut the lines on the kitchen counter. My nostrils sting, my throat is numb, and my eyes widen with energy. I check my phone—Casey called about eight times last night and has been calling all day. I put the phone down and clean the kitchen, making sure to get the dirt that's stuck in the cracks of the floor and table. I'll have to call her back later. There are other things I have to tend to.

I don't answer when it rings again. I just let the musical tones resound off the walls. Sitting on the floor with phone in hand, I watch the display light up with her name. The room smells like lemon and bleach, and I pick at a spot on the floor with nervous fingers.

What am I supposed to tell her, that I've found a shovel at the bottom of this pit and started digging deeper?

It rings again. I let out a sigh of defeat.

"Hey," I mumble.

"Why haven't you been answering?" Casey demands, fear in her voice.

"I didn't want to upset you," I tell her quietly.

"Upset me? Why? What did you do, Alana?"

"Nothing. Just forget I said anything, okay?" I plead with her.

"Yeah, no. Alana, I'm not stupid." Her tone changes from scared to pissed.

We both fall silent for a long moment. Neither of us want to be the first to break it. The only sounds between us are our exaggerated breaths on either end.

"Sorry," I finally say.

"Don't—" She pauses, reconsidering her words. "Alana, I don't know how much more of this I can handle."

The words sink in like acid. They chew away at me and slam into my chest. "What are you saying?" I know the answer to my question, and I'm not sure why I asked. "Please, don't do this. You're everything to me."

"Are you sure? It seems like the drugs are a step above me," she says quietly.

"They're not."

"Then quit."

"I don't think I can," I whisper with guilt.

"Then what the hell am I supposed to do? Every morning I wake up worrying about you. Did she get kicked out yet? Is she sober? Who is she with? Is she alive?" Casey doesn't speak for a long moment. "I can't do this right now. I do love you."

"I know." My words are empty. "I love you, too. Let me make it up to you?"

"How?"

"Let me take you out. One last time. No drugs. Just give me this chance. If you're sure you're done, then I'll give you space."

I hear her sigh deeply on the other end. "Fine. Where will we go?"

"I don't know." I try to wrack my brain for ideas. "Camping? I'll be there soon." I hang up the phone and wipe the tears that had formed in the corners of my eyes.

Stripping out of my clothes, I jump into the shower, making the water as cold as possible. I scrub my body of its lingering toxins and shave my legs, arms, and head. After I dry off, I pull on a pair of leggings, a long-sleeved shirt to hide the bruises, and a pair of combat boots. I don't put on any makeup and leave my jewelry on the counter. However, I do stuff a small baggie of heroin into my sock.

I am a slave to my foul spirit.

Baseball cap on my head, I grab the keys to the family pickup truck, and stick my license into my bra before leaving the house. The thought of writing a note for my parents crosses my mind, but I'll probably be home before they are. Besides, they have to be used to me disappearing. It isn't out of character.

I play classical piano music as I drive to Casey's house. Back roads and the green scenery of trees surround me on the way there. Her house is outside of the brick city, and it's always nice to see nature when I make the trip to her mom's place. I pull into the paved driveway and park behind a black sedan. Their ranch home with its manicured lawn and perfectly trimmed bushes is inviting. It feels more like home than my own does. I walk through the front door and close it behind me. Kicking off my boots, I place them with the other shoes on the mat.

"Hey, guys!" I announce my presence.

Casey's mother appears from behind the corner and her face lights up. Her cheeks have a natural pink tint, and they rise with the happy curl of her lips. She steps forward and embraces me in a tight hug, her honey brown hair brushing against my neck and shoulders.

"Alana," she exclaims and kisses my cheek. "You look sick, honey," she comments with worry. "You're so thin."

"Yeah, I don't gain weight," I lie.

I do a lot of drugs and I don't eat.

I love drugs and I hate food.

That's the real answer.

Casey shows up quickly and jumps around her mom. "We'll be home tomorrow sometime, okay?"

"Of course." Her mother hugs her. "Just be safe."

CHAPTER TWELVE

We drive around with nothing but radio repeats to drown the silence. It's the same song for the third time, and neither of us make a move to change the station. The windshield is streaked with droplets of water from the misty fall of rain, and the engine roars gently as I continue down the road. Casey just stares at the dent in the dashboard. Her eyes don't stray from the mark that Xavier's fist put there a few years ago. I can't remember why he was angry. I just know that he punched the dashboard until it cracked and paid my father later. It was never fixed. I watch Casey from my peripherals as we twist down the winding roads in the small pickup. A tear begins to make its way down her cheek as she looks ahead.

My chest tightens and my heart drops into my flipping stomach. I pull the vehicle over to the side of the road and watch her helplessly.

I did this.

I made her feel like this.

"Come here," I mutter, untangling her from her seatbelt. I undo mine—it flies back with a snap, clipping my shoulder—and hold her close to me, kissing her forehead, cheeks, and hands. She buries her face into my chest, and her hands rest on my stomach. I can feel every movement of her body as her sobs lessen and her breathing slows. Casey unwraps herself from her curled position against me. She holds my hands in hers and lightly presses her forehead against mine. I free a hand and use my thumb to dry her tear-streaked face.

"Hold still," she commands, pulling away from me.

I gaze at her and remain as still as sculpted ice. She presses her lips softly against mine, and still I do not move. With the tips of her fingers, she begins to trace me. Her touch is light as she glides her hands along the curve of my cheeks, the bones of my jawline, the stillness of my lips. She closes my eyes and traces softly over them with her fingers before slowly guiding her hands against my fingers.

"What are you doing?" I murmur with my eyes still closed while she traces my lips for a third time.

"Memorizing all of you that I can," she whispers.

I take her hand in mine and kiss her fingertips. "What for?"

She doesn't respond.

"You're never going to lose me," I tell her quietly. "You know that, right?"

"You can't promise me that." She presses her head against the cold window, staring out into the black sky.

The emptiness returns to my stomach, and that dark pit creeps back up into my chest. Compulsive urges make my fingers shake as old, faded thoughts of self-harm slither into my head. I could open my skin and release the pressure of this moment as if it were a wound.

I remember the bag in my sock, and the urges become nothing but whispers. I turn the truck back into drive and accelerate down the road until we come to a park. It only has a pavilion and a winding path that snakes around it. There's a thick patch of woods behind the pavilion that local stoners tramp through for a safe place to smoke. They set up campsites and sleeping areas for those who want to spend the night. I gather a large blanket from the back seat and hold it close.

Casey jumps out before I do and leads the way into the woods. She walks along the concrete path until it turns left. When it does, she turns to the right, into the grass and into the trees. We stomp down fallen branches and get snagged a few times on thorn bushes along a narrow, unkempt trail that opens into a clearing. It has a fire pit with stones surrounding a pile of gray ash, seating areas made of fallen trees and random garbage—broken lawn chairs and cracked stools—found in the woods, and a lean-to next to a large oak tree to sleep under.

It's still raining softly, but under the small shelter it's relatively dry. I lay the blanket down and pat it, inviting Casey to sit beside me. It's dark among the trees against the night, but the sky is lit up with tiny, brilliant speckles of white flames. The candles of the universe are flickering just for us.

"We should build a fire." Casey stands up. "Right? That's what we're supposed to do?"

"Yeah, I think so."

Together, we gather twigs, fragile branches, and dry leaves. We build a tipi-like structure with the branches and fill the hole in the center with the twigs and dry leaves. I use my lighter to set it aflame. The dry brush ignites, devoured as if a hungry beast is consuming it. The fire crackles beautifully against the backdrop of the night. We duck back into the shelter and watch the blaze. Casey curls up on the blanket and falls asleep, shadows playing along her perfect face.

I poke her cheek to make sure she's indeed passed out. She swats my hand away and rolls over with a groan. Silently, I take my shoes off and retrieve the heroin tucked inside a small square of yellow wax paper. With careful fingers, I open it. I retrieve a dollar bill from my pocket and roll it up to snort the brown powder.

It takes more than a few seconds to hit me. My eyes flutter, and I detect euphoria easing into me. There is a calm, floating feeling in my blood and bones. With a grin on my face, I stuff the evidence back into my sock and settle on the blanket. I stare up at the roof of the lean-to and watch the fire from the corner of my eyes. For hours, I fight sleep, not willing to leave this high. Eventually, it gets the better of me, and I slip into a dreamless slumber.

CHAPTER THIRTEEN

I call Casey's mom the next day and let them know that she's safe and at my house—she will be home soon. She's in the shower to wash off the smell of fire and dead trees. My parents are back home and in the kitchen, conversing about their latest adventures. I nod politely, trying to act interested while all I want to do was duck into my room and snort lines of sparkling bliss.

As each day passes, the monster kills another part of me.

I wonder if my parents know, but don't know how to acknowledge it. The conversation would be full of rage, confusion, and pity—all of which I don't need.

When Casey emerges from the shower, I take her hand.

"Hey, excellent story, guys, but we have to go now." I look at Casey.

"Yes," she quickly exclaims. "Yes, we do."

They tell us to be safe, and my dad throws me the keys to the sedan. He warns me not to let an angry Xavier into this car; he doesn't need another cracked glove box. I chuckle at the remark.

"Where are we going?" Casey asks as we climb into the car.

"I have no idea." I shrug and turn the key. "I just didn't want to listen to them anymore."

I flip through the radio stations as we drive around aimlessly before deciding on one that's playing rock music. The speakers thump with bass, and the words are sung clearly. A groan of frustration escapes my lips when a slow-moving car pulls in front of us.

"Ten miles under!" I scream through the windshield.

I lean on the horn and do not let up. Casey laughs as I bounce around with a smile on my face. The blaring sound encompasses everything, and the turtle-paced driver eventually pulls over. He gives us a stiff middle finger, and Casey shouts at him through an open window. I speed recklessly past, wildly whipping the car around the streets until we come to the town's main park. I drive carefully through the grass towards the large pavilions with picnic tables and charcoal grills. My headlights find sleeping silhouettes of three people I really don't want to see there as dusk settles around us. They're curled up on the grass, still sheltered under parts of the roof that overhang from the concrete floor of the pavilion. I turn the headlights off, not wanting to wake Skylar, Xavier, and Michelle—who is protected under Xavier's arm—just yet. Casey looks at me and frowns.

"My dad usually keeps candy around." My eyes are locked on them. "Check the glove box please."

"That's random." Sure enough, there are two bags of skittles. She hands them to me. "What are you going to do?"

"You'll see." I step out of the car.

I rip the skittles bags open and pour the candy onto their chests, waiting for them to wake up. They're light

68

sleepers, and the falling candy does stir them awake. When Skylar's eyes open, I smile.

"Why are you asleep on the ground?"

"We're tired and have nowhere to go." Skylar yawns and sits up. "Why are you pouring skittles on us?"

"You can stay at my place," I offer. "It's free of charge. There's no fancy hotel amenities, but we have Wi-Fi, so that's cool."

Xavier picks himself up and rests a hand on my shoulder. "Thanks, Alana. It means a lot."

Michelle teeters on her feet, leaning against her oldest brother.

I wave my hand, and we pile into the car. Before I make it onto the main road to head back to my house, Xavier's phone rings from his back pocket. We go silent so he'll be able to hear the other end. He mostly just says the words 'okay' and 'I understand.'

"Alana, take us to the hospital," Xavier demands and hangs up the phone.

"Why?" My stomach sinks. I've always feared one of the brothers would be beaten beyond saving. "Missing a leg? Took too many Viagra?" I have to calm this with humor. I have no drugs left on me, and my emotions are holding strong. "Are you having an erection that has lasted for more than four hours?"

"Fuck, Alana, no! Dante is awake and ready to come home. We have to go pick him up before our dad gets there."

"Dante's awake!" Michelle shouts. "Finally!" she finishes with an exhausted sigh, arms crossed at her chest. "Come on, Alana, let's go!"

I turn down the road and drive at high speed until we make it to the gray building with large white letters that spell out 'Augustine Emergency.' I keep the car idling while Xavier runs in to retrieve his brother.

Dante has stiches above his left eye. It's still swollen and dark blue. There's a yellow bruise along his jawline and two on his collarbone. He doesn't speak. He doesn't look away from the windshield. His breathing is shallow and slow.

He is completely silent the whole ride to my house. It's as if we picked up a corpse.

My parents greet us without looking up as we walk through the front door, the bells jingling to announce our entrance. We duck into my room and sit on the bed. In one corner of the room is a new bass guitar that Dante keeps hidden here. He picks up the instrument and plucks away at the thick strings. Dante ignores everything around him and lets his fingers dance. Xavier and Skylar remain at his side, staying close. Xavier keeps apologizing for not being there. Skylar is taking the blame, saying that it should have been him. Michelle rushes out of the room, muttering something about her brother under her breath.

Dante tells Xavier and Skylar to shut up, that he'll beat them if they keep up their pity. They don't listen, and Dante doesn't lift a finger away from the strings. Michelle comes back and plops down beside Dante, squeezing herself between him and Xavier. She found Band-Aids and places them one by one on Dante's many wounds, kissing each bandage as she makes sure they're in place. I lie on the bed, staring at the blank ceiling as a strange energy rushes through me. The emptiness still lingers in the cavities of my chest and ribs, but something is rising within me.

The brothers, Michelle, and Casey spend the night. Xavier, Dante, and Skylar all curl up in the guest bedroom with their sister, and Casey stays with me. They leave early in the morning. Casey offers to let them stay at her place, but they decline. They have to go back home eventually, and the more they put it off, the worse it'll be. After they leave, I pull together an outfit and apply on makeup.

I feel confident, and the monsters within me are damn near forcing the smile that appears on my lips. I call Creature up to warn him that I am on my way. I want the drugs to match this elevated mood. The sun is bright, and the sky looks extraordinarily blue. The green of the trees is nearly glowing, and I can taste sweet pollen on my tongue. I'm grinning from ear to ear as I walk to Creature's rundown apartment.

"You look happy." He pulls me inside.

"It's a good day," I tell him. "I just need some coke to make it better, ya know? Oh!" I inhale. "Could I get some more heroin, too? Do you think I should just get the coke though? I don't have enough money on me for both." The words spill from me like waterfalls. "I could just pay you back I guess, and—"

"Sunshine!" Creature shouts. "Shut the fuck up."

I stop and look at him. My hands twist together.

"You can pay me back later," he says. "What can you afford and what do you want?"

"I can afford an eight ball." I count my bills. "I want everything you have."

"Seriously?" he raises an eyebrow. "I'll give you the eight ball and a bundle of heroin. Need rigs?"

"Yes." I nod, bouncing on my feet.

"Are you high?" he asks as he gathers the drugs.

"Nope." I feel like I am though.

What the hell is happening? I was empty and now I'm full.

"Whatever." He hands me the goods, takes the money from my fist, and counts it. "Okay, you'll owe me one hundred for the bags and thirty for the rigs. You have one week or I find you, good?"

"Yeah, perfect." I shake his hand, hide the merchandise, and leave.

I snort a little bit of coke in the hallway and walk on clouds the entire way home. I don't sleep that night. I don't really sleep for *three* nights. I stay awake, locked in my room, in a cocaine dreamland. I allow myself to become vaguely sober for a few hours each day and vacate from my room during those times to hang out with my parents. I listen to their stories and talk rapidly about my day, careful to leave out the details of my bad habits.

I learn two things: my father wants me to see the mountains of Colorado and my mother wants me to eat a full meal.

I have dinner with them while the beast starts to tear at my head. It seems to please my mom that I finally eat something substantial.

Then I lock myself back in my room once midnight hits. My brain is delirious from lack of sleep, and the shadows of the room distort and create black beetles that scatter across the floor. Shutting my eyes tight against them, I try to make the hallucinations disappear. I gather a rig and some heroin, set up my space—drawing the curtains over my windows to farther seclude myself. I grab a lighter from my dresser and bring flames to life on the wicks of the candles I have scattered around. The lavender and eucalyptus smells will ease my troubled mind more than the drugs. The illusion consumes me. I pull the drugs into the syringe and tap the crook of my elbow, just like Tiger has taught me, to find a suitable vein.

The plan doesn't work. I still don't sleep. Not fully. I become lost in that place between sleep and reality. My body shuts down, but my mind continues to wander around valleys that are dark and desolate. I am stuck in that void as the energy balls in my chest and fights against the drugs. My muscles twitch beneath my skin as my fingers scratch methodically at the wood floors. My mind and emotions swell like a festering wound begging to release infection. I am paralyzed to the spot, incapable of moving. All I can do is blink and breathe in this euphoric energy as night comes and goes. The morning brings toxic sunshine.

CHAPTER FOURTEEN

Stomping angrily around the house for the eighth time, I throw things around as I search each and every crevice. My mind jumps wild with panic in the confines of my skull and a ball of rage burns in my chest, creating tightness in my muscles.

"What are you looking for?" my mother asks.

"Yeah, you've been freaking out all day," my dad adds with concern.

"I still can't find my fucking wallet!" I shout, throwing a pillow.

"It'll show up. Don't panic," my mom reassures me.

"Where is it?" I look under the couch cushion again.

Someone must have stolen it. Did I leave it somewhere?

I'm going to be killed. Natural recoil runs through me as my parents close in and sit me down on the couch.

"Breathe," my father instructs. "Calm down, Alana."

I don't say anything. I just fold my hands over my knees. My focus intertwines with my shaking knuckles as they bounce with the motion of my legs. The strange monster that lives inside of me has only come in aggravated gasps over the week. I have enough to keep her at bay. This anger though—this isn't me. I want to punch through the walls, destroy the house, and scream. I take deep breaths as my father suggested and try to calm myself; I'm still shaking. The rage won't subside. I have to shove it down into another part of me where I can drown it later. My thoughts continue to circulate around the money I still owe Creature. I need to pay him so he can pay the other dealer for the things I bought from him. If I don't get the money to Creature in time, the other guy will probably kill him. Which ultimately means that if I don't give Creature his money, he will kill *me*.

My parents remain with me for as long as I can stay unmoved. My legs bounce up and down, and my hands interlock with one another as my mind flips in rapid circles. The bells over the door soon break the strange silence around us.

"Alana?" I hear Casey call out first.

"Alanaaaaa!" Dante sings dramatically, drawing out the last letter of my name.

I look at my parents, and they smile sweetly. "We're going out anyway. You guys have fun here."

The moment my parents leave, the brothers and the girls make themselves at home. Lily lies in Dante's arms as he smokes a cigarette. Casey cuddles up close to me, her knees pulled to her chest. Xavier puts Michelle down for a nap in the guest room, and he sits in the recliner, observing us like an over-protective hawk, munching on a bag of popcorn while we watch the news. It's not something we usually do —mostly because none of us can really stand the bias that's obviously present on each network. It doesn't matter which news channel we switch to; we're being spoon-fed lies as they try to brainwash us into mindlessly picking a side.

"I can't stand this!" I throw the remote.

"What? Why?" Casey asks.

"The news. Why isn't it used to give us important information? I don't care what celebrity got a DUI. I don't need to know if that person's comment was racist or not. If it has to be debated, it is. We need to know what's really going on around us." My thoughts and words are tumbling. "Like, what is being implemented to help our addiction to destroying the Earth? Not some broken-down, washed up, feel-sorry-for-me pop star." I lean forward a bit as I speak.

"Well, some people have an interest in those things," Xavier comments and catches a piece of popcorn in his teeth.

I throw myself back against the couch with an exaggerated sigh. "They can watch some other channel for that stupid information then. Pop culture shouldn't be on the news." I wrap my arm around Casey again before fidgeting into another position. "We're being blinded by shiny rocks so we don't see what's really going on." I'm not sure where my thoughts are going, but I can't stop talking.

"The damn commercials annoy me the most. *Buy this! Buy that!*" Dante keeps up with my energy. "The whole thing feeds off of the tiniest insecurities and exploits them for profit."

"Yeah. Fat? Take this miracle pill and eat these miracle meals!" Skylar says with an announcer's voice. "Skin too dry? This lotion is made of unicorn blood! It'll make your skin softer than a baby's bottom!"

It amazes us that he's actually paying attention to what's going on.

"And god forbid they sell something without sex and women with flawless bodies made by airbrushing and photo editing." Lily rolls her eyes. "Really, what does a half-naked woman have to do with cars and shit?"

Xavier laughs at us. "What are you guys even talking about?"

Casey shrugs, and we continue to talk about topics that melt and braid together in a chaotic mess that doesn't make much sense. Dante and I lead most of the conversation, feeding off one another. We talk into the darkest hours of the night, and everyone exits the house when my parents return.

Retreating to my room, I can't bring myself to sleep. Shadows dance, morphing into people that hide in the dark corners and bugs that scurry along the floor. I blink to try and make it all go away, but they continue to haunt me.

CHAPTER FIFTEEN

I end up finding my wallet the next morning hidden in my sock drawer. It feels like my feet have wheels on them as I glide across town to an alleyway behind an old tool store, hoping to find a dealer. I know I'm supposed to pay Creature back, but I can worry about that later. My brain is running with thoughts of suicide and the urge to hurt myself. I need to make this beast completely silent.

I find someone and waste my money on an eight ball of cocaine and two small bags of heroin. My home is empty once more, and I snort a line before Xavier sends me a text. He's made a reservation at the restaurant in town.

Why won't he stop trying to save me?

Eating out all the time is not going to make me better.

They're at my house in minutes, and I inhale another line and clean up before they can make it into the living room. Xavier and Sarah don't come inside. Skylar is silent, but gives me a knowing look. Dante slips me an ecstasy pill before walking back outside with Lily and Michelle, telling me to make sure Xavier doesn't find out. His younger sister holds his hand tightly and follows him like a shadow, looking up at him in awe.

"Tell Xavier I'll catch up," I call after Dante before the door closes.

"Whatever," he yells.

"Yeah, whatever!" Michelle echoes.

"No," Dante scolds. "You're not old enough to be mean yet."

"Sorry."

The door clicks shut, and I work mechanically, needing to stop the heightened clawing that still tears at my ears. My hands shake with paranoia as I lift the floorboard and retrieve the drugs. Skylar watches me blankly while I roll him a joint and make two more lines for me. Once the stimulants are in my system, I pour two shots of alcohol and down both of them before refilling the glasses and giving them to Skylar. He tilts his head back to slam the liquor down.

No reaction.

Seriously. Can he even taste it?

I lie on the floor, arms sprawled out at my sides like wings as the monster's screams become weak and bearable. My eyelids spasm, and my breathing is fast while my heart races in the confines of my chest. Once I can feel my tongue again, I scramble to my feet, lace up a pair of boots, and grab Skylar. We walk arm in arm through the misty air. Xavier and Sarah are waiting for us outside of the restaurant.

Sarah frowns and tries to put her hand on my shoulder. "Alana."

"Don't." I pull away. "Don't touch me."

She was concerned. I don't really blame her. I was withering away. My thin hands shook with the drugs, and my pupils looked like large black holes.

79

Xavier guides us through the maze of booths. The circular table holds us tightly together. We are the knights at the round table, ready to serve King Arthur. Casey laces her fingers through mine and grips my shaking hands. I gaze at her beauty, soaking it in and letting myself swell with love. The others clash their glasses together and laugh. My mind wanders off, and I have no idea what they're excited about.

I don't really care.

I do, however, take notice of the large-breasted black-haired waitress going out of her way to make Xavier extra happy. She pours an additional shot into his drink and gives him a free sample of mozzarella sticks.

"Don't you remember me?" she finally asks, twirling a strand of hair around her finger.

"No," he says flatly without looking up. "Let us eat." A loud clang echoes around us when Xavier stabs his plate with frustration. He's hiding something.

"How do you not remember me, X?" she nearly shouts in hysterics. "We had sex the other night."

We all stare at Xavier with wide eyes. Sarah crosses her arms and tilts her head, challenging him to start talking.

"So that's what I did," he breathes out the realization. "Whatever that shit was, it is dope!" He turns to the waitress. "That wasn't an actual thing. You know, that right? Leave me alone, okay?"

"You said you loved me!" the waitress screams.

"Yeah, seems I lied. Give us the check."

The waitress storms away, and I can't help but crack up.

"Dude." Dante shakes his head, grinning. "You're so screwed."

Everyone but Sarah and Xavier heads outside. They are going to cover the bill and talk about what Xavier has done.

I know Sarah will forgive him. He doesn't deserve it, but she will.

The man deserves to be punched in the damn nose.

CHAPTER SIXTEEN

We all go back to my house after Sarah lets Xavier know that she still loves him, but he needs to shape up. Dante and Skylar both call him stupid. My parents invite the group in with open arms. My mother offers glasses of lemonade, and my father talks to the brothers, bonding with them. Their own dad doesn't bother them with father-son conversations —not like this. Their father's idea of "bonding" is screaming incoherent drunken rambles. He doesn't have it in him to be humane to his own sons.

And we've never told my parents where the bruises come from.

The last time they were in foster care, the siblings were all separated and Michelle ended up being poorly taken care of. We thought Dante was going to kill the family that took her in. They all misbehaved until they were back under their own hellish roof. After that, they vowed to never let it happen again.

Casey and I lie out on top of the roof over the porch, legs crossed over each other as we watch dark clouds swim slowly across the sky. The effects of the drugs are beginning to wear off, and my stomach sinks with the weight of an anchor as the thought of angry dealers quickly speeds across my mind.

"Shit," I mutter, lips barely parting.

"What?" Casey asks, sitting up.

"I forgot to pay Creature." I pull myself up as well.

I didn't forget to pay him. I chose to pay someone else.

She looks at me, confused and waiting for an explanation.

"I owe him money—he can't pay his guy. His guy doesn't get paid, and Creature doesn't have a good day."

If Creature doesn't have a good day, then I don't have a good day.

"That's really bad, isn't it?" Her expression drops.

"Very." I exhale and kiss her cheek.

She cuddles close to me and kisses my neck. I shiver under the touch of her soft lips and rest my head against hers.

"I wish you weren't so stupid," she says against my skin.

"Yeah, me too."

The moonlight vanishes, and the dark clouds release their rain. I open the window behind us and help Casey back inside. My legs scratch a bit against the windowsill when I crawl into the room behind her. We lie on my bed, my arms wrapped around her stomach. I breathe in the scent of her tea tree oil shampoo and her rose petal perfume. I listen to my heart and focus on my chest as it rises and falls until I fall asleep.

When I wake up, Casey is gone.

I find her in the kitchen with Xavier, Sarah, Skylar, and Michelle. They're eating eggs and bacon; the smell of breakfast floods the house.

"I don't like bacon!" Michelle complains and tries to put

it onto Xavier's plate. He grabs her hand and pushes it back to her dish before she's able to release her food.

"What about my bacon?" he offers her.

She takes a small nibble. "Yes."

He shakes his head with an eye roll, gives her his bacon, and takes hers.

"Where's Dante?" I ask, nibbling on a single slice of greasy food.

"Yes." Michelle looks around, fist gripped around the slab of meat. "Where's Dante?"

"Asleep," Skylar states in a bored tone. "The door to the room he slept in is locked."

"Mmnah go wahak him uhp," Xavier mumbles through a mouthful of eggs.

"What?" I laugh as Michelle tries to mimic him while giggling.

"I'm going to wake him up." He pushes himself away from the table and sprints down the hall.

We listen from the kitchen, wondering how Xavier is going to get through the locked door. Something thick and dark is hanging overhead. I can't put my finger on it, but it's suffocating and sinister. It works its way into us, and I can feel the aura of negativity surround our group. Michelle seems to be the only one at peace with the situation. She smiles and pushes her eggs around, dividing them into halves as if to share with an imaginary friend. She steals more meat from Xavier's plate and lays the pieces carefully over half of the eggs she has piled up, giggling to herself. She doesn't touch that half.

"Come on, time to wake up!" Xavier pounds on Dante's door.

No answer.

"Dante! Wake up! Let's go!"

Nothing.

"You're not funny, dude!" Xavier shouts. "Wake up!"

Silence.

"Fine, I'm kicking the door down!"

I cringe as the wood of the doorframe splinters under his force. My parents won't mind a broken door on a room we never use.

I hope.

More silence follows. The air is still. I pull Skylar to his feet and drag him towards the room. "We'll be right back."

We walk cautiously to Dante's room. Anxiety fills me as the worst thoughts circulate in my head. The atmosphere is evil for a good reason: Dante's body lies unmoving under Xavier's sobs.

"Xavier..." Skylar is shaking as he stumbles into the room. His legs contain nothing but jelly.

Shock fills me as I look at Dante's lifeless face. His wrists are stained red and blood floods the floor like a stagnant river. He hid his pain so well. He smiled and laughed and cracked such stupid jokes. He put on the perfect act, and we had no idea how alone he felt once the day was over. I try not to beat myself up, but how can I not? I allowed Dante to die. Why wasn't I there for him?

Why didn't he talk to me? Or anyone?

I want nothing more than to rewind time and pause it while he was still alive. I'd hug him and tell him how much he is loved.

My eyes swell with pain and tears. I bury it quickly. I have to be strong for Xavier, Skylar, and Michelle. I turn on my heel and head back downstairs. Words won't form when I see them. My tongue twists, and my throat has too many stones in it, but tears make their way down my cheeks without my consent.

Casey gasps, and Sarah looks at her.

"Dante's uh...he's uh...dead." I shake out the words like I'm removing thorns from my skin.

They embrace each other, and I realize I have no idea how to comfort them. Michelle bursts into tears and hugs Casey, begging for her favorite brother to come downstairs. I run back to the room, sensing that I'm just an awkward presence in the kitchen.

Xavier and Skylar's expressions are blank, and they're trembling. Their eyes are red and puffy.

"Hey, talk to me." I shake Skylar.

"About what exactly?" Skylar spits.

I brush it off, pull my phone from my boot, and call 911. I tell them my friend is dead—that he's killed himself—and then give them my address and name. They say they'll be there in no time. Once they hang up, I call my parents and tell them what's going on. They ask me if they should come home. I somehow convince them that we'll be fine. The fact that the cops are coming probably eases any doubt they have about whether or not the situation will be handled properly.

"Are you okay, Alana?" My father's voice is small.

"Yeah," I lie, biting my cheek and wanting to scream.

Before the police arrive, I make sure all of my paraphernalia is out of sight. The house still smells like eggs and bacon, so any odorous traces of illegal substances are hidden. Even so, I follow the officers closely as they walk through my home. My brain clouds, and every word they say sounds foreign. Xavier ends up taking over and talking to them.

Michelle hugs Skylar's legs. "Everything is okay, big brother. Dante is safe now." She's still crying, but the sound is silent.

My heart shatters at her words. My chest caves in under their weight. Sarah stares out the window, waiting loyally for Xavier to return. Casey runs into my arms, presses herself into my chest, and lets the rest of her tears fall. I pat her hair and kiss her head.

After a while, I speak up. "I think you guys should go find Lily and tell her what happened." It'll be better if they go. Xavier, Skylar, and I won't be helpful. We only want to become numb and messed up.

"I want to be with you right now," Casey whispers into my chest.

"And I want to comfort Xavier," Sarah murmurs. "He's falling apart."

"Please let me handle them alone." I look at Sarah.

Her large brown eyes plead with me, but I hold strong. Xavier won't want to be hugged and held. It isn't his style. He'll want to get so wrecked that he won't be able to walk straight.

"Alana's right," Skylar whispers. He's on his knees, arm around Michelle. "Wanna go with them?" he asks softly.

She wipes her face and nods. A small smile begins to creep onto her dirty face. Casey pushes herself away from me and walks towards Sarah. She pulls her away from the window and holds her hand.

"Let's go tell Lily," she encourages.

"No! Why can't we just bring them with us?" Sarah pouts.

"They want to be alone!" Michelle stomps her foot.

"Okay, okay." Sarah easily gives in to the toddler.

They leave the house and jump into Sarah's run-down sedan. Xavier grabs Michelle's car seat from his vehicle and quickly puts it into Sarah's. He cradles Sarah's face in his hands and kisses her long and hard. He murmurs something and encourages them to leave and comfort Lily.

I can't let this sadness fill me. When I hear the car pull out of the driveway, I run to my room and shut the door, locking it. I prep some of the heroin, draw it into a needle, and fill my bloodstream with it.

Picking myself up, I sneak past Xavier and Skylar. There's a handle of whiskey in the kitchen somewhere. I know there is. My father always keeps it on hand. It's just hidden now.

Again.

It isn't hard to find—he only has it under the sink.

I grab it and find the two brothers sitting on the floor, staring at the carpet. I sit with them, open the bottle, take a swig, and hand it to Xavier. He grasps the neck, tilts it back, and takes a healthy gulp before passing it to his brother.

Neither of them shiver like I do. It's like drinking water to them.

Is the ability to drink alcohol without tasting it a genetic thing, or am I just bad at it?

We drink in silence for a few moments before Skylar opens up the conversation. "Remember that time Dante stole sandwiches from the deli so we could eat? It was like he brought home another Christmas." He looks at Xavier, who grins weakly.

"Yeah, he got Michelle a cookie." Xavier takes another swig before handing the bottle to me. "He got you out of trouble a few times, too."

"More than a few." I drink. "And his stupid jokes!" I laugh.

"What's green, has four wheels, and would kill you if it fell out of a tree?" Xavier stares at us.

"Hm?"

"A pool table. I lied about the wheels." He chuckles to himself while a few tears escape.

I met Dante at the same time I met Skylar in elementary school. We traded drinks because I wanted the chocolate milk and he had never had a juice pouch before. He had only had the small boxes that leave a cardboard taste lingering in the straw.

We talk of our memories. We talk about his life. We talk about the parts we wish we saw. The ones we overlooked. The spaces between the conversations are stuffed with silence and tears.

We talk until our lips run out of words, and we drink until the bottle runs dry.

CHAPTER SEVENTEEN

When I wake up, the television is playing, and the scent of pizza dances around us. I pull myself up onto my elbows and see my parents sitting on the couch. The empty bottle is by my feet. Xavier is curled up beside the couch, and Skylar is awake under the table, staring at the bottom of it. He turns to me and attempts to smile, but can't find the muscles to turn his lips.

"Your daughter is awake." Skylar looks at my dad and stares back up again.

"I'm sorry." I look at him. "We needed this though. You have to understand." My stomach flips and my head is pounding.

"I'm not mad," he says softly. "I understand. I bought pizza, but Sky and X don't seem to want to eat. Please have at least a slice. Convince them to do the same. Please." He sounds desperate. He doesn't know how to handle a situation like this.

Neither do I.

I can't process it. I want something to make me numb. My body shakes from more than just the hangover. Still, I wobble my way to the table and grab two slices of pizza. I sit beside Skylar and move the table away from him with a push of my hand. I give him the slice, and he gets up to nibble at it mindlessly. I wake Xavier again with a nudge of my foot. When I hand him the slice, he shakes his head.

"It's not a request, Xavier." I shove the plate into his hands. "Eat."

Grabbing two more slices, I sit beside my dad and give him one. I rest my head on his shoulder and curl my legs up on the couch. I can only bite at the corner. My stomach won't allow food to enter it.

An hour passes, and the bells above the door sing. Michelle is first to find her way into the living room. She cuddles up in Xavier's lap, and he tears up some of his pizza for her. Casey and Sarah are close behind, their faces downcast.

"Lily said she wants to be left alone," Casey tells us.

So, that's it.

With Dante gone, Lily vanishes. Like smoke against a gray background, she becomes invisible.

The monster inside of me is slashing away as the screaming reverberates around my skull. I pull myself away from everyone, go to my room, and get dressed. A small baggie of heroin is stuck neatly in my bra before I walk back to them.

Michelle is sitting with my father when I return, and he's changed the channel to cartoons for her. Xavier, off the couch, holds up a set of keys when he sees me enter. My father tells us to have fun while Skylar forces himself off the floor, groaning dramatically.

Skylar, Casey, and I push ourselves into the back seat while Sarah calls shotgun. We pull out of the driveway and ride in absolute silence for what seems like an eternity before Xavier turns the radio on and accelerates at a terrifying speed. He turns up the radio as he weaves in and out of cars and the speedometer rises bit by bit.

There's anger in his eyes when he glances at us through the rearview mirror before refocusing his vision. My adrenaline rises and boils just behind my ears and I stomp my foot a couple times and holler with excitement. I encourage him to go faster. He has a white-knuckle grip on the wheel, and he shoots me a look through the mirror. A smirk forms on his face, and he pushes the car even further. There's a sharp curve up ahead that will divert us away from the traffic and towards a bridge. Xavier's racing for it, and shows no intention of slowing down.

"Xavier, knock it off!" Sarah cries. "You're scaring me!"

Xavier just laughs. At the last second, he slams on the brakes and slides the car around the corner before stopping at the bridge. He pulls over to the curb and steps out. We follow suit and slam the car doors behind us. I look around, and the realization of where we are hits me. We would come to this bridge as kids and jump into the water long before we met Sarah and Casey. Dante was the first to bring us here and the first to launch himself into the water. He didn't jump off the edge of the bridge because he was following his friends.

He was leading them.

It's been years since we've stopped here.

I look at Xavier, and he shoots me a sly grin, shaking a hidden finger at his side. I give him a single nod to let him know that I know where we are.

"What the hell was that about?" Sarah screams, shoving Xavier.

Well, she tries. Xavier doesn't budge.

The bastard is made of steel—she can't move him.

He kisses her forehead and lights up a cigarette. Smoking it quickly, he walks to the edge of the bridge. Xavier climbs onto the concrete ledge and peers down, his toes teetering. He spins on his heel, flicks his cigarette into the air before him, and falls backwards in time with the descending ember. The sound as he crashes into the water is eerie. Sarah is shaking. I almost feel bad.

Almost.

Skylar snaps out of his stupor. "What just happened?"

"Xavier jumped off a bridge. Poor guy never stood a chance." I keep my eyes down.

Does Skylar not know where we are? Has he dissociated here too?

"You're such a jerk, Alana!" He marches up to me and pushes my shoulder.

Casey goes to the edge of the bridge to looks down. She's the only one brave enough to act upon the morbid curiosity that boils within each of us. The same feeling a person gets when they drive past a gruesome car accident.

No one will actually admit to this, but everyone slows down to get a good look at the damage.

"Oh my god!" She spins back around with her mouth covered and her eyes wide in shock.

I rush up to her and glance over the concrete ledge. I have to bite the inside of my cheek to keep myself from laughing. Xavier is waving at us with a huge smile on his face. He puts a finger to his lips, points to Casey, and then to himself.

"I'll make sure she's okay," he mouths dramatically.

"Never thought hitting water would make this much of a mess," I sigh deeply while shaking my head. "You wanna do this?" I say in a low tone to Casey.

"I trust him," she whispers.

She climbs up and leans forward as if examining the scene in more detail. I send her over with a push to her butt and watch her until she hits the water below. Xavier swims to her and asks if she's good. She's nodding and beaming with excitement. Casey hugs Xavier and giggles into her hand.

"Well, that's one less bill to pay." I shrug.

Not that I pay any of her bills.

I don't think she even has any bills.

I wink at Skylar and plead internally that he'll finally remember where we are. I see his eyes light up seconds before he's sprinting for the ledge. He leaps over it and dives into the water below.

"What is going on?" Sarah is in hysterics.

I turn my back to her and look down. The others aren't paying attention to me, and Sarah has her head buried in her hands. I seize the opportunity to take the baggie out of my bra and snort it into my system. I do this quickly and throw the tiny bag to the ground.

"Sarah, come here," I call to her.

"No!" She looks up with fury.

I roll my eyes and grab her by the arm, pulling her up and dragging her to edge of the bridge. She struggles against me, but it doesn't do any good. Once we get to the ledge, I pick her up, set up down on, and push her over before she can jump down. I watch as she falls and Xavier smiles wide. Once she surfaces, she screams at Xavier and the others. She gives me a middle finger, slaps Xavier, and splashes Casey and Skylar. I turn my back to them and take out my phone. The monster is still rearing its ugly head. One small dose just isn't enough. Leaning against the wall, I dial Creature's number.

"Hey?" he answers with a cough.

"Hey, it's Sunshine." My words tumble out of my mouth. "And?"

"I need something to knock me out." I kick a rock across the road with my foot.

"Meet me later tonight. Need any more rigs?" he asks casually, like questioning whether someone needs needles is normal.

"Not now. I'll see you later." I hang up.

I'm glad Creature is high because he doesn't ask about the money I still owe him. It won't take him too long to remember though, and I'm going to cheat him out again. I don't have a choice—I am running out of money.

I can stop doing drugs.

I won't, but I can.

I'll pay him for the drugs he's going to give me. I just won't pay him back for the other stuff. Not yet.

I put my phone in the car and run to the ledge. Like Skylar, I launch myself with a vault into the water. Wind sweeps through me, and adrenaline spikes my heart. Only seconds pass before I plunge beneath the cold surface. It shocks me for a moment before I swim towards the light that breaks through the rippling up above.

Before long, we climb out of the river and back to the car. Piling in, we laugh and joke and speak rapidly. We talk about Dante and how he jumped off that bridge without knowing about the water below. When he surfaced, the rest of us had jumped in at once.

Xavier drives Casey home first, then Sarah. He picks up Michelle from my house, and they reluctantly walk back to their hell. At home, my parents are zoned into the television with full wine glasses in their hands. A bottle of red wine sits on the coffee table. I don't say hello, I only sweep past them silently. My mom's purse is on the kitchen table, open and inviting. With stealth, I snatch three twenties from her wallet.

She won't notice.

She'll just think she spent it on food or wine.

I run to my room, grab a purse, and nearly sprint out the door before I can be spotted. Still wet from the dive, I go back to the car and drive to I head to the bridge before calling Creature again.

"Do you know where the bridge is where Dante discovered you could jump off and not die?" I ask before he speaks.

"Yeah," he responds. "Why?"

"Can you come here instead?"

He sighs heavily, annoyed. "Fine."

I wait for him on the concrete ledge, my legs dangling over. My boots are sitting on the sidewalk, and my feet are bare, the cool air fluttering against them. When he arrives, he sits beside me. He hands me a black plastic bag. I peek inside to see a bottle of cough syrup, four baggies of heroin, and an eight-ball of cocaine. I close the bag and smile at him.

"You know me so well."

"Yes," he says. "Yes, I do. You want all of it?"

"You act like that's a real question." I look into the bag again as if I'm gazing upon an ancient relic that will turn me into a queen.

"It's $180 then."

I dig into my purse to pull money out from the bottom, count out what I have, knowing I'm short, and hand him the wad of cash. With that, he jumps down and leaves. I sigh with relief when he takes the money without counting it. The bottle of cough syrup makes my insides turn as I gulp it down. I leave the rest for later. It will take a while for the high to kick in, so I stare at the water below patiently.

Within a half hour, my head begins to feel heavy and full of fuzz. My stomach rolls, and I don't attempt to prevent it from emptying into the river. Once it escapes my gut I'm done, my world spins and pulses; it warps, turns, and distorts. Slowly, I climb off the ledge to the sidewalk. I have to sit down and carefully pull on my boots. My limbs are filled with air, and walking is like stepping on marshmallows. A smile stretches my lips and spans across my cheeks, and I am sure my pupils make my eyes look black. Knowing that driving the metal death machine is not an option, I walk. I'm not sure where I'm going. The hallucinations from the dextromethorphan in the cough syrup make me wander aimlessly around the town, searching for a final destination that will never be found.

CHAPTER EIGHTEEN

"Hey, wake up." The raspy voice barely makes it to my tired ears. I'm shaken. "Honey, wake up."

"Yeah, I'm up." I try to stand up and hit my head on the bench I'm half under. "Don't touch me, okay?"

It's dark out, and the sky is touched with stars. My vision is still blurry and I feel sick. I swallow hard and rise to my feet, doing my best to steady my balance and act as normal and sober as possible in front of the stranger. I don't know why. Sober people don't pass out under benches in the park.

"Sorry about that," he apologizes. "You all right? Do you need any help?"

The stranger is tall and thin, with hollow cheeks and bags under his light green eyes. He has a crooked smile that shows a missing tooth. There's white and gray scruff on his chin that doesn't match with the long brown hair on his head.

"I'm fine." I sit down, my world still spinning recklessly. I'm not high anymore. Just sick. Or I am still high, *and* sick. It's hard to tell.

"You might wanna ease up a bit, no? You'll end up like me." He chuckles humorlessly. "Homeless and alone."

Ignoring his comment, I make sure that my drugs and wallet are still hidden in my purse before I walk off. I can find my way home now. If anything, the high is at least wearing off. The weight of depression on my chest is like a stone, and the hooks of the monster in my head grows deeper with each step. I retrieve a baggie of heroin from my purse and snort it with a rolled up dollar bill. My eyes feel heavy, and my body is fills with exhaustion. My stomach churns again, but it's too empty to expel food. Stomach acid burns my throat as it forces it's way up my esophagus and onto the sidewalk.

I struggle to stay awake long enough to make it through the front door. No bells jingle.

Did I enter the right house?

I look around and smell cigarette smoke and beer. This is Skylar's house. I fall twice on my way to their living room, praying that their parents aren't home. I don't need their father's drunken rage or their mother's psychotic outbursts right now. Chances are I'm wrong, but I'm not leaving. I won't make it to my place anyway.

I don't feel like passing out on the streets again. It gives off the wrong impression.

Sarah is curled up on the couch, clutching a pillow to her chest and crying. I'm sure it's because of Dante, but Xavier could have done something stupid again. She sees him as a saint gone astray. Really though, he's just a whore —and kind of a jackass. We still love him though.

I stumble to the couch, banging my leg on the coffee table upon my arrival.

The blanket from the top of the sofa snags on something

when I rip it down and wrap it around me. Laying a pillow down on the floor, I collapse onto it. My world falls around me as I drift into a dreamless slumber, curled up into the fetal position on the dirty ground.

CHAPTER NINETEEN

A pillow hits my face twice before I fully come to and I swat at the air in frustration. "What?" I groan.

I open my eyes a bit to see Casey standing over me with her fist clutching her soft weapon of choice. I lift myself up enough to grab her around the waist. She kicks off her shoes and wiggles her cold feet to rest between my calves. Content and snuggled up against her, I fall asleep once more. Xavier shakes us awake at noon and informs us that his dad is spending the day at the bar, and their mom is passed out cold in her bed. We sit on the couch and stare at the television set. I ignore Xavier and his mindless channel-flipping as Michelle yells at him each time he passes a colorful cartoon. After a few minutes, Skylar stumbles in from his room. He sits down on the other side of his brother and snaps his fingers in front of his eyes. Xavier doesn't respond. He just keeps scanning through the channels. Skylar jumps up and starts to punch at his older brother's face, his fist only inches from him. He laughs and bobs around; Michelle cheers him on with claps and giggles filled with glee.

Xavier glances up at his brother with confusion on his

face. He moves in a blur, throwing the remote down and tackling Skylar to the ground. They wrestle around for a bit with grins on their faces as the three of us sit on the couch and watch.

"Boys are stupid," Michelle scoffs at her brothers.

"Yes, they are," I agree.

Xavier throws Skylar down to the floor and sits on his chest, holding his arm up with his wrist in a lock and threatening to bend it forward.

"What's up, Sky?" he says nonchalantly. "You okay down there?"

I can't ignore the sharp talons of my devil any more. The dark cloud is coming back, and I am craving the numb sensation that comes with the drugs. I zone out, away from the brothers, as I try to fight away the evil in my head. Casey grabs my hand and leads me into the dirty kitchen. She tries talking to me, but I can't seem to focus on the words. Casey glides around the kitchen and opens cabinets until she finds a loaf of bread. She checks it for mold, pulls out two slices, and sticks them into the toaster. Her feet slide along the tiles as she dances around the room.

I watch her, and a smile worms its way to my lips. My chest expands with love.

"Why do you stay?" I finally ask, rather quietly.

"What?" She doesn't stop moving as she speaks.

"Why do you stay with me? I'm not going anywhere in life. This addiction is eating me alive. Why do you stay? You deserve so much better."

She stops and looks at me with a hurt expression in her eyes. "Are you trying to break up with me, Alana?"

"No!" I grab her shoulders and press my lips to hers. Mine are dry, and hers are soft and taste like mangos.

"I love you." She sighs, pries my hands from her shoul-

102

ders, and kisses my knuckles. "Even your flaws. I know what you're really capable of. *You* just need to realize it. I'm here for the whole ride. Bumps, spins, crashes, and all. I just get overwhelmed sometimes. You worry me."

"I love you, too." I can't think of how to respond to the last statement. It makes me feel empty, yet full of bubbling anxiety.

The cravings begin to start at my chest, and slowly make their way up my neck. My head echoes with deathly a shrill. I frown at Casey, and she waves her hand at me before turning back to her task.

On the top shelf, towards the back of the cabinet, is black coffee cup, where I hide a small stash of cocaine. I take a small baggie from it and sit back down on the counter and snort the white powder into my nose through a cut straw and it goes down like a smooth drink.

"I think Xavier just vowed to behave," Casey says, trying to make the situation as normal as possible.

"Shocking."

CHAPTER TWENTY

We end up walking around outside, inhaling the fresh air. The only thing to do around here is trudge from one end of town to the other. We can admire the few tall buildings with walls made of tinted glass and hang out at the local park. It's no wonder most of us do drugs to pass the time. Being bored while sober sucks, but being bored while high is tolerable. Well, at least to me. The minutes are blank and pass by unacknowledged. We find ourselves at the aforementioned park, sitting in the bed of the pickup truck. I notice Skylar staring at a girl that is sitting in the pavilion, her nose is buried in a book. His eyes are glazed over and have an almost dreamy look to them. I jump out of the truck, and dart for the girl.

Sitting beside her, I move closer until our shoulders touch. She has wavy red hair, pale skin, and freckles that spot the skin along her nose and cheeks. She is small and skinny; her shirt hangs loosely off her frame. I stare at the words on the pages until she looks at me.

"Hello?" Her voice sings like wind chimes. "Do I know you?"

"I'm Alana," I tell her. "Now you know me. I think my friend likes you." I point to the truck full of rowdy morons.

"Well, I'm Emily," she introduces herself. "And which friend?"

"The one with the blond hair." I admire a small colorful tattoo behind her ear that she reveals when she tucks a strand of hair behind it.

"Is he okay?" she says with alarm.

"Hm?" I look at him and see that he's trembling.

I jump to my feet and give her Skylar's number. When I get back to my friends, Sarah and Casey are keeping their distance as Xavier is holds Skylar by the shoulders, attempting to stop the shaking. He smacks his brother's face a few times to try to get him to snap out of it. Finally, Skylar glares at him finally and cocks his head to the side.

"Don't fucking touch me!" he screams, clawing at Xavier's face.

What is going on?

Xavier lets go of him and Skylar falls to his knees, still shaking. The tremors are become more violent as time progresses. He tilts his head back and laughs as if Satan has escaped his lungs.

He's finally snapping.

Tearing apart at the seams.

"What do I do?" Xavier looks at me in a panic. "Alana! Help me! Please!" He grabs my arms. "Please! I don't know what to do."

To see someone as strong and steadfast as Xavier begging for help is unbearable. I kneel in front of my best friend and cup his hands in mine. He stares at me with blank eyes. I'm not sure if he's even in there.

"Skylar, listen to me. Calm down." It isn't like I know what I'm doing either.

His eyes begin to dart around to each face in the group. I detect them examining us, silently begging us to somehow break him free. He laughs again, and begins to curling into himself.

"Skylar, focus!" I grab his face so he can only look at me. "Don't focus on them. I know you're scared, but you need to relax. Breathe."

He takes a deep, unsteady breath, and tears begin to fill his eyes. Then he pushes me aside and vomits. I rub his back and repeat to both him and Xavier that everything will be okay. Skylar collapses forward, his face inches from the mess.

I look up at Xavier, who throws his head back with a defeated groan before scooping up his brother to throw him into the truck. Unsure of what to do, and completely at a loss of words, we drive him to the hospital. Maybe someone there can give us an explanation about what is going on. The ride is silent, and Xavier drives well over the speed limit to get us there as quickly as he possibly can.

The hospital is well lit with thin carpeted floors and seats that have a layer of padding worn down from too many people sitting for far too long. We stay in the waiting room with Skylar barely coming back to the world. He isn't dying, nor is he really a danger to himself, so we wait. A nurse finally calls us back, and we follow like well-behaved children.

She escorts us to a small room and pulls the curtain around us. It takes a few minutes for a doctor to appear. He's shorter than Xavier by nearly a foot with black hair cut short and squared off at the top. His brown eyes droop with exhaustion and I wonder how often he sleeps. It probably isn't much. The man is stocky and holds himself high, as if he believes that he is as big as someone like Xavier. He introduces himself as Doctor Zaltman before talking to Xavier, who talks with confused panic.

He doesn't know what's going on with his brother. None of us do.

Doctor Zaltman tries to touch the stethoscope to Skylar's chest, but Skylar snatches it and yanks it out of his hands, throwing the instrument onto the ground.

"Don't fucking touch me!" he growls.

"I don't want to hurt you." Zaltman picks up his equipment and tries again.

Skylar thrashes at him, and the doctor stumbles back. He picks himself up and walks out of the room. Doctor Zaltman returns with four bigger guys—two of them in police uniforms.

Xavier turns to us. "I think I can handle it from here, thanks." He begins to usher us out, glancing back at the officers and his brother. "You guys should go."

"Are you sure?" I ask.

He turns his back to us, so we leave.

Sarah calls a ride home, and Casey takes up the offer to join her.

For the longest time, I just stand outside the hospital, unaware of my surroundings as I try to wrap my head around what's going on inside. Has Skylar really just hit his absolute breaking point? Will he be able to snap out of it and come back to us? The wailing inside of me has become unbearable. I just want all of this—the dark clouds that hang over me, the screaming that slashes at my head and chest, life itself—to stop. Addiction is a battle with all losers and no winners.

This can only end one way, and I just wish the end would hurry up.

With shaking fingers, I dial Tiger's number. Creature

isn't going to cut it this time. Besides, I don't feel like asking for favors from someone who I owe money to.

"Hey." His voice comes through quickly.

"Yeah, hey." My words are shake more than my hands. "It's Sunshine. Creature said he had rigs, but I uh... I trust yours more."

"No problem. Meet me at the park."

All business.

A deep sigh escapes from my lips, and I have to force my legs to walk me to the given location. Tiger is already waiting when I get there.

Can this guy teleport?

He has abandoned his usual casual businessman attire and is wearing a gray hoodie despite the humid weather. I assume he just ran out quickly without regard for how he looks this time. He has a backpack on the bench beside him, a lit cigarette held carelessly between his fingers. I sit next to him.

"Can you do this by yourself yet?" he teases me.

"Shut up." I scowl at him and hold out my hand. "I'm not in the mood."

He chuckles and takes out the supplies. He hands me an old spoon and some of the brown mixture. I light a lighter under the utensil and coagulate the drugs in it. Tiger grabs the needle and pulls the liquid into it. I take it from him and find a vein in my arm quickly. When the drugs release, I fall over with the needle still in my arm.

"Too much?" He stands over me laughing, tugging and takes the needle from my skin.

"Nah, man. Just enough."

I hop to my feet and give him a hug. I love this feeling. It's like the sweet beginnings of addiction all over again.

"Just be careful, Sunshine." He touches my shoulder. "Remember, if you need anything—anything at all—don't hesitate to call me."

CHAPTER TWENTY-ONE

I float home, no longer aware of the mess that circulates around in my head like a tornado. Xavier and Skylar are both there, sitting on the couch. Skylar looks out of his mind with a stare that drills through the wall in front of him.

"What happened?" I ask.

"They suspect dissociation of some sort." Xavier looks at his brother. "They don't really know, so they gave him something to calm him down for now."

"He doesn't need to be admitted?"

"I can hear you, Alana." Skylar turns to me slowly. "I'm high. Not deaf."

"You didn't need to be admitted?" I glare at him. "You lost it, man."

"I'm good now." He smiles stupidly. "We should go out. You still have those fake IDs?"

"Yes!" I jump around before running into my room and snatching them.

Creature knows a guy. He introduced me to said guy. I never found out his name. I just know his fake IDs worked.

"Should you really be drinking on this?" Xavier is concerned for his brother. He's already lost two, and he'll be damned if he loses another.

"How about you don't tell me how to medicate." Skylar sticks out his tongue.

Xavier rolls his eyes and leaves with us. He drives to the club that hangs in the middle of the small city. We show the bouncer our IDs, but he hardly glances at them. This whole place is illegal—drugs fly around here more than the liquor does.

Sped-up pop music blares from the DJ station, and a large crowd of people writhe on the dance floor in rapid motions, like palm trees caught in a hurricane—none them can really dance. Booze and drugs will make anyone think they can move like fluid ocean waves. My adrenaline is soaring. Along with the high, I feel on top of the world.

I am completely invincible.

When I spot Tiger by the bar, my heart flies out of my throat.

I need uppers—something to make me go completely out of my own head. Before I can get to him, Xavier beelines for my drug dealer. They talk to one another, making animated gestures as if they're old friends. After several minutes, Xavier makes his way back to us. He hands each of us a single, tiny paper tab. Skylar stares at his as if he is looking at a tiny dancer in his palm.

"It's acid, you idiot." Xavier pops his onto his tongue.

Skylar and I follow his lead down into the rabbit hole.

"Have fun, kids." He bids us a farewell and disappears into the crowd.

I look at Skylar and shrug. We make our way to the bar, pushing past people covered in glow paint and smelling of both heavy cologne and fruity alcohol. I make sure we find a spot near Tiger. As Skylar orders our shots and drinks, I turn to the man beside me.

"Again?" He lifts an eyebrow.

"No." I shake my head. "Snow."

We talk to each other with our heads ducked down. Each word is nearly shouted into the other's ear so we can hear one another over the loud music.

Tiger nods and pulls a small baggie from his pocket. "This is all I have on me."

"I'll take it." I pull a ten from my pocket and we make the trade.

I manage to tuck the loot into my bra before Skylar taps my shoulder. Tiger is soon yanked back into another crowd of people. He will be pulled into several different directions here, and he will leave a rich man.

Well, he'll at least leave with more money than he came in with.

"I got us whiskey and liquid marijuana." Skylar hands me a short glass with ice and dark, honey-colored liquor and a shot glass filled with bright green, almost glowing courage.

We pour the shots down our throats and sip on the whiskey. He orders two shots of the same thing, and these two quickly turn into two more. We sit on the stools and sip our drinks until the bar spins and pulses. Skylar turns to me with a stupid grin spread from cheek to cheek. I try to hold the laugh that wants to escape from me, but it pours from my mouth in a fit of giggles. I put my hand up to cover my lips as if that will hold the sound inside.

The light fuses with the music, and they sway with an array of beautiful colors. Solid things buzz and vibrate around us. Objects and people that move do so in slow motion, leaving a trail of evidence behind them.

It is a gorgeous and chaotic mess.

I push my way to a door. Skylar follows close behind as we weave our way through the distorted patrons of the bar.

The large, hairy bouncer clad in black doesn't let me leave. I want to see the sky, but he blocks the exit. I just make a 'meh' noise and twirl my way back into the crowd, Skylar at my side.

"Why do you think they hired a gorilla as a bouncer?" Skylar looks over his shoulder.

"What?" I glance back, but can't see it. "Don't know."

Without the option to step outside instead and being surrounded by sweaty people who can't properly locate the beat to the music that is pumped into them, my trip descends into a fiery hell pit. The crowd's eyes turn black, and they have blood in their mouths, staining their teeth and seeping from the corners of their lips. The music spits lyrics that come out backwards and in guttural gasps. I hear conversations around me as people shout to one another about the night—their words sound Latin. I grab Skylar's shoulder. His eyes are black as well, and his skin becomes paler. I gaze at him with wide eyes.

"It's me." He cups my face and smiles. "Need to get out of here?"

"Yes."

He scans the club looking for an exit that isn't blocked by a gorilla. Finding one, he takes hold of my hand and leads me to a small door just behind the bar. We duck past servers and bartenders, acting as if we belong there.

We only need to leave. The air outside is damp and cold. I spread my arms out and invite it in, letting it wash away the dark entities playing in my head. It doesn't work, but I feel lighter without the walls imprisoning me. The clouds are warped and black, but the stars shine through them like portals beckoning me towards another world.

I hold my hand out in front me and watch the trails that it leaves behind as I wave it around with wonder. Skylar wraps a hand around my forearm and turns me towards him.

His eyes are black, but I know who he is. I watch the shades of his skin morph and bubble. He is pale before he gives off a hint of green that glitters into purple. Either this is the strongest hallucinogen I've ever tried or it's laced with something out of this world.

"How the hell are you doing that?" I wonder aloud.

He chuckles. "Doing what?"

"Your skin is glowing." I make a motion as if to tell him it's blowing my mind.

"I do that sometimes." He looks at his arm and back at me. "Let's get you somewhere safe."

"Good plan," I agree.

How is he handling this so well? What is he seeing that I'm not?

We make it to his house, tripping over our feet along the way. The walk is a blur, and I don't quite know where we are at first. He sneaks me inside, careful not to wake up the sleeping drunkard on the couch. Skylar locks his door and turns on the television, keeping the volume low. I can't hear it, but I don't care. I'm too busy trying to quiet my mind. He curls up on his bed and turns his back to me, falling asleep within a few seconds. Sunlight is beginning to peek its way through the clouds, lighting the sky with subtle shades of pink and blue. I can hear the chattering of a few birds.

The hallucinations are distant and nearly gone, but my stomach hurts. I wrap an arm around my waist and lie in the dark, shaking. Feeling the contents of the bar making their way to my throat, I drag myself to the bathroom. I keep the lights off and close the door behind me, locking it. My arms wrapped around the toilet, I begin to puke out the night. Once I think I'm done, I huddle into the fetal position on the floor, groaning in pain. I crawl my way to the shower and turn it on as cold as possible, undress, and sit down under the stream of water before turning it so hot it makes my skin sting. I breathe and feel better. When I turn off the water, I have to rush for the toilet again, heaving up more of what my stomach wants to evict. I stay enveloped around the porcelain throne until I pass out on the cold, and dirty tiles.

CHAPTER TWENTY-TWO

I wake up to a light knock at the door.

"Alana." The voice comes through like feathers grazing my cheeks and ears. "Alana, are you alive? Wake up." There is panic, but he keeps his voice soft. "Come on, Alana, wake up. Xavier will kill me if you die in there."

I reach for the door and tap it. My mouth refuses to form words. I stand up and immediately fall back to the toilet. Bright yellow bile expels itself from me in painful gasps. With my stomach completely empty now, I find difficulty in standing up straight. My insides bend in half to protect themselves.

From what?

From me of course.

"I'm alive," I say as I stumble out of the room. "Your dad here?"

"Yeah, but we're safe," he assures me. "You look dead."

"I *feel* dead."

We gather our shoes and head out the door into the warm morning sun. The rays caress our skin and bring life back into us. Well, sort of. I still have to walk with an arm wrapped around my stomach as I focus on not dry-heaving or vomiting more burning bile. We walk, slowly, to the park where we find our group. Casey holds my head to her chest and calls me stupid. I nestle my face into her breasts and smile contently.

If this is what happens when I'm being stupid, I should be stupid more often.

Her hair is pulled back into a loose ponytail, and she wears a black and zip-up hoodie with dark jeans. She smells like cedar wood and smoke. Xavier is lying on a picnic table in the sun with his shirt over his eyes, but he has a keen ear turned toward Michelle, who's swinging a few feet away, and singing a song at the top of her lungs.

"Was he already here when you got here?" I ask Casey, pulling away from her and sitting up straight.

"Nope," she admits. "I found him in my living room. He was passed out with a bag of chips on his lap and salsa on the floor next to the couch."

"What?" Skylar nearly splits himself in two with laughter.

Xavier walks up to us and groans.

"Fun night?" I ask him with a mischievous grin.

"Shut up." He presses his fingers between his eyes. "I don't know what happened between the club and Casey's house." He scratches his head. "I don't know why I ended up at your house. Tell your mom thanks for not freaking out and making me breakfast."

"Did you tell Sarah?" Skylar asks, holding his hand out to ask his brother for a cigarette.

"Fuck no." Xavier throws his head back and hands Skylar what he'd silently requested.

Hours fly, and we recall our night. Skylar begs me to tell him what I had seen during our trip. After a while, I cave. I tell them about the dark forces I witnessed taking over the bodies of those around me. I describe the black eyes and how every word was said in Latin or spoken backwards in phrases I couldn't make out. Xavier compliments my strong will and is impressed that I was able to make it through the night without going to the ER. Casey thanks Skylar for keeping me safe.

We both leave out the part about me passing out in the bathroom, puking my brains up because I combined too many drugs and then attempted to wash them down with torrents of booze.

Our group laughs and jokes with one another until Sarah storms over to us with her arms crossed. She takes a seat beside Xavier, and her face scrunches.

Xavier raises an eyebrow. "What's up?"

"My parents!" She stomps her foot. "God forbid I do anything bad! I was out past curfew, and now I can't borrow the car! I pay rent, so why do I have a curfew? They're completely insane! I can't stand them."

"That's it?" I glare at her. "You have to walk? Tough life. Move out."

She turns and shouts, "No one asked you!"

How the hell does Xavier put up with her all the time? What does he see in her?

Xavier howls with laughter, incapable of holding it in.

She crosses her arms and stomps her foot again. "You guys just don't get it! They're so pushy!"

Xavier looks at me with wide-eyed frustration, he's begging for help. I just watch. She's his problem to deal with. I am my own problem; I don't need more. He turns back to Sarah and presses a stressed hand onto the back of his neck. At this time, Michelle has returned from the swings and hugs Xavier's legs before climbing up on the table to sit beside Skylar and show him a rock she's found. He acts as if it's the coolest thing he's ever seen. With pride, she presents it to Casey and me—we coo over like it's a diamond.

"It's for Dante," she whispers softly, staring at it. She goes back to sit with her brothers, sticking her tongue out at us.

"Your parents aren't bad." Xavier sits beside Sarah on the wooden table. "They're stable. They're there and the most they're asking is for you to be home at a decent hour. Have you tried asking if you could maybe text your mom and let her know you're safe so you won't have a curfew?"

"It's not that easy, Xavier!"

"Consider yourself lucky. Skylar here failed a test and got a black eye." Xavier turns to his brother. "How many times has Dad been in jail?"

"Lost count."

"How about Mom in the psych ward?"

"Lost count."

They hardly ever talk about their mother. Last I knew, she'd been placed in the psych ward and hasn't been out in weeks. Apparently, she'd been stabbing the couch and screaming. Michelle is unfazed by all of this, she's squishing ants beneath her fingertips.

"You're being dramatic, babe." Xavier kisses Sarah's forehead, and she pushes him away.

"No, I'm not."

"Give it up, X," I say. "It's like talking to a bag of bricks."

"Alana, fuck you!" Sarah gives me a middle finger.

Michelle's eyes widen, and she looks at Skylar, who gasps.

"Sarah, seriously?" Xavier's voice is rises. "Watch your

mouth! Michelle is right there." Not that it really matters. Their father curses like a sailor who's broken his leg.

Casey's phone rings, breaking the awkward tension that hangs around us in that moment. She quickly puts it on speaker, knowing it will calm the air. Her mom wants her to go out to lunch with her to a new restaurant down the road. She asks how Xavier is doing and tells him to take care of himself. Casey grabs the keys to the car, gives me a passionate kiss that lifts me to my feet, and runs off. Not receiving the validation she craves, Sarah storms off behind her, asking for a ride. Xavier lies back down and puts his shirt back over his eyes again. I follow Skylar as Michelle drags him to the playground. After an hour, I tell him I'm going home. He nods, but doesn't give me any more acknowledgement than that.

The monster is loud.

I feel sick, and I only want to poison myself.

CHAPTER TWENTY-THREE

My body is getting thinner and weaker. Addiction shows on me like a cancer. My skin hangs on my bones like cold rags, and my ribs are daggers piercing against my lungs. I am dying, and nothing can be done about it. There is simply no escape when you've fallen this far. I could drag myself out of my own grave, but I'm too tired. I'm too high.

I start most days with a mountain of cocaine and end them with a handful of heroin. I've been told that mixing the two can be fatal, but I'm still standing—even if I don't want to be. My hands are shaking when I call Creature. My fingers hit the numbers as my stomach flips.

"What?" he answers.

"You know what." I hope he understands.

"Come over." He hangs up.

I shove my phone into my pocket and head to his place on foot. The cool air keeps me awake as I walk to the rundown apartment building. I'm let in before I even knock. Does he have a camera hidden within the halls to alert him when customers or cops are about to show up at his doorstep? Within seconds of being there, drugs are up my nose, and a needle is placed promptly in my arm. Before long, I am lying on the dirty floor, incapable of moving away from the high's deathly grasp.

"Can I have another hit?" My mind is jumbled, and my mouth is dry.

"No can do, Sunshine." He shakes his head and lies on the floor next to me. He laces his fingers together and places them on his chest. "If I give you another, you'll die, and then Tiger will kill me."

We stay there, on the thin, dusty carpet until our highs begin to fade. Only then does he give me another hit. I take enough to see black and pass out. I wake up already turned on my side with my cheek in vomit. Picking myself up, I sit on the ratty couch. Creature hands me a towel to clean up, not mentioning the mess.

Several days blur by at Creature's apartment. They're filled with getting high and passing out. Food tastes like clay and is hard to stomach, so I don't eat while I'm there. I turn my phone off to ignore the concerned calls and texts from my family and friends. After a nice fat line of cocaine, I head to Creature's bathroom to clean up. I use his chipped sink to wash my face, hands, and arms. I can shower at home. Besides, I need to shave my head and the rest of my body.

When I come out of the bathroom, Creature presses the cold metal barrel of a pistol against my temple. I turn around slowly with my hands up. My chest starts to pound harder than it already is from the cocaine. My heart is about ready to leave its captivity and run out the door.

"Eight-hundred dollars!" He screams, his face almost purple. "The guy threatened to kill me! You'd better think of something fast, Sunshine!"

"What are you talking about?" My voice trembles as I play dumb.

I almost did forget that I owe him money. I don't think it's that much. Is $800 really worth murder?

"You know damn well what I'm talking about!" He hits me over the head with the butt of his gun.

The world spins around me in dizzy waves, and my vision blurs under the impact. Still, I try to take a swing at his face. He hits me again.

And again.

And again.

I taste blood on my tongue, and I can feel it streaming down my face. My body pounds as I struggle to defend against his attack. He screams obscenities at me while his shoes collide with my ribs. I hold up a hand and scream for him to stop. I tell him I'll get him his money. He grabs my arm and yanks me to my feet.

"Walk to the car." Creature spins me around and presses his gun against my spine.

He hands me the keys when we get to his small vehicle. I should drive off and escape while he walks to the passenger's side, but my fear keeps me paralyzed. I can barely see as I fade in and out of consciousness. I am a puppet attached to his strings.

"Drive to the bank," he murmurs, turning up the stereo up to a deafening level—the bass fills my bones.

My head pounds so badly that it makes me sick. I swallow my vomit so I won't make him angrier by puking in his car. I can feel black bruises beginning to show along my skin. Blood travels down my face and pools in my lips, the taste of copper leaves small puddles on the tip of my tongue. I drive to the bank with his gun pressed into my ribs. It takes everything in me to keep myself composed.

"Pull up to the ATM," he demands over the music.

I do as I'm told. With shaking hands, I take out my

wallet, shove the card into the machine, and punch in my number in, surprised I can remember it. Unable to think of anything other than being shot, I take out eight hundred dollars and hand it to Creature.

"I'm driving. Get out."

With my head down, I switch seats with him. He snags my wallet and steals the card and the receipt. I open my mouth to tell him to give me back these two things. He doesn't need them. I can't get the words out before he strikes me over the head again. He leans over my half-conscious body, opens the door, and shoves me out of the car. When I hit the cold cement, he speeds off. I just lie there, crying and bleeding.

I drag myself home, hoping that no one will be there. I find the hidden key among the rocks in the garden, fumble with the door, and crawl inside. Leaving a trail of blood behind me, I make it to the kitchen before collapsing. Sobs wrack my body as pain shoots through me. When I finally force myself into the shower, ice-cold water washes the attack from my bruised skin.

In a desperate attempt to seem like I'm fine, I try to cover the bruises with makeup. I nearly succeed, but can't quite figure out a way to conceal the gashes. I want this whole situation to become a vague, and faded piece of my pathetic past. The stereo speakers crackle a little when I turn them on to drown out my thoughts. The music flows over me as I pull a stash of cocaine from behind the light switch in my room and I take the contents to the living room where there's more light.

My body is aches, and my head feels like it's on fire. The cocaine will make me numb. Soon, I will not know physical pain.

I hear the bells over the door sing and quickly inhale the

last line. I shove the straw and razor blade under the floorboard and crawl onto the couch, where I curl up and stare blankly ahead.

"It is I!" I hear Skylar announce.

There is no use hiding from them. They will see me in this state eventually anyway.

If only I had succumbed to the attack and died under Creature's gun, then they wouldn't have to see me in all my cocaine-fueled glory any longer.

Even with the coke in my body, I still sense a darkness washing over me. Before Skylar and company walk through the house and into the living room, I hobble to my bedroom. Still soaring, I dig around my room until I find a needle and the heroin. I shoot up, hoping it will stop my heart.

CHAPTER TWENTY-FOUR

I don't remember much, but I wake up in my bed with my shoes off and a blanket pulled over my body. When I sit up, I look around my room as it slowly fills with sunlight. Skylar is lying on the floor, staring up at the ceiling, hands folded at his chest.

He peeks at me. "Good morning, Alana."

"What? How long?" I mutter with confusion.

"Two days," he confirms. "It's okay. I'm the only one who saw the bruises. What the hell happened?"

"Nothing," I lie and climb out of bed.

"I cleaned up the blood," he says.

I step over him and shuffle to the bathroom. Death hangs on me when I turn on the shower. My wounds pulsate, so I take a couple of my mom's Vicodin from the medicine cabinet, swallow them with faucet water, and sit in the tub. Naked and shaking, I let hot water beat against my skin. When I step out, I hear my father speaking with Skylar, but I can't make out what it's about.

Shit.

How am I supposed to explain this to them?

My mind spins, and panic in the deepest crevices of my chest bubbles to the surface. I sneak through the hallway to my room and get myself dressed. Slowly and steadily, I apply makeup. My hair is starting to grow back, showing itself in a fuzzy, soft layer. I know I need to shave, but I'm too high. I hear Skylar leave and curse him under my breath.

How dare he make me face them alone!

Perhaps he's punishing me.

Forcing me to show my parents what I have become: a monster.

I take a deep breath and walk out into the kitchen. I can't look them in the eye, and I keep a keen focus on the floor by my feet.

"Oh, my god!" My mother embraces me in a tight hug. She holds me back at arm's length and inspects me. "Are those track marks, Alana?" I can hear the shock and hurt in the syllables of her words.

There is nothing for me to say. I can only glance at my father. Fear and disappointment make him appear helpless.

What am I doing to them?

"What happened, Alana?" my father presses. "Something is wrong."

"I owed someone money and they stole my card," I admit.

"Who?" my father demands.

"I don't know his name." Here's an important rule: never rat out someone who beat you with a gun.

I can't stand to look at them any longer. I shove past, ignoring their commands for me to stay put. The door slams behind me as I rush away from the house. The last thing I hear is my father urging me to cancel my card as soon as possible. My chest pounds while my mind grows dark and fuzzy.

I walk around aimlessly, head pointed at the ground before calling up Creature.

How stupid am I?

All I can think about is getting high.

Why don't I just call Tiger instead? He didn't beat me and steal my money.

My voice shakes when I hear him pick up on the other line. "Creature? It's Sunshine."

"What the hell do you want, cunt? Don't call me. If I see you again, I will kill you. Understand?"

I listen to the dial tone in shock. I should have expected this. I should have seen this coming from miles away. It makes my thirst to achieve a high greater than the peak of Everest—and it's getting stronger. One would think a death threat would slap me in the face with some sort of sense, but it doesn't. Not even a little bit.

Persistent internal screaming bounces around my brain as I continue along the dark streets. I dig my nails into the inner part of my wrist when I see someone lying on the side-walk on the opposite side of the street. Part of me wants to just keep walking past the poor soul, but I'm pulled towards him by both pity and curiosity.

"Oh god," I mutter.

Xavier's left eye is swollen and black. The whites have turned blood red. A round knot protrudes from his fore-head, and there are hand-shaped bruises around his arms; the fingers wrap around his biceps like snakes. His lip is split open, and his breathing is labored.

"What the hell happened, X?" I help him to his feet and start guiding him to the hospital.

"Dad got out." He coughs and holds his head. "I'm so dizzy."

"He was in jail again?" I question. "Does Skylar know?"

"Yeah. I was hoping it would stick this time." He chuckles without humor. "But I've been wrong before. No, Sky doesn't know yet. The bastard and I just so happened to meet here." He stumbles.

When we get to the emergency room, Xavier nearly falls through the doors. He just knocks on the desk, incapable of saying a word. The nurse glances up, takes one look at him, and gasps. Another nurse comes through the doors immediately. Xavier grabs my arm and stares at me pleadingly.

"She comes with me." His words are laced with finality.

The nurse nods and motions both of us forward. "Can you walk, sir?"

"Yes." Xavier sways on his feet. "Alana, call Noah." He hands me his phone. "Skylar should be with him."

I follow behind them as I scroll through his contacts list, looking for the correct name. The nurse sits him on a cot and begins taking his blood pressure. Another enters to give an IV in his hand. He doesn't flinch. His eyes flutter, jumping in and out of consciousness.

Finally finding the name, I hit the call button and wait for the other end.

"Hey, Xavier," answers a familiar voice. "What's up?"

"Tiger?" How does Xavier know him so well that they refer to each other by name—their *real* names? "Your real name is Noah?"

"Yeah..." His voice is slow and cautious. He knows the rules: keep your name to yourself. Handing it out makes you a victim a lot faster. So says Creature at least. "Sunshine, how did you get Xavier's phone? How do you know my real name?"

"Calm down. Xavier told me," I clarify. "He's in the hospital, and he told me to call you and Skylar. Their dad got out again. He's worried about you, I guess?" My suspicions perk. "Why is Skylar with you?"

"We're just hanging out." He pauses. "Xavier's the one in the hospital and he's worried about *us*?" I can almost hear him shaking his head on the other end. "Typical. We'll be there soon. Thanks, Sunshine."

"Alana," I correct him with a knot in my chest.

"Alana." He hangs up.

I take a deep breath and collapse into the chair by Xavier's bed. A nurse hooks him up with morphine to ease his injuries into something more tolerable. Xavier will never admit he's in pain, but we can see it in the quivering of his eyes and the twitching of his muscles. He lies on his back and inhales deeply, trying to stay awake. I intertwine my fingers and dig my nails into my palms to try to focus on something other than my own rapidly twisting mind.

CHAPTER TWENTY-FIVE

I wait for Skylar and Noah outside. I am halfway through my second cigarette when they appear. Noah walks a few paces behind Skylar, who looks worried. His face drops when he sees me standing outside—as if my being away from Xavier's bedside automatically means that Xavier is in trouble. I stub out my cigarette on the side of my boot before slipping it back into the pack.

"He's fine," I reassure him quickly.

Skylar exhales with relief, and Noah rests a hand on his shoulder, shaking him a little bit and smiling. Noah looks me over and gives me a quick nod, which I return. I lead them back to Xavier's room through the long halls that smell like death and bleach. Noah steps towards the bed first. Xavier holds up a fist and Noah bumps it with his knuckles.

"You alive with all this?" Noah jokes as he examines what's in the IV bag.

"More now than I was then." Xavier's words slur a little.

Skylar stands still, scanning his brother. His breath

catches in his chest; I can see the panic fading in and out of him as he does his best to hold it inside.

"Hey, it's okay." Xavier grabs Skylar's hand and pulls him forward, "Really, I'm fine. You're not allowed outside by yourself for a while though."

"What?" Skylar raises his eyebrows. "I'll be fine. I don't need anyone's protection."

"I'll be back later." Noah gives Xavier another fist bump and lets himself out.

How long have they known each other?

Is Xavier aware of the extent of what Noah does?

"Yeah. I know," Xavier says softly, turning his attention back to his brother. "At least make sure Michelle is safe."

"Always," Skylar assures him.

Xavier encourages us to go do something else. He'll be released in no time. He's more than capable of moving around with all those painkillers, so he isn't sure why they're even holding him here.

It's probably because he refuses to tell them who did this to him.

Skylar mumbles an 'okay' under his breath and I follow him out of the room, back through the obnoxiously bright hallways that make me dizzy, and outside to the fresh air that smells like asphalt and gasoline.

"Are you scared?" I ask Skylar.

"Yes," he admits without expression.

Noah is sitting on a curb at the end of the parking lot, wisps of light gray smoke ascending from the end of his glowing cigarette. He lights two more and gives one to each of us. We sit beside him and smoke, taking in the noisy silence of cars zipping past and the bustle of people shuffling through the automatic entrance. Noah rises and offers us both another cigarette. Skylar politely declines, but I take one from the pack and stick it behind my ear.

"Keep in touch, okay, Alana?" He looks at me before turning to Skylar. "Keep your eyes open, kid."

Skylar doesn't respond, and I too keep quiet. Noah walks off, not turning back as he holds his phone to his ear. His conversation drifts into the air and becomes lost. Skylar and I wait on the curb until they let Xavier out. I need a distraction from the howling that shatters apart the inside of my skull, so I decide to spend my night at Casey's.

With caution, Skylar and Xavier make their trek to their own house to sneak Michelle out before going to Sarah's.

No one's home is safe.

CHAPTER TWENTY-SIX

A couple weeks have zipped by in a blur of colors and noise. I spend most of my time at Noah's house getting high. I cut ties with Creature, and Noah provides me with what I desire now. The only difference between the two is that Noah actually cares about his customers.

A dead customer won't make him any money.

Casey is staying the night at his place. We spend the day in his living room smoking until we reach a hazy plateau. Ending up in the spare bedroom, we wake up to birds chirping outside and sunlight inching over the edge of the windowsill. She squirms against my grip and I hold her tighter, burying my face in her hair.

"Alana, I want to get dressed," she exhales.

I groan and let her escape. Following her lead, I throw my legs over the edge of the bed and pull on the dress that's still lying on the floor from last night. I shove on the combat boots that had been tossed to the side and flop back down onto the bed with my arms outstretched. My nose is itching for cocaine. My body is begging for heroin. My brain doesn't care, as long as I get high—and fast.

Casey wants to talk about why I'm staying at Noah's so often. She wants to know if I've told my parents where I am. She asks if I've considered getting help.

I keep my eyes closed with my face towards the ceiling.

"Noah has acid. I can buy us some if you want to do any." I sit up and look at her.

"You didn't answer a single one of my questions." She crosses her arms, hurt and fear in her eyes.

Casey turns on her heel and leaves. I follow behind her through the house like a sick dog—I suppose I sort of am. She walks with her head high through the carpeted hallways and the living room that houses a black leather couch and chair. A large flat screen television rests on a stand, and Noah turns around from his seat and watches her head to the front door. Casey glances behind her shoulder at me as if offering a second chance.

I don't take it. I just stand still—frozen in place like a statue in a courtyard waiting to be torn down.

I turn to Noah and slink down beside him. We stare at the television for a long moment before either one of us speaks.

"So, what do you have?" I ask.

"Drugs." He laughs. "I have drugs."

He lifts the top of his coffee table to reveal a stash hidden beneath in a small cubby. There are a few large packages of marijuana, a couple bags of cocaine, and a handful of bundles of heroin. There is also a book of LSD and a sack of shrooms. It's the first time I have seen his hidden jackpot. My jaw hits the floor and my eyes light up with thirst.

"This is only a quarter of it." He smirks, watching me. "Don't bother looking for the rest. If you steal it, I will shoot you."

I can't tell if he's being serious.

I don't want to believe that Tiger would do something so sinister. Still, an internal part of me knows that he's perfectly capable of it. The reality of in gnaws at me, making my stomach twist. I know that if I *really* steal from, him like I did Creature, he'll have to answer to someone much higher on the food chain. It'll be his life or mine, and I won't blame him if he picks his own.

My heart pounds rapidly when I see the cocaine. My brain goes for the heroin, begging me to take more. I begin to feel sick. My stomach turns, and my head grows hot. Have I already developed a dependence on that brown substance?

"What can't I have?" I ask with wonder.

"The mushrooms," he states matter-of-factly. "They're for Skylar and Emily."

"Emily?" I ask. Skylar has never mentioned Emily. "Oh!" The realization hits me. The girl from the park.

We pass the hours by snorting lines of cocaine off the coffee table until our nostrils are raw with the drug. I take three lines and start cleaning the tabletop and polishing the legs. When that wears off, I take three more and clean something else. Inhale. Exhale. Repeat. The energy that courses through me is impossible to contain. I need to keep busy to release the drug like a poison caught in my lungs. The sudden knock on the door sends me into a paranoid alarm.

"Christ, Alana. Every time." Noah gives me annoyed look. "I have customers. Calm down."

Easier said than done.

Emily glides in like the wind and sits beside Noah with her hands in her lap. Her red hair is pulled back into a knot, and her long, wispy bangs tickle just past her eyebrows. Her raised cheeks are pink, and her light amber eyes watch him with interest. Noah digs out the mushrooms for her and

136

Skylar. Their small dome heads upon long spindly stems jump in the bag as she moves them around.

Noah pulls out a square black electronic scale and sticks an empty bag—the same size as the one that holds the drugs—onto it. He zeroes it out with the bag before putting the mushrooms, still contained, onto the platform. With satisfaction, Emily hands Noah the cash, takes the bag, and leaves.

She doesn't acknowledge my presence, and all she says is 'thank you' to Noah.

My jaw jitters with adrenaline from the cocaine still working its way through me. Noah hands me a packed bowl and a lighter, urging me to calm down again. My eyes dart around, and I curl my vibrating body onto his couch with the bowl to my lips. The smoke is harsh as I inhale a cloud into my lungs. I hold it, counting down seconds in my head before exhaling in a satisfied sigh. I pass the piece to Noah, and we smoke the rest of the day away, trying to let our devils ascend above us in the wafting wisps over our heads. We don't move until we have to load up a rig. Then we travel even higher.

CHAPTER TWENTY-SEVEN

Noah eventually kicks me out of his house. I don't blame him. Putting up with me for long periods of time allows people to realize that I am nothing more than a nuisance. I am only here to take advantage of his generosity anyway. I stopped paying for what I'm taking. Now, I owe someone else money. Still, he gives me a bundle of heroin and a baggie of cocaine, but only after I scrub his house and plead.

My mother embraces me tightly, kissing the top of my dirty head when I step through the door to my home. I can't remember how long I've been gone. I know I don't look the same. My skin hangs on my skeleton like an oversized jumpsuit. Who needs food when you have coke? The scale says I weigh a mere ninety pounds.

My father calls Skylar and lets him know that I've finally showed up at their door.

Skylar and Xavier come over with Michelle in tow. She grips Xavier's hand like a lifeline. He doesn't talk about the bruises or the burns on his arms. Skylar holds me tight and tells me he loves me.

"You look dead," he states flatly.

"I don't look dead, Sky," I tell him. "I *am* dead."

Michelle takes my hand and beams up at me. "No, you're not, Alana."

I just smile back at her, forcing my mouth into the shape of happiness. We head outside and sit on the porch, swaying on the swing with cigarettes between our lips. Michelle picks dandelions in the grass with my mom while my dad sits on the steps. His back is to us; light gray smoke billows from his own cigarette. No one talks. We're too scared to acknowledge anything beyond the silence. My phone vibrates in my pocket, breaking me from a trance. I try to ignore it, but it goes through its cycle a second time, urging me to answer.

The number is unfamiliar. Holding the phone to my ear, I don't say anything. I just wait for the other person to speak first.

"Sunshine?" It's Noah. Why is he using my nickname?

"Yeah," I exhale. "What?"

"I'm in jail." His words tremble.

"What?" I shoot up and pace the floor, taking a longer drag of my cigarette. "How did this happen? Why did you call me?"

"Honestly? I don't know. I couldn't think of who else to call." He pauses. "Someone snitched. My house was raided. They found my stash." Noah sighs, and I can hear the phone move on his end. "Give the phone to Xavier. I know he's there."

"Yeah," I mutter before handing over the phone. "It's Noah. He's in jail."

Xavier grabs it, presses the receiver to his ear, and walks off the porch and into the yard for some privacy. I can't hear what he's saying, and I don't care enough to attempt to read his lips. Not that I can.

"Noah's locked up?" Skylar asks.

"Who is Noah?" my father ponders aloud.

"A friend," I say and look at Skylar. "He's there for reasons."

He makes an exaggerated 'O' with his lips.

Xavier comes back and returns my phone. "We're safe. He'll be okay."

I take a deep breath of relief. Though I used Noah for his abundant, never-ending stash, I almost think of him as a friend. Yeah, I stole from him, but I'd still help him out in a pinch if he really needed it—especially since he never did shoot me. Unlike Creature, who I will never release from a bind, I like Noah. I trust him. More than I should. Trusting people while trapped in this life can get a person killed.

I'm more concerned about not having a dealer anymore. The handful of drugs that weigh down my pocket will barely last me a few days.

I guess there's always Rabbit.

Lighting up another cigarette, I take a seat on the concrete step next to my father. We watch Michelle and my mother make flower crowns from the dandelions Michelle has eagerly plucked from the ground. My father rests his head on top of mine and tells me he loves me. My breathing rattles for a moment, and I can't respond. Of course I love my parents—even if they are absent a lot, even if my mother goes off on rants about her ex-husband from years ago. One I don't know. One I don't care to know. I know all of his flaws, but I just don't know which flaws are fantasies concocted by her brain. I shake the thought from my head. It's not my story to tell.

The demon inside of me is screaming. My high is wearing off, and I have no way to escape from my friends and my parents. I'd been gone for so long.

Was it only days?

Had I been gone for weeks?

It feels like a lifetime, and all I can think about is leaving again.

My father asks the brothers and Michelle if they want to spend the night. He is pretty sure he knows what waits at home for them. He has tried to help before, but they keep getting dragged back into the same environment. I bite the inside of my cheek until it's raw. I can't turn them away just because the screaming in my head is hardly tolerable. I can duck into the bathroom if I really need to.

Skylar gazes at his older brother with a wary look. Xavier nods as if he can read his mind. They don't speak about their exchange, but Skylar seems to relax a little.

"Michelle!" Xavier yells.

She jumps a little, but immediately turns around. "Yes?"

"We're spending the night here, cool?"

She bounces to her feet and hugs my mother, who twirls her around. Her face lights up like fireworks during a festival, and she sticks the flower crown on my mother's head. Mom takes it off and replaces it atop Michelle's fine hair, encouraging her to dance in the sun.

I stand up without a word and trudge into the house. Skylar is close at my heels, his silence like a weight over us.

"What are you doing?" he finally asks as I shut my bedroom door.

"The fuck you think?"

I can't bear to see his face as I lay out a couple big lines on my dresser. There is a cut straw stashed in the top drawer

—I use that to inhale the drugs. My head spins with bliss as the cocaine makes its way through me like wild rapids.

Finally turning to Skylar, I hold out the straw. He stares at me hard for a few long seconds, eyes boring into my skull while the look of disapproval slowly fades. He grabs the straw, I pour out more of the cocaine, and he takes a hefty line, back arching with the intake. He shakes his head and bounces a few times before handing the straw back to me. I breathe in two more before examining what is left in the bag.

Rabbit has to have more.

I need to reach that higher existence that lets me taste colors and see music like a kaleidoscope. I need to find out how to re-wire my brain so the monster isn't so loud.

I need more.

Skylar jumps around me. "Let's go for a run!"

I beam at him, pull on a pair of sneakers, and follow him out the door.

We push past his brother, ignoring his demand for an explanation of where we're headed while my mother just urges us to be home by dinner. We run down the first street and bank a left, weaving through the roads and parks, our sneakers hardly hitting the ground beneath us. It's difficult to keep up with Skylar. He is much healthier than I am. He has muscle beneath his skin, and I have only bones. We reach the park where he and Xavier often find refuge, and he stops, hands on his knees, panting. I collapse on the ground at his feet, chest heavy as it caves in and out. I gasp for air, incapable of speaking.

"I'm worried about you." He sits beside me. "We all are."

"Me too," I sigh and grab a fistful of grass. "Me too."

I am going to die. I am going to become another statistic,

vomiting and convulsing on the streets until the overdose claims my last breath. Alana is already dead.

I am Sunshine.

I am the malignant monster.

We walk home as the sky begins to change colors and the sun slowly dips below the buildings. We'll be late, but we don't care. It isn't like we're going to eat anyway.

CHAPTER TWENTY-EIGHT

Xavier passes out on the floor near the couch. Michelle curls up on the cushions with a blanket tucked around her tiny body. Skylar and I stay awake, trading a bottle back and forth in the kitchen. He mustn't be too worried about me if he keeps sitting in the grave beside me. Only difference is that it's not *his* grave—he can climb out if he wants.

Together, we fade in and out of existence, our eyes struggling to stay alert.

"I need to find Rabbit," I say absentmindedly.

"No, you don't." He takes the booze from my hands and sips before setting it down on the floor. "Your dad is going to kill us." He looks at the bottle of disappearing liquor.

"Yeah." I giggle and stand on unsteady feet. "Seriously. I'll be back. Get some sleep."

I hear him mumble beneath his breath, but can't make out the words. He wobbles into my room; the closed door muffles the sound of him flopping down on my bed. I hold on to the counter to regain my senses.

I feel sick, but it isn't the alcohol. Not entirely. I force myself into my room, opening the door as silently as possible. Skylar would not stir if I unleashed a moose on him. He's snoring, sprawled out on top of the covers with his feet on the pillows. I glance at him for a moment, expecting him to shoot awake and scold me.

He doesn't flinch.

I retrieve a razor blade from my dresser and use the corner of it to remove the light switch panel next to the door. Taped to the other side are two hits of the brown substance. Opening the small wax squares in my palm, I grab the straw and snort the contents into my system. It slams into me quickly, making me feel a bit more human. It doesn't fly me to a cloud anymore, but it makes the sickness subside.

I'll have to do more to feel bliss.

Empowered and slightly high, I bury the evidence in the trash bin next to my dresser. I give another backwards glance at the unmoving, unconscious body of my best friend and sneak into my parents' room. They, too, are passed out. I tiptoe to my mom's jewelry box and steal a gold ring with a blue stone sitting on top of it. I pocket the ring and leave the house with shame.

The morning air is misty and suspends on my skin like ice.

Is it really cold out, or am I just incapable of producing body heat now?

I walk steadily down the path where Creature had driven Noah, Casey, and I to see Rabbit for the first time. Twice, I lose my way, only vaguely familiar with my surroundings. The deeper I travel into the depths of the city, the worse the conditions of the houses grow. Battered frames with boarded windows envelope me. Grass as tall as the chain-link fences give the cracked streets an eerier feel.

I walk until I stumble upon a small, run-down strip of storefronts: a local pizza place where cops and stoners hang out in harmony, a smoke shop that holds an array of tobacco products and bongs, a comic book store, and a pawnshop. I head into the pawnshop, and the lights blind me. Old guitars, guitar cases, and other random objects hang from the ceiling. Little knick-knacks and jewelry sit in the lit-up glass display of the countertop. I wait at the register, twirling the ring between my fingers. It has to be worth something. The imprint says it's twenty karats.

An overweight man with a comb-over and a wiry beard emerges from the back. "How can I help you, miss?"

"I just need to sell this." I hand him the ring.

He looks at the gold in his palm and then at me and frowns. "Bad breakup? Men are jerks, huh?"

"I'm dating a woman," I tell him flatly. "I think..." I add under my breath.

Just give me the damn money! I don't need your pity. I need cash!

He rolls his eyes and turns to grab a pair of glasses. He looks at the ring closely, examining the band and the likely fake sapphire rock affixed to it. The pawnshop man clicks away on the old laptop before looking back at me. "I can give you $150."

Fuck. That's probably not enough.

I remove my earrings and give them to him. I got them as a gift from my grandmother years ago. She says they were rather expensive when she bought them, and I can only hope she's right.

He takes them reluctantly, avoiding eye contact as he examines them. "Fifty bucks."

"Good enough," I breathe out.

I take the money and shove it into my back pocket, determined to find Rabbit's house and leave with something heavier. I bolt from the pawnshop, waving my hand vaguely to say thanks.

A flutter of bugs create a home in my stomach when I find Rabbit's place—or what I assume is Rabbit's place. Am I nervous? Excited? Stupid?

Definitely stupid.

The U-shaped latch on the fence hangs limply, broken and unable to attempt to lock the rusted door. I follow the cracked concrete path shrouded by weeds and overgrown grass. The door is closed, but not locked. I take hold of the loose knob, about to just walk in before I think better of it and tap on the dilapidated wood. I wait for what feels like hours.

Rabbit answers cautiously, only poking his head out of the frame. He's wearing a black backwards cap, and his eyes are wide and sunken in. "Sunshine?"

"Yeah." I stop bouncing. "I...uh...do you have any to spare? N-Tiger is in jail, and I need—"

He opens the door wider. "Say no more." He waves his long, thin arm. "Come in."

The hardwood floors are worn from hundreds of footsteps and covered in a thin layer of dust. The walls are dirty; I'm sure they would be a different color if only someone cleaned them. One would think that a tweak house would be scrubbed down to the frame. The couch has a tear in the fabric, and the table before it is covered in round, swollen water stains. Two other people are sitting on the couch, controllers in their hands with their pinhead pupils fixed on the video-game.

The girl has thin hair pulled back into a ponytail. Her fingers are painted a dark pink and shaped into rounded triangles. There's a tattoo on the side of her hand, and I can see track marks on the inside of her elbow. The man next to her has a shaved head and he's wearing a white collared shirt with dress pants. He is clean-shaven, and the sweet allure of his cologne fills my nose.

Drugs really don't care who they attack.

I stand nervously beside the television.

"People," Rabbit speaks to the two who aren't listening, "this is Sunshine. Sunshine, these are people."

I lift my eyebrows. "Do they have names?"

He shrugs. "Probably."

Rabbit leads me past the living room and into the kitchen with cracked, peeling tiles on the floor, but clean and organized counters. The tops of the burners on the gas stove are black, but the center is spotless. Everything on the countertops has a specific place, and each item has a spot that it calls its own. There isn't much: a coffee maker, a small jar of sugar, and a square container that houses a spatula, a wooden spoon, and a whisk. Two pots, a skillet, and a pizza pan hang on the wall from nails. Rabbit opens up a door that tips down slightly when pulled too quickly. He digs around the random contents until he grasps a small box from the back. Rabbit flicks it open and pulls out a bag of clear rocks that look similar to crystals a person would buy at an overpriced new age store, convincing themselves they will heal them of any ailments possessing their mortal bodies.

This will heal me. Or kill me. Whatever.

"Do you have H? Or snow?" I ask sheepishly. I haven't taken meth before and I'm nervous.

Strange. I want to be high, so why do I care what it is? It'll do the job, won't it?

"No." He holds up the bag. "This is all I have to offer right now. Take it or leave it."

"Yeah, I'll take it." I roll my eyes. "What's your price?"

"Eighty dollars."

I dig around my back pocket, nick my hand on a forgotten razor blade, and pull out the money.

"Want to do some here?" He offers his pipe and I take it graciously.

We load up a small amount and light the dirty glass. I take a deep inhale at his command and hold it in my lungs, letting the poison burn its way thoroughly into my body. A huge plume of smoke escapes my mouth with a series of coughs. I soar into the sky above us and my heart thumps wickedly in the cage I call a chest. My skin is on fire, and a grin tears apart my face, stretching my cheeks away from one another. Rabbit takes a hit and his lips crack into an upward turn. He hands me the pipe and tells me keep it. He knows I don't have one.

"Anything else I can do for you?" he asks.

"No, not now." The words tumble out of me. "Let me know when you get more or when you go to pick up. Can I come with you? How long does this last? Will you have more later?"

"Sunshine, breathe between sentences. It will help." Rabbit laughs.

I gasp and nod. My hands shake, jaw clenched beyond my control.

"I'll let you know when I pick up. That hit will last about ten hours."

"Got it." I jump around him before heading towards the front door. "Bye, strangers." I wave to the well-dressed man and the thin lady beside him.

No response.

I'm walking on clouds as I wrack my brain for the way back home. The sun has risen above the treetops, and the cold mist has completely disappeared. I am soaring with gods beside the sun. I have to get home and tell Skylar and Xavier that I will be okay—that I can survive.

A feeling deep within my gut lets me know that I can walk through the fires of hell and come out on top.

A goddess above mortals, I am untouchable.

CHAPTER TWENTY-NINE

When I get to my house, Casey is sitting on the porch steps waiting for me. She looks up through her long hair and rolls her eyes. "Fucking Christ, Alana."

"What?" I ask, fingers fumbling to light a cigarette. I can't sit beside her. I can barely stop bouncing.

She extends her arm and lights it for me with a swift flick of the lighter. "You're so high right now."

I don't respond. Of course I'm high. I'm *always* high. It's not like it's a new thing. "You said you were done with me," I state, watching the ash fall from the cigarette and onto my boot.

"No," she corrects me. "I said you didn't answer any of my questions."

"Oh, yeah. Right."

"Did you ever tell your parents where you were that whole time you stayed at Noah's?" she presses, still looking up at me.

"No."

"Are you considering getting help?" She grabs one of my cold, bony hands. "We're worried about you."

I wish people would stop telling me that. They're worried about me. No, they're not. They're worried about the person I used to be. The person I killed for a hit. I can't answer her question. Some days, Sunshine is quiet in my head and I feel as though I should run and seek a therapist or lock myself in a rehab center until my system is clear of this dark, vile thing, but most days though I just want to be high. I don't care about the consequences.

Casey just shakes her head, stands, and makes her way back inside. Xavier allows her to pass before stepping outside with Skylar.

"What did you take?" Xavier asks. He settles a palm against my forehead, holds back my head, and opens one of my eyes with his thumb.

"Fuck off." I swat him away. "And don't worry about it."

What does it matter to them?

Skylar doesn't ask questions, staring at me in curiosity. I'll probably share with him later. My teeth are chattering, and I pace along the porch now, my heart doing its best to escape while my lungs find air in short, hurried bursts. My world begins to cave. Everything around me is suffocating, and I can feel fear building from my toes. It wraps icy fingers around every fabric of remaining muscle and brings me to a halt. Black swirls around my eyes and my vision tunnels. My chest tightens and can't find enough air. I stare into the distance, eyes fixed on a dark spot at the edge of street.

Am I dying?

Is this it?

I grip the railing, knuckles white as I begin to accept death.

Skylar clamps a hand on my shoulder. "You're okay," he coaxes. "Breathe. Deep breaths. Inhale for four seconds." He inhales, and I follow. "Hold for seven." His voice is strained. "Exhale for eight."

I follow his lead as he carries me through the exercise a few times. My breathing steadies, the grip around my muscles loosens, and my chest no longer feels tight and hot.

"What?" I look over at him and Xavier.

"Panic attack," Xavier states flatly. "You took too much."

I sit down and hold my head in my hands. My skin feels like it has ants beneath it, crawling along my bones. I shake off the feeling and stand up to pace along the porch. If I move, the anxiety seems to stop.

With her hair pulled back into a messy bun, Emily walks up the path to my house. Why does everyone gather here? Why is my house the place of refuge when I only want to escape it?

"I found the house!" Emily shouts and runs to Skylar, who offers her a cigarette. She declines with a shake of her head. She glances at me. "You're high," she states flatly.

"When am I not?" I point at her enthusiastically while she rolls her eyes. "Park?" I suggest, wanting nothing more than to get away from this place.

They agree. The brothers have only one condition: they want to retrieve their instruments from their house. I don't know why it's so important to them. I can't figure how plucking away at a few strings helps them ease their troubles and mask their pain. Not really.

But who am I to judge? I attempt to destroy myself in order to do the same.

Casey and Emily take Michelle to the park while the brothers and I head to their piece of hell. The front door is locked, and the hidden key has been taken inside. We walk around the perimeter of the property, trying the windows until we find one that's unlatched, which leads into the dirty kitchen. It is too small for the brothers to fit through, so they stare at me for a second before I shrug and step forward. Sliding through the opening, I crawl over the sink awkwardly, tumbling to the stained floor with a thump. I jump back to my feet and look around cautiously while Xavier watches with wide eyes. I don't move or breathe for a minute before I give them a thumbs up.

Hope, with a slice of impending doom, allows me to believe that their father is asleep in a drunken coma.

The lights in the living room are off—probably blown out—and the once hidden key is sitting on the dusty end table by the door. I undo the bolt lock and let them inside. Xavier shakes my shoulder as if to tell me 'good job'. He's too scared to speak.

Noise could awaken the sleeping villian, and I have already made enough noise.

Cautious steps take Skylar and me into his room to fetch his guitar. I watch Xavier's shadow slip into Michelle's room to grab the ukulele she keeps hidden beneath her bed. Dante had gotten it for her years ago, drawing pictures on the back of it with her to make it her own. The shadow of Michelle's door stretches across the hall like a ghost as it slowly closes and latches shut. My breathing hitches when I hear the heavy footsteps of their father coming down the hallway towards us. Skylar isn't paying attention and his door remains open.

"Sky..." my voice trails in soft waves. I bite my bottom lip to get my teeth to stop chattering. The sound feels like gunshots in my head.

He nods, frozen, staring at his guitar. We hear a fist pound on Michelle's door, but it quickly gives up. In that second of silence, Skylar pushes me aside with an open stretch of his arm, lunges across the room, and slams his door shut. He keeps his back pressed against it with his head towards the ceiling. The door vibrates behind him as his father pounds away on the weak wood. Skylar presses his palms against the door, and he begins to mutter to himself while still staring at the ceiling. I shake myself from my stupor and take a spot next to him—pushing my limited body weight against the barrier as well.

"Go away, go away, go away," Skylar keeps softly repeating.

"Open the fuck up!" The words shoot through the walls. "Skylar, open the fucking door! I need to talk to you!"

"Fuck off!" I scream.

Skylar unlocks his gaze from the ceiling and glares at me. "Dude."

"That whore is with you?" The words are needles.

They make me laugh, the sound escaping my lips like a foreign language. "The hell do you know?"

"Alana, shut up," Skylar warns under his breath.

The closed entrance pounds behind us again. Our bodies jerk with the force, but we hold our ground. We hear the door across the hall slam open and the battering stops with a groan from Skylar's father and a grunt from Xavier. Skylar opens the only thing between him and his father, and we watch Xavier struggle with the monster. One arm is locked around his father's neck, the other hand pressing against his eyes.

"Go!" Xavier yells when his father throws him against a wall.

Skylar runs out down the hall and I follow, but we don't leave—we can't. We head into the kitchen, and Skylar grabs an empty glass bottle from the trash bin. I grip the pepper shaker from the table, unscrewing the cap and throwing it behind me. We fly back to Xavier's aid. His dad has a forearm against his neck, forcing him against the wall. Xavier does his best to relieve the pressure so he can get a breath of air. All the while, his dad scolds him for missing curfew and not calling to tell him he's abandoning his family.

With a war cry, Skylar bolts down the hall with the bottle raised. He hits his father over the head with it, breaking skin and drawing blood. The bottle doesn't shatter as I stupidly expect. Instead, it bounces off his head with a hollow *thunk*. Xavier is released, and their father turns around, a hand over his wound, eyes on his youngest son. I run up to him and shoot the pepper into his face. As he sneezes and attempts to regain himself, we make way out the front door, slamming it behind us. Xavier rubs his neck and coughs.

"Thanks," Skylar whispers.

"Yeah." Xavier stands up straight and hugs his brother. "Thanks, Alana."

"Anytime." I nod. "You know, if you guys want, you can just stay with us."

"We'll think about it," Skylar answers.

I know what he's thinking. They don't know if they can bear to constantly watch me wither away. They don't know if they're willing to expose Michelle to that. If there is one thing their father did right, he doesn't beat his sons in front of her. And he doesn't raise a finger to his little girl.

Without another word, we head to the park to meet up with the others. Emily and Casey are playing with Michelle on the playground while Sarah looks on from a wooden bench. Xavier sits beside her, kissing her cheek. Skylar and I sit on the grass closer to the playground so Skylar can keep a close eye on his sister. He rests his guitar on his knee and plucks carelessly at the strings, allowing the melody to break through the tension still enveloping us. He stares straight ahead, his gaze unfaltering. I'm not sure what he's looking at. It isn't Michelle—she's behind the slide using an old toy walkie-talkie to talk to Casey on the other end.

He doesn't blink or glance down at his moving fingers. My jaw is slowly beginning to stop chattering. I scratch at my arms until I'm tearing the skin a little. My stomach, empty, turns and I grab fistfuls of grass and throw them ahead, eyes darting back and forth across the park. The energy claws away at me, seeking an escape through my skin.

I just have to let it out, but I can't.

Something stops me. I feel like my butt is glued to the grass beneath it. My head spins; I have to take bottomless breaths of air to make the panic swallow itself deeper inside of me. I poke Skylar's shoulder.

He doesn't respond.

I poke him again.

He looks over and stares at me blankly, still playing his melody. "What?"

"I need to get sober." The words tumble out of me like vomit. I know they're true, but I'm not sure I can really do it.

I said I *need* to get sober, not that I *will* get sober.

Words matter.

"No shit." He blinks once. "Will you?"

"Fuck it."

That's it. I'm getting sober.

CHAPTER THIRTY

It's early—too early for even the birds to screech their songs to persuade the worms to squirm their way up from the dirt. My parents open their arms to Xavier, Skylar, and Michelle. They clear out the spare room for them, and Xavier and Skylar both opt to sleep in the living room so Michelle can have it to herself. The brothers clean the house, Michelle following at their heels with the broom, as their form of rent.

Everyone is asleep.

I sit in the kitchen with the lights off, watching the sun cast colors across the cloudy skies. While they sleep, I do lines of coke in the bathroom. As I watch the sky, I pull back on a syringe and slam heroin into my veins.

I told Skylar I'd get sober.

I told Skylar a handful of lies.

I am a lost cause.

Rabbit told me absentmindedly that mixing uppers and downers will kill me. I'm not sure what I'm expecting: the screaming to cease its control, or death? Either one would be nice.

As the drugs work through me, I slump to the floor, my back against the cabinets. I can feel a pressure inside of me, colliding with my skin and attempting to escape. My moods begin to shift with the drugs. I feel on top of the world, the cocaine making me indestructible. I also keep envisioning opening up my throat with the nearest kitchen knife each time I catch darkness when I blink. I take deep breaths, counting them as Skylar had instructed before. Still, the visions cloud me and the pressure keeps building.

As if something else has taken control of my body, I watch from the outside as my own hand grabs one of the knives from the butcher's block. I stare at the inside of my arm for a long moment, eyes grazing over old scars before locking onto my thigh. The blade glides along my flesh in fluid movements and a breath of relief escapes my lungs. I make more thin slices from my hip to my knee in quick successions, adrenaline rushing through me with each drop of lost blood. My thigh is now coated in crimson, and I am still outside of myself. Forcing myself from the floor, I rinse off the knife, throw it in the sink, and hobble into my room —careful to keep any blood from dripping onto the floor.

It had been nearly a year since I'd last self-harmed.

There are still some ace bandages stowed away under my bed from my earlier days of self-mutilation. I wrap a bunch around my thigh and pull on a pair of jeans. At least with the bandaging, the blood won't seep through the fibers of the denim. My emotions have completely ceased. My hands shake, and I all I can seem to feel is the physical pain of my thigh.

The pain I created for myself.

Oh yeah, and the drugs as they fight in my system.

My stomach lurches as a warning. Vomit travels up my throat, demanding an escape. I shoot up and barrel for the bathroom like a bull, locking the door behind me. All I can expel is yellow and green bile that burns as it exits. I fall beside the toilet, shivering, and press my forehead against the cold tile. My stomach turns again, and I am forced up like a bullet, arms cradling the bowl. Despite my face being buried in the toilet, bile staring back at me, all I can really think about is getting more.

I need help.

If only I can keep getting high first.

The cycle never ends. I'll get up to fall right back down.

The endless war in my head rages on. The beast is clearly winning.

I pull myself off the ground, clean my pale face, and brush my teeth. Morning brightens the house with rays of light and the sweet smell of pancakes and bacon fill the air. It takes everything in me to hold my stomach in place.

"Good morning, Alana." My father kisses my forehead. "You gonna cut your hair anytime soon?"

"Yeah." I feel my own head. The fuzz has grown quite long. "Can I use your razor again?"

"Of course, dear." He chews on a piece of bacon as he speaks. "Hungry?"

"No."

My head spins with the scents. I can feel the burning slices on my leg with each movement, but keep my face straight as I sit with everyone at the table, only sipping on a cup of hot, black coffee.

"You should eat something." Xavier looks at me with a stern expression.

Shit.

Does he know?

"The pancakes are yummy!" Michelle chimes. "Alana, please?" She holds out a piece for me.

160

"Michelle, don't use your fingers," Xavier scolds. "Use your fork to feed Alana."

I roll my eyes.

Michelle takes the torn pancake piece and sticks it on her fork before offering it to me again. I take it and smile at her with closed lips, stretching my face apart with fake pleasure. The pancake feels like clay between my teeth and I use a swig of coffee to force it down my throat. I stare at the steam afterwards from my mug, not wanting to look up.

Xavier has to know.

He usually does.

Or I'm just paranoid.

While they talk and laugh among one another, I can only think about getting a hold of Rabbit. Maybe he can get me more of whatever he had last time. Or some cocaine. Or anything. I just want drugs, and Rabbit has a connection. I don't know if I could pawn anything else right away without being obvious. Mom will eventually notice that her ring has gone missing.

Although it's not like she's ever said anything about the money disappearing from her wallet.

The monster within screams, slashing at my skeleton, begging for another hit. The cuts on my thigh sting beneath my bandages like a beckoning call to ruin myself further.

"You guys planning on going to college?" My father's seemingly out of place question makes my head poke up and rejoin the table.

"Yeah," I mumble. "Eventually." I haven't applied to any schools.

"I still have a few high school classes left, but I'm just going to take them online," Skylar adds. "I'll probably apply to community college and go from there."

Skylar is still seventeen and should have graduated with

me, but had to miss school due to bruises or violent mishaps at home that required his attention.

"What about you, Xavier?" my father presses. "You're nearly twenty. You thinking about going back to school?"

Xavier's eyes widen, and the legs of his chair screech as he pushes himself dramatically away from the table. He stands up, eyes still shot open, and bolts out the door.

"Uh...what?" I look at Skylar, who only shrugs.

"I like school," Michelle says with a mouthful of food.

"Chew first, then speak," her brother corrects her.

She swallows. "Sorry, Skylar."

We clean up, throwing the dishes into the dishwasher. Michelle wipes down the table, and Skylar cleans the countertops. They are grateful for the sanctuary my parents are providing, but there is a fear around us that none of us dare to speak aloud. Since Skylar and Michelle are minors, they will eventually have to go back to their own house. Xavier only sticks around to protect them as much as he can, taking the brunt of most of their dad's punishments. He has been trying to learn how to gain custody of them.

I wait until everyone begins to make their way outside to enjoy the morning sun as it warms the concrete and grass before grabbing Skylar by the arm and pulling him into the kitchen. If I don't tell him now, I'll probably keep destroying myself—or at least the part of myself that is left.

CHAPTER THIRTY-ONE

"You don't seem to be zoning out and being all strange anymore," I note as I jump up onto the counter top.

"Yeah." He sits beside me. "Meds."

"Oh, good."

"So, what's up? Why are you acting weird?"

Am I acting weird?

I sigh deeply. "I need help."

"Yes." He nods and lifts his eyebrows. "We've been over this, but you keep pretending you're made of steel and nothing can kill you."

"No, you've got it wrong." I laugh. "I hope *everything* can kill me. I want to die—except when I don't."

"I don't follow." He lifts an eyebrow and I can feel him shift closer, his shoulders slump with the weight of what I had said. His breathing shatters for a moment as he exhales a heavy sigh.

"I don't know, Sky." I look down. "Some days I feel great and on top of the world, and it's like I'll do anything to stay there. Like, imagine the happiest you've ever felt and triple it. And then, at times I feel like absolute trash. And I do drugs to make this voice in my head be silent for a moment or two. I don't know what to do." I'm not going to tell him I hurt myself again.

"I already knew you weren't staying sober. Xavier knows, too. I think your parents might be a little naïve though." He grabs a glass from the cabinet behind him and fills it with water from the sink. "Xavier told Casey, and that's why she hasn't been back here. She loves you, Alana. She can't see you like this."

"I know." I look up at the ceiling. "What do I do?"

"Get help." He takes a swig of water and hands it to me. "You look awful. You know that, right?"

"Yeah, I know."

"Listen, I'll help you get help. We'll sign you into a rehab facility tonight. While you're gone, X and I will clean out your drugs."

"You'll never find them," I scoff.

His face turns to stone. "Floorboard by the living room table, mug in the back of the cabinet behind me because no one uses it, underside of the toilet tank lid, behind the light switch—"

"Okay, I get it," I stop him. Perhaps he pays better attention than I give him credit. "I can do this, right?"

"Of course." He jumps down. "We need to tell your parents. They're good people, and they deserve to be informed."

"Yeah, shut up."

I hop down as well and shake off the nerves. The flutter of anxiety beats in my chest like a bird flapping its wings, desperate for an escape from this cage of bones. Skylar walks beside me through the house and lets me ahead of him when we reach the outside. He lights two cigarettes and hands one to me. I stand beside my father, watching Michelle and my mom work in the garden of flowers and herbs. I don't speak; my words catch in my throat and leave a bad taste on my tongue.

"You seem troubled." Dad looks down at me.

"She is." Skylar sits on the steps in front of us. "Talk, Alana."

I shoot him a look that would turn him to stone if I only had snakes for hair. "Dad," I start. "I want—no—I *need* to go to rehab."

"I know." He embraces me tightly, wrapping his arms around me and holding me close to him. He rocks me back and forth. "I just needed you to say it. I love you. You know that, right?" I can hear him sniffling back his emotions with shaking breaths. "I love you so much, Alana. I'm so proud that you're doing this." He holds me back at arms-length before embracing me again

I nod and hold back the tears. I don't want to feel this. I don't want to burden my soul with the guilt and stabbing pain of disappointment. My parents know. They always knew. They just couldn't acknowledge the fact that I'm being destroyed by my own hand.

I want drugs. I want to find Rabbit and throw myself into a whirlwind of stupidity. I want to snort lines of coke from a kitchen table until my nose bleeds and I can't stand.

I'm getting help.

And I still want to die.

My father keeps an arm around me when Xavier runs back up to my house. "I did it!" He's holding a letter in his fist. He goes heads towards Michelle and picks her up, swinging her around with her feet behind her.

She giggles and laughs, lips stretched across her cheeks in joy.

"Did what?" Skylar stands. "Steal someone's mail?"

"No." He puts Michelle down and jogs up to the porch, placing the letter in Skylar's hand.

"I'm going to college."

"Oh, nice!" Skylar hugs his older brother.

"Congratulations, Xavier." My father shakes his hand.

"Good going, X." I smile weakly at him. "Will you be the first in your family?"

"Yup." His face falls for a moment. "Everything okay? You look upset."

Skylar explains to him that I am finally going to get the help I should have sought long ago. Xavier holds me close to him, wrapping his large arms around me as he buries me into his chest. He thanks me for figuring out what they all knew then tells me how proud he is of me and how he will never give up on me. I push him away, wiping the tears from my eyes before they fall too far. I hate feeling anything but that euphoric intensity that visits me from time to time. It's much easier to find with stimulants.

Without a word or a backwards glance, I walk off. I put my cigarette out on my boot and throw it into an ashtray at the end of the property. Michelle calls after me, but I ignore her small voice. The ghouls are making my brain swell while I walk through town with my head down. My fingers hover over Rabbit's name on my phone.

No. He isn't who I need to see now.

Not really.

I click on Casey's name and pray that she'll pick up.

"Yes, Alana?" Her voice is flat.

"Casey!" My cheeks light stretch. "Meet me at the bottom of that bridge."

"Why?" she demands.

"Please, just do it," I beg.

"Fine."

"I love you." All I hear is the dial tone.

I walk quickly, forcing my injured leg to move as fast as it can as the cuts rub against the bandages. I make it to the bridge and look over the edge, considering jumping into the cold water below. If I do that, my wounds will be exposed, and I can't let anyone see them. I'm not seeking attention. I'm only seeking relief from the pressure building inside me.

Instead, I slide down the bank to the quiet river below, muddying up my shoes and the bottoms of my pants. I stare at the water as I wait, the current gently massaging the banks. The complete serenity of nature and the calming effect of the water clash with my raging emotions. I want to throw my head back and laugh manically while ripping open more of my flesh, but I hold back, staring hard at the trees and river. Finally, I hear Casey making her way down to me. She stands behind me with her arms crossed, not looking in my direction.

"What do you need?" she asks, choking on her words.

She still cares. She cares enough to not see me kill myself.

"I don't need anything," I tell her. "I'm going to rehab."

Her arms drop, and she finally looks at me. Her smile is slow, accompanied by tears. She kisses me with soft lips and tells me she loves me.

"Spins, bumps, crashes, and all." She pulls away.

"Spins, bumps, crashes and all," I repeat with a weak smile.

Casey holds my hands; mine are made of ice and hers are warm. The water rushes, and droplets of rain drizzle from the clouds overhead. We can hear a few small animals scurrying back to their homes, away from the rain no matter how slowly it falls. We stay there, holding each other and watching the raindrops hit the water. The silence away from town wraps around us as we let time fade away.

CHAPTER THIRTY-TWO

I walk Casey home, the journey taking a toll on my underweight body—I don't let her know that though. I keep the exhaustion hidden behind a forced smile. I love her, and I am going to get help.

Right after I meet up with Rabbit.

I text him as we walk, keeping the screen tilted away from her view so she can't see. I let my fingers linger in Casey's palm before she walks up her driveway to the front door. I stay on the sidewalk, watching her hips sway before walking away myself.

I meet up with Rabbit at an old building a few blocks away from what I assume is his house. Maybe I'm wrong. Maybe Rabbit doesn't have a house and just journeys from one old abandoned home to the next. This one has a fence covered in vines with the gate thrown into the front yard. The windows are boarded up, and the stairs leading up to the door are missing a step at the top of the railing. I don't bother knocking; I just walk inside as if I've been here a thousand times. It smells like cheap alcohol and vomit.

As long as I can get high, I don't care if there is a dead body in the front room.

I walk through the poorly lit place until I see Rabbit sitting on a couch. There's no television or radio playing. Someone is in the kitchen watching a pizza cook in the oven. It's the same well-dressed guy from the other place. He looks like he can afford something more high class. Why does he hang out with the likes of Rabbit?

Furthermore, how does he fill himself with drugs and still keep a career? At least it looks like he keeps a steady job. That, or he just likes wearing suits and looking good. Although, despite filling myself with toxins, I was still able to keep a 4.0 and never skip class when I was still in school.

"Sunshine!" Rabbit stands and greets me with a handshake. "How are you?"

"What do you have?" I skip the formalities. I don't want to waste time telling him how I am going to get sober.

After I get high.

"Only H." He frowns. "I can get coke or even crack later if you want."

"No." I shake my head and sit beside him. The cushions cave in around my legs as I sink in.

He works on the drugs and the rigs as I watch. His white hands and long fingers measure the heroin with careful eyes. He hands me a syringe before slowly guiding his own into a vein in the crook of his elbow. I shoot up in my leg, pulling my pants down a little after having trouble finding a vein in my arm.

Rabbit doesn't ask about the cuts. He doesn't give a damn. Everything slowly begins to fall into place. The gnawing in my head lessens and I sink onto the thin, matted carpet. I feel numb. I feel wonderful. A stupid grin is plastered on my face like the paint of a twisted clown. All I need is more. I need to keep going until I can feel the tingling behind my eyes.

I can't move, so Rabbit shoots me up then tells me he has nothing left through a whisper. I just lie on the floor, staring at the ceiling fan. Rabbit slowly makes his way to the carpet beside me. Our heads are next to one another with our feet sprawled in opposite directions. Hands at my sides, I close my eyes, letting this feeling fill every bit of me.

Maybe I don't need to get sober.

This is so much better.

Not even the slamming of the front door swinging off its hinges snaps me from my stupor. Rabbit, however, sits up with his hands on his legs as he watches through the hall.

"Rabbit!" The deep voice sounds far too much like Xavier's, but I still don't move. There is no way he could have found me here. This isn't even the same place that Casey had seen.

Rabbit stands up and sways, waiting. I don't open my eyes, so I can't see whose footsteps end up in the room.

"This kid is supposed to be going to rehab, you piece of shit." His voice is getting closer.

Shit.

It *is* X.

Rabbit laughs. "Business. It's all business. I don't give a fuck about her and she don't give fuck about me."

I pop my eyes open and look over, still unable to get up. I'm not sure if it's drugs this time that keep me glued there or the fear that the giant, angry man will kill me if I'm not already dead.

Xavier grabs Rabbit by the throat and throws him against the wall. "People are not profit!" he yells.

"Who even are you?" Rabbit raises an eyebrow. He can't feel anything that Xavier does to him.

"Xavier. Tiger sent me." He lets go of Rabbit and grabs me by the arm, pulling me to my feet.

My mouth makes an O at the realization that Noah gave me away. It was Noah who told Xavier about Rabbit. Does Rabbit have the same spots? How many doors did Xavier break down until he came to this one? Did Noah tell him not to use his real name—that it could get him into trouble?

He probably doesn't care.

Nothing is worse than facing his own father.

Xavier pulls me out of the house, fingers wrapped around my bicep. He opens the passenger door of my parents' car and throws me in, no sound escaping his tight lips. I can't form words. I'm too high. I nod in and out of consciousness as we drive. The ride is silent. He doesn't speak on the way to our destination and keeps the radio off. The windows are down, and the only noise that fills the air is the whipping of the wind, cold and beating against my numb skin. We park in a large, well-lit lot next to a large brick building with lots of doorways and big windows. He gets out and picks me up, throwing me over his shoulder.

"I just want to sleep," I mutter. I am too weak to fight him.

"Shut the fuck up, Alana."

The doors open at his footsteps. He places me on a bench by the window, and I immediately lie down. I don't hear what he tells them at the front desk and I don't care. I've stopped moving, and that makes me happy.

He gives me one last glance and walks back outside. I sit up and watch him leave. Where is he going? Why am I here? Where the hell did he leave me?

Two middle-aged women in scrubs approach and coax me up with gentle words. They call me things like 'sweetie' and 'dear'. I glare at them with venom. They each grab one of my arms and lead me down the hall to an empty room with nothing but a bed and a window that doesn't open.

"You need to sleep this off," they tell me.

I lie down on the floor, staring at the dark corners of the room, not looking over at them.

Xavier must have dropped me off at the facility without my permission.

I'll have to thank him later.

If I don't die first.

CHAPTER THIRTY-THREE

I lie on the floor, staring at the ceiling. There are thirty-seven tiles lined up above me; four tubes of light, two each are encased in rectangular plastic pieces. The bed has a slab of foam padding and a thin sheet with a single pillow. There's a toilet and sink to the left, against the wall. Sunlight slowly seeps in and covers me. I can see speckles of dust floating in the rays like little bugs. I don't move. I can feel the high leaving me.

In isolation, my phantoms scream, gnawing at the confines of my body as if they can escape and suffocate me themselves. I want to run and jump and shriek.

I am fine.

I am dying, but I'll be okay.

I just lie there.

My heart is poundings hard, and I breathe against the inside of my chest. My breathing comes in deep gasps as beads of sweat form and run along my skin. The crash comes quickly. At the very least, it seems that way. I might have been lying there for hours, allowing the drugs to work their way through me. I try my best to ignore the nausea that comes with the nagging need to gather more drugs to fill myself with.

Just not heroin.

I'd rather have cocaine.

Or meth.

Maybe crack.

It doesn't matter what it is. I want an upper. I want something that will give me the energy and strength of ten men who visit the gym on a bi-hourly basis.

But I know I can't get more, so my stomach flips, and my demons shriek relentlessly. Suicidal thoughts come rushing in, making it hard to close my eyes again without seeing bubbles of red and swollen cuts. I press a hand against my thigh and exhale.

I don't need rehab. I need a coffin. If only I could move myself up off of this damned floor. I know this is my last chance to survive. I have to stay. If I can't make this work, I will die.

I know it.

Part of me is still okay with that.

Alana would be dead, and the devil named Sunshine would reign as supreme ruler of this sack of flesh.

My door slowly creaks open, and a woman with lots of freckles and shoulder-length red hair peeks around the edge. I just flutter my eyes in her direction. She walks up to me and hoists me to my feet, keeping her hands on my shoulders to steady me. She smells like strawberries, and her hair is still a little damp from a last-minute shower. The name-tag on her green scrubs says 'Aztec.' We are the same height, but I'm so much smaller than her. She smiles warmly at me and lets go of my shoulders. I just stare at her, unsure. She takes the stethoscope from around her neck and presses it gently against my chest.

"Deep breath," she instructs in a soft voice.

I do as I'm told, my lungs shaking.

She moves to my back, pressing in three different areas, and tells me to repeat the breathing.

"Do you have any thoughts of suicide or self-harm?" she asks me within that same gentle tone.

"Yes and yes." Lying won't get me anywhere. Besides, my leg is covered in cuts that have not yet healed.

"You'll be assigned to a therapist and group," she notifies me.

I nod. There has to be more. They can't just keep me in this one room by myself, can they? As if reading my mind, she tells me that I will be relocated to the main area. I will have a roommate as well. She's another recovering addict and her name is Rachel. She's twenty-five and has been in and out of rehab a few times.

We walk along the halls, and she keeps providing me with information on what will happen. The corridor is lit with the same fluorescent tubes in plastic casing as the isolation room, and the floors are made of speckled tiles. Wooden doors with numbers line the halls. A few scattered people hang out, leaning around or lying on couches in the lobby. A television plays cartoons, and a couple people play cards at a round table.

I refocus on Aztec as she begins to rattle off names. A guy named Doctor Andres leads the group therapy I will be attending; one on one therapy will be with a guy named Doctor Cameron, and my psychiatrist's name is Amber Rizzo. Apparently, they want me to see a psychiatrist first, but considering the situation and how few openings there are, they're opting for me to do group therapy before seeing the psych nurse.

Nurse Aztec gives me my first dose of methadone after

she opens the door to my new room. She motions me inside and keeps the door open as I stand in there, dumbfounded. There are two small beds, and in the room each one comes with a little table. The carpet is dark beige, and there's a bar light on the ceiling, the switch next to the door. I pop the magical withdrawal drug and immediately fall in love with the taste. The orange hexagon tastes like citrus and pine trees—like if Pine-Sol had a flavor. My new living buddy is nowhere to be found, so I am left alone again. I lie down on the bed that doesn't have anything on it and stare at the ceiling. I feel calm, at ease, and dizzy.

Really dizzy.

The tiles begin to bleed into one another, and the mattress suddenly feels like it's made of water. I roll myself off and onto the cold floor below, landing with a weak thud. The floor doesn't sway me around as much, but the fall makes my stomach turn. I stand up and throw myself into the bathroom that's to the right of the room, I slam the door behind me, and quickly learn that it doesn't lock. The contents of my stomach force their way through my throat. My vomit is bright orange like the methadone, but the smell is nothing like it. I lie on the floor, unable to move without my head spinning and my stomach flipping. I place my head on the tiles and cover one eye with my hand. It seems to work, but even the smallest movement sends me back to the toilet, vomiting and dry heaving until my stomach muscles cramp and I have nothing left to give.

CHAPTER THIRTY-FOUR

As I'm sprawled on the floor, forehead against tile, muscles spasming, the door opens slowly. A girl with intoxicating curves and long, white-blonde hair with electric blue underneath steps into the bathroom. She closes the door behind her and slides down until her butt is on the tile. Her knees are up, and she places her arms on top of them, hands dangling in front of her. She cocks her head to one side and looks at me as if I'm a bug in a case. I want to tell her to piss off, but if I so much as breathe too deeply my body will attempt to expel the nonexistent contents of my stomach.

"Methadone won't help if you don't do heroin most of the time," she states matter-of-factly. "I'm Rachel by the way. You must be Alana."

My eyes travel in her direction, but I can only manage to groan.

She stands up and walks out, coming back in a few seconds with a plastic cup full of ice chips. She sits beside me and helps me sit up. I want to refuse, but I'm too weak.

She places the cup in my hands. "Eat some."

I look at the cup and then at her, not wanting to pass anything through my lips.

"Trust me," she encourages. "I've been where you're at more than once."

Reluctantly, I place an ice chip to my mouth and let it melt on my dry, cracked, sensitive lips. The cold sensation makes my stomach relax a little, and the room stops spinning just slightly. I place a few on my tongue and let them melt in my mouth, satisfied as the cold liquid slides down my throat. We sit beside one another in silence. She watches me as I stare ahead, one hand still over my eye. A moment passes before the nausea kicks in again. I turn around and puke the water out of my body and into the toilet.

"Fucking hell!" I shout into the bowl.

"Eat more ice," Rachel instructs.

I shake my head.

"Please," she insists. "It will help. I know it doesn't seem like it, but if you have nothing in your stomach to puke, you'll just keep hurting yourself."

I take a piece of ice and let it melt in my mouth, but stay close to the toilet. She leaves me there, claiming she has to go to group. She offers to take me with her, but I can only vomit in response.

She just laughs.

Once I'm sure my body has nothing left inside of it and the cup of ice is empty, I stumble my way to my bed and collapse on top of the sheets. I curl up, knees to my chest, and shiver.

I don't want to experience withdrawal—I don't want to be here—but I don't get a choice. I have to make this work.

I'm not sure how long I'm in that bed, shaking like a wet cat, but I do notice Rachel going in and out and sleeping every so often. Have days passed with no one checking up on me, or is Rachel reporting that I am just fine? I don't feel that way. I feel like my body is playing a game of chicken with a mac truck and losing. I don't attempt to eat—not after Rachel offers me a few strawberries and my vomit looks like thick blood mixed with tiny seeds. I know I'm losing weight; my legs wobble even more when I have to force myself to the bathroom to relieve myself of my body's pesky needs.

When Aztec finally comes to visit me, she sits at the foot of my bed with a dose of methadone. I shake my head violently and push away from her. I love the smell of the orange drug. I love the taste of it as the pine tree citrus finds its way down my gullet. But I can't take any more vomiting. I can't take being that sick again.

"It will help," she tells me gently.

"Like hell it will," I scoff. "Why does it hate me? Why am I withdrawing? I didn't do that much heroin, did I?"

"According to your friends, you did a lot." She fixes me with a stern look. "And it could very well be because of the amount of other substances you took."

Those bastards—my friends—ratted me out.

I lie back down and turn my back to her. I'm not going to take the methadone, and there is nothing she can do about it.

She sighs and stands. "Very well. You'll be expected at group tonight."

"Yeah, okay," I say to the wall and listen as her footsteps fade out of the room.

I should be grateful they're allowing me to occupy one of their beds. I should be happy they paired me with someone who isn't completely intolerable. I guess I should thank them for even considering allowing Xavier to drop me off at their doorstep, half alive.

All I can think about is getting high.

The raging war in my head is powerful, and I need the battle to stop.

I suppose I feel well enough to trudge my sorry ass to this magical group. I envision them sitting in a circle with their heads bowed in addiction-riddled shame as they speak in whispers of their woes. I don't really want anything to do with it.

Someone sits on my bed and I curl up further into myself, not moving my gaze from the wall.

"Alana?" It's Rachel.

I sit up and grab the pillow, clutching it to my stomach as if it'll help contain all of the madness seeping out of my skin. She turns and crosses her legs, staring at me with bright emerald eyes and rosy cheeks.

"Group time," she blurts and jumps to her feet, taking my hands so she can help me to mine.

With legs made of jelly and a stomach doing more flips than a gymnast, I drag myself behind her. There's a smell of lemon in the air that seems to leak from the shining tiles. I hold an arm around my stomach as the smell reminds me of that beautiful destructive drug I'd been given when I first came in. I stand in place, taking deep breaths to make my body stop reeling. Rachel stops and turns around, concerned. She takes one of my hands and walks beside me, swinging our arms back and forth.

"Please stop doing that." I hold my arm stiff and pry my fingers from hers.

She frowns. "Okay, I just know how you're feeling right now." She locks her arm with mine.

I doubt that. Perhaps she knows a sliver of the dark cloud that lives within me, but she can't know the full weight. I allow her arm to stay looped through mine as she leads me into a large conference room at the end of a hall. A long table—surrounded by a handful of people—sits in the dead center of the room. One person, who I assume is Doctor Andres, sits at the head. He has olive skin and matching olive eyes. His head is bald and shines under the lights like a freshly polished bowling ball; there is gray and red scruff along his jaw. He's wearing a blue button-up shirt and his hands hover over a notepad, a pen balanced between his fingers. He smiles at us when we enter.

"Finally decided to join us today, Alana?" he says with a tease on his tongue. "Thank you, Rachel."

"I didn't have a choice," I mumble, sitting next to Rachel on the other side of the table.

He doesn't respond. I'm sure he's had more than a few people reluctant to step into his sessions. I keep my head bowed, staring at the back of my hands as he begins to address everyone.

I can only think about cocaine.

CHAPTER THIRTY-FIVE

I don't want to talk. These people don't care about my situation, and I doubt Doctor Andres actually gives a shit. I half-listen to a guy named Sean confess to selling a ring to buy a rock of crack. I smirk because I've done the same a few times.

I'm not alone.

For some strange reason, my stomach flutters, and I suddenly feel just a hair lighter.

"Alana?" Andres' voice cracks through me. "Care to share?"

"Nope." I look at him and lean back in my chair. "Not really."

"Will you speak about why you're here at all?"

"Probably not." I lean forward again and rest my forehead on the table, wrapping my arms around my head and plunging myself in darkness.

The banshee is loud, and the storm inside of me rages like a tornado. It rips my brain apart, and it's starting to make me feel empty. Sitting here, I'm becoming hollow. I hardly noticed how silent it is. I look up slowly, still leaning over the table. Everyone has their eyes on me, waiting.

"What?" I growl, looking at each of them in turn.

I don't know if I expected to sound or look threatening. I could be blown over by a light breeze. There is a possibility that I will puke all over the conference table, yet I'm trying to stare these people down.

Of course they don't budge.

My eyes lock on one person. I know him. It's the well-dressed man from one of Rabbit's tweak houses. His head is freshly shaved, and his suit has been replaced with jeans and a t-shirt. His brown eyes look heavy, and his cheeks are sunken in. He must've gotten here right when I did, but he looks better off.

"Come on, Sunshine," the man from Rabbit's house presses. "We'd love to hear it. We've all shared."

My eyes narrow, and rage boils over from somewhere within the empty confines of my gut. "Do not call me that." Poison spits from my tongue.

"Why not?" Andres puts down his pen, all his attention on me.

"He knows." I don't look at the doctor.

"Fine." The once well-dressed man crosses his arms. "*Alana,* share your story. It can't be worse than any of ours."

He's probably right.

I know all of these people must have the same monsters I do—if not the same, pretty damn close. They're all probably related in some way. They all dance with drugs, balancing on the thin line that separates life from death.

All eyes are still on me.

"Fuck it." I sit up. "Sunshine is what I call myself out there," I gesture towards a large window with the jerk of my head, "so they couldn't find out who I really am. Creature taught it to me when I was like, fifteen."

"Who is Creature?" Andres presses.

"An asshole," the tweak-house man interjects.

I giggle. "Yeah."

"How did you get here? How did all of this," Andres sweeps an arm over the table, "come to be?"

The shrieking in my head gets louder as I twist my fingers together. I don't want to be here. I want to be high. I want to taste the elixir of a deadly concoction. Still, I also want to muster the courage to tell my story. It's why I'm here after all, right? I make eye contact with Andres.

"Um...I was twelve the first time I got drunk. I was with a friend. I was maybe fifteen the first time I really got high. Maybe I was younger? I don't know. It was with these two random dudes. I met them somewhere, but the details are blurry. They just told me that everyone experiments with drugs." My voice is growing softer, and I find myself looking at the table again as I speak. My hands shake as I let my tale unfold. "The high haunted me, you know? I needed more of it. Like, if I didn't have it, I would go insane. So, I called them back."

I look up for a second, turning to Rachel, who smiles to encourage me to keep going. My stomach is turning and my chest is tight. If I blink, I see rigs filled with brown liquid and lines of toxic snow.

"I told them I wanted something stronger than what they had first given me. I started doing basically anything that was handed to me. Honestly, I couldn't tell you half the shit I've inhaled, ingested, or shot up." I laugh even though the facts are far from funny. "Cocaine is my mistress though." Sunshine is screaming for a hit as I speak. "I can't get enough of it. Still, if I need to, I'll substitute it with whatever the dealer has."

"What was your turning point? Or greatest regret?" Does the guy from Rabbit's rundown homes of horror generally lead these conversations? "Mine was having my kid find my rigs and playing with them."

"I honestly don't know about my turning point. Hell, I was held at gunpoint and still kept going. I felt indestructible. I still do from time to time. That or empty." I'm rambling, so I make the final call and stand up. "I'm done sharing."

Doctor Andres ends the session.

Were they really just waiting for me to open my mouth?

I could have spewed any story and they would have probably believed it. All I did was comb the surface of what had blossomed in my head. I catch the once well-dressed man in the hall and stop him.

"What's your name?" I ask. "You know mine, so it's only fair."

He grins. "Steven." He holds out a hand. I take it, and he grips firmly, shaking my limp fish with vigor. "Nice to meet you finally."

"Yeah." I tear my hand away from his, almost embarrassed by the weak shake. "Do you know where I go for one-on-one? I think that's next, and Rachel just disappeared." I'm rambling again, my words tumbling over one another. "Or is the psych doctor next?"

"Slow down, it's fine. Everyone's lost on their first day. You probably need to see the psych next." He points down the hall. "Go to the stairwell, go up, turn left, tell the lady at the desk who you are, sit and wait." The instructions are straightforward and simple.

He walks me to the end of the hall, not saying much of

anything, but his presence is nice. He wishes me luck as I head up the steps, trying to keep my head straight. It's spinning, and my stomach still aches with the effects of the withdrawal. I am sure this sickness will never end.

I let a lady with gray hair bunched on top of her head know who I am. She tells me to have a seat and that someone will be out to see me in a moment. The chairs have a thin padding to them—an illusion to trick the mind into believing the metal frames are made to be comfortable. My feet tap nervously on the floor, and I dig my nails into my palm as I stare at the floor. There's a hallway ahead of me—opposite of the front desks—blocked off by a large door made of blue glass.

A voice breaks into the silence of the waiting room. "Alana."

I poke my head up. A woman in a ruffled blouse tucked loosely into her black business slacks is standing at a doorway that leads into the hall. She has black, curly hair and soft gray eyes framed with thin-rimmed glasses. A chain leading from one side of the eyeglasses to the other hangs loosely at the back of her neck.

She smiles at me, dimpling her rosy cheeks. I stand up and look around as if I don't know I'm the only one in the room. I walk up to her, and she guides me through the doors and into that hall. She has me stand on a scale to the right and doesn't say anything when the digital numbers read only ninety-four pounds.

Hell, at least I gained some sort of weight despite throwing up everything.

We walk down the hall a little more, passing a few doors on either side of us. Still, she doesn't talk, but she seems friendly enough. She holds a door open for me that has the name 'Amber Rizzo' on a plaque above the meshed window.

"After you," she says, waving me in.

She takes a seat behind a small wooden desk scattered with paperwork. There is a monitor on top, the tower tucked neatly underneath, suspended from the ground via a stand. She takes out a few papers from a printer to her left and silently looks them over, peering at me every so often as if trying to read me.

I sit on one of the over-sized chairs on the other side of the desk. I feel like I am at an interview and I have to say the right things so I won't have to stay any longer than necessary.

I have to lie.

Staring at her, I wait for a single word to escape her lips. For the longest time, she just gazes back through her glasses as she skims my file.

Is this how psychiatrist appointments are supposed to be? A desk between two people while you have a staring contest—trying desperately to seek out the dark parts of the other's soul?

"So, Alana, what brings you here?" the woman, Amber Rizzo, says. Her words are gentle and smooth, like a wave against sea glass.

"My friend dropped me off at your doorstep."

Like an unwanted cat.

"No, what seems to be the problem?" she presses. "I know Xavier dropped you off here."

What the hell? How many people did Xavier talk to?

"I have a drug problem," I state flatly. "I know that. I just can't seem to stop."

"That," she points at me and smiles, "is why you're here. Are you feeling depressed? Anxious? Any thoughts of suicide or self-harm?"

"Depressed, yes," I confirm. "Thoughts of suicide, yes.

Self-harm, yes." Why am I being honest? The words just keep somersaulting from my tongue.

"Do you have a plan on how to kill yourself?"

"No."

"When was the last time you self-harmed?"

"Two days before I got here." I look down, ashamed.

"Okay, for now I'm going to put you on a low dose of antidepressants." She begins typing away at her computer. "It's called Lexapro, and you can pick it up at the window in the lobby area. The nurses will administer your doses, and when you leave here, you'll take one a day. Understood?"

"Yeah." I want to leave.

She looks up. "Cameron will see you next. I'm sending him a message now. He'll meet you in the lobby."

I spring myself from the chair and head back to the sitting room to wait for my new therapist. In the meantime, I stare at the clock, my feet tapping nervously against the floor as I wait for my next doctor to tell me how I'm feeling and what to do about it. More people begin to spill into the room from the doors that lead outside and to different parts of the hospital. They each go to the front desk first to check in before taking seats around me. Most of them only give me a passing glance, quickly looking down when I catch their gaze. There is one woman sitting across from me who stares head on. Every time I look over at her, she hasn't moved. She has a head of tight blonde curls and too much blush smeared across her cheeks. Her clothes are too baggy, and her eyes look beady. The third time I catch her gawking, she just laughs.

"What?" I finally ask.

I want to curl into myself, away from her prying eyes and the harmless gazes of the others. I want to become invisible, a speck upon the floor for people to ignore without a second thought.

"You are so skinny," she blurts out, the words meshing together to make one.

"Yes." I can feel my eyes widen as I try to scoot my chair away from her without being too obvious.

Where the fuck is Cameron?

"Why?" She stands up and takes a seat next to me.

Why can't I disappear? Why can't I just turn sideways and slip through one of the cracks in the floor? Why does this person have to single me out?

"My name is Desi." Her grin is toothy.

"Alana!" A voice booms into the room as my response.

I jump to my feet and scurry to the sound as if I am making my way to the last lifeboat as the Titanic sinks. The man who called me has a dark-blond crew cut and bits of scruff along his chin and jaw. He wears a light gray button-up shirt that hugs at his large chest and arms. His pants are black without a speck of dirt, dust, or hair on them. His shoes are shined and could probably double as mirrors should he ever need it. He towers over me. His hazel eyes dart from me to the girl who calls herself Desi and I see the corners of his lips quiver for a moment.

"Follow me." He leads me back through a door that opens to a stairwell. We walk down the three flights until we get to the bottom floor, where we weave through the cold halls until we reach an office with the number 224 on the door.

He opens it for me and closes it only when I take a seat on the couch pushed against the wall. The cushions are a bit too soft, and I don't feel like I can get comfortable. He takes a seat at the armchair on the other side of the room, a laptop on a desk next to him.

"My name is Cameron." He reaches out a hand.

I shake it, trying to be as firm as I can with only bones. "I know."

"Ask me a question," he encourages.

This feels different. I had been put in therapy when I was really young because my mother couldn't handle my attitude, but I can hardly remember what happened. I vividly recall one man giving me cupcakes because I wouldn't talk to anyone.

"Did you ever do drugs?" I force myself to ask, fingernails digging into my palms.

"Yes," he admits. "I was around your age, probably younger. I took painkillers when I was about fifteen."

"I started drinking when I was about twelve at a friend's house, then I stole my mom's painkillers when I was fourteen." I'm happy that I'm finding common ground. "I drank a bottle of cough syrup soon after and fell in love." So, I lied a little during group. They don't need to know all of it.

"Did you stick with cough syrup?" he presses.

"No." I snigger. "My parents got me a prescription for Adderall when I was about fifteen because I would have these fits of hyperactivity and I abused the hell out of them. I slowly graduated to cocaine, and then whatever happened to fall in my lap, but coke is my go-to." I take a deep breath, fingernails digging deeper.

"Why did you start?" he asks. "Really think about it. It's okay if you can't think of an answer right now."

We sit in silence for a long time as I let my thoughts circulate like a hurricane in my head. He's patient, watching me intently. Not once does he pick up a notepad or pencil. He doesn't glance at the laptop or at the door with silent indications that he wants me to hurry up.

"I wanted to kill myself," I can't look at him, "so I drank

the bottle, but I only got high and I loved it. The depression completely faded away."

He nods.

I stare at a spot on the floor near my shoe. It looks like a face. "A friend gave me a couple lines of coke at her apartment. I couldn't find it, and my parents had taken me off Adderall. Another friend gave me a gram for a Christmas present about a year after that. I supplemented with cough syrup, painkillers—anything I could get my hands on." I take a deep breath, the face in the floor morphing into something wicked. "I always had to be this shining example. Straight-A student, work hard, look good, you know? Make everyone happy, bend over backwards for the those around me. Drugs helped me escape that stress and then I just laid in the grave I'd dug."

I am just beginning to peel the skin from my bones, exposing bits of myself that I leave buried.

Still, I don't speak up about my self-harm scars.

I won't mention my struggles with the demons that rear their ugly heads in my mind, or the mood swings that feel like I'm being thrown off a cliff and how I attempt to control them with a balance of cocaine and heroin.

"Alana," Cameron finally says after I'm done rambling, "I want you to let this sink in while you're here." He leans closer, both feet planted on the ground. "You are not responsible for anyone's happiness but your own."

Scoffing, I don't speak again.

CHAPTER THIRTY-SIX

I sit outside, following the few people from group that night after the meeting with the nurse that gives me my first dose of Lexapro. So far, it isn't making any sort of difference. I'm not sure what I expect. It's not cocaine or meth, so it's not going to hit me like a freight train.

The air outside in the courtyard is cold and the wind feels a little icy. I'm wearing a hoodie that Xavier threw into a bag he'd given to a nurse the day after I was dropped off. I hug it tightly around me, the sleeves drowning my arms and hiding my hands. The locusts scream in the nearby trees despite the cold. Like us, they refuse to die.

The guy named Sean, who has greasy hair and a pointed nose, sits with Rachel at the table next to us, chattering rapidly. Others—some I notice from therapy, and others I haven't seen around yet—linger around in scattered groups, enjoying the clear night sky and sobering air. Conversations between them spark and die just as quickly, like a broken light flickering. I keep my head down, tying the ends of the sleeves in knots to encase my frozen fingertips.

I am not here to make friends.

Hoping no one will bother me, I sit at a picnic table underneath an open blue and white umbrella by myself. Someone takes a seat next to me.

"Hey, kid." His voice is low and steady.

"Hey, Steven." I look up at him, hands still tied inside the sleeves.

He doesn't look like he belongs in here with us. He is built with slivers of muscle, his hair is trimmed and neat, and his skin is clear. What he doesn't have is light in his eyes, so perhaps he is just like the rest of us.

Dead.

Addiction is funny like that.

It doesn't care who it destroys.

He's wearing a gray t-shirt and black sweatpants. He lets the still air between us linger for a while. Maybe he just needs the company. Perhaps he's happy, somehow, that someone else here has experienced the same circle of fucked up people.

"Rumor has it that Rabbit and Tiger are pretty high up on the food chain." He breaks the silence. "We got out alive."

"We're not out yet." I state flatly. "And Tiger's in jail."

"Oh."

I pull a hand underneath the table and press it hard against my thigh. My wounds are healing quickly, but they're tender, and I can still feel pain if I try hard enough. I don't want to think about Noah being in jail and how I've used him. I don't want to think about Rabbit feeding me drugs until I couldn't move or speak.

I was only profit to him. I could've died on his floor and he would have just picked me clean and rolled me outside for someone else to find.

I press harder on the wounds, trying to clear my head of everything except the pain.

"What are you doing?" Steven's voice breaks my trance.

"Nothing," I lie and put my hands back on the table, digging a finger into the wood until I find a splinter. "What are you going to do when you get out of here? When they deem you well enough?" I keep the subject away from me. I don't need him prying.

"Take my kid to the lake." His eyes sparkle. "It's been a long time. I'll get a job and prove to my fiancé that I can be the provider I promised I could be."

He already broke his promise, so what makes him think she'll believe him? How many times has he been in here? He didn't look like someone who could keep promises to a wife and child when he was wide-eyed and twitching on Rabbit's couch.

"What if you relapse?" I ask.

"I won't." He sounds so sure of himself. His words have finality to them. "What are you gonna do?"

"Propose." The word gushes from my mouth like a waterfall. I can't gather it up and shove it back into my brain.

"Who?" he asks.

"No one." He doesn't need to know. He is part of this stupid drug game, and I don't need her name thrown around in it any more than it already is.

Besides, am I really ready to ask Casey? She probably won't accept it. I keep proving to her how trash I am.

"Well, best of luck."

He lets the silence return, hanging over us like a cloud as I wait for him to leave me alone. Still, he sits there, side turned to me so he can face the door. He watches people pass by in silence, elbows on his knees. I keep knotting and unknotting the sleeves of Xavier's hoodie. Steven slowly stands slowly and sighs loudly.

"Going to bed," he states. "Why the look?"

"It's just my face." I must seem annoyed.

Is there a reason he had to announce to me that he was going inside? I guess he's just being nice and I'm made of stone. My hands are shaking in my sleeves as I bite my lip to prevent tears and I stare back down as he walks away.

I messed up.

I don't feel like this one instance of rudeness will keep Steven from trying to be my friend. I'm sure he'll bother me again. The flood of emotion comes from deeper within. I let my friends down. I let my parents down. I let Casey down. I let my self-hatred consume every last piece of me.

I am going to change.

I can feel it.

CHAPTER THIRTY-SEVEN

I don't sleep during the night. I can't. Really, I don't sleep for three days. I feel tired, but resting is a waste of time. My mind races and flips, swan diving into crystal clear lakes. It's like a switch has been flipped in my brain. I don't feel empty anymore, or filled with black clouds. I am filled with light and happiness. My mind spins with ideas of what I can do both in here and when I get out. I talk to Rachel more, telling her stories of Skylar, Casey, Xavier, and Michelle. I may have told her a bit too much about Dante's suicide, but I can't make my mouth stop spurting confessions. A few times, I catch Rachel asleep as I continue to speak to her. Then I seek out Steven, who also doesn't sleep much. We talk about future plans, his kid and fiancé, and how we had come to meet Rabbit—they went to college together. He doesn't talk too much, but he stays awake. I move my cot around the room a few times, trying to find the perfect spot, and finally decide it's best where it started.

I draw complex mandalas on scrap pieces of paper and map out how I can most effectively rearrange my room back home so that I gain the most optimal sunlight. I will enroll in college and take as many classes I can while working. I'll clean the house for my parents and take Michelle on walks and teach her about the town and the city it's tucked within. I'll escort Casey to the fanciest of restaurants and provide her with the finest of meals.

I have plans.

I just can't sleep.

When I'm scheduled to see Cameron, I wait for him in the lobby while tapping my feet impatiently, eyes darting around the room, trying not to lock onto one person for too long. When he comes through the door, he can barely part his lips to say my name before I shoot up. I am happy to see him. After all, he is helping me, isn't he? He'll be proud of me. I'm making progress. However, his smile looks troubled. I can't bring myself to frown or match the worry that begins to fill my chest.

"What?" I ask, my damned mouth still stretching into a smirk.

"Nothing." He returns the expression.

He leads the way through the halls—not that I need him to. I have to restrain myself from rushing ahead of him and making my way to his small office with the plush chair and too-soft sofa. His door is open, and he closes it behind us after turning on the small speaker on the floor in the corridor that hums white noise so our conversations will remain private. I sit on the couch opposite of his chair, and we stare at each other for a moment. My knees bounce, and my feet are jiggle, fingers knotting themselves together as I bite the inside of my cheek.

"Well?" he finally presses. "What's new?"

I begin to tell him how I plan to do such wonderful things as soon as I am able. I tell him that I'm finally becoming friends with my roommate instead of holing myself up in a dark pit of depression. Unable to sit still any longer, I stand up, decide that's silly, and sit back down. I'm practically crawling out of my skin with energy. My words tumble over each other gracelessly as my tongue struggles to keep up with my brain vomit.

He listens to me babble on and on, nodding but never smiling. His expression is one of concern.

Why is he so worried? I am happy! I am energetic! I've felt this before—I have experienced these ridiculous bouts of energy before—and it's the only thing that will keep me sober. I don't need to chase the high. The high has found me instead.

"How long have you been awake?" he asks when I take a breath.

"Three days."

"Any sleep at all?" he questions.

"Like an hour." I shrug.

"A night?" He raises an eyebrow.

"No, total." My head shakes quickly.

He leans closer. "Have you ever been diagnosed with ADHD?"

"When I was a teenager, yeah." I nod. "It didn't stick though. I would get this excited and unfocused for a few weeks and then dive into suicidal depression. This is good though, right? It's better than being depressed. This has to be better. I feel so alive!"

"Alana, are you hallucinating?" He doesn't answer my question.

"No."

"Do you have feelings of grandeur?"

I have to struggle to focus on his words and not interrupt him with my own. I bite my lip to prevent myself from talking over him. "I feel like I'm meant for something greater than this—than what I've been doing, yes. I feel like I have some untapped talent begging to be released."

"Have you ever been diagnosed with bipolar disorder?"

I stare at him for a moment. "No. I don't get that bad, though." I'm not sure why I'm defending myself. A rock forms in my stomach as my heart begins to beat irregularly. I'm starting to feel dizzy, but keep it to myself.

"There's different types of bipolar disorder," he starts, calm.

Can he see how nervous this makes me? Do I really wear it on my skin like a new outfit?

"There's bipolar 1, which would bring you more detrimental manic episodes and depression. Bipolar 2 has upswings of hypomania, which is mania, but it generally doesn't last as long and isn't as damaging. Depression is the hard-hitter in bipolar 2." He pauses, watching me fidget on the couch. It's starting to make sense. "There's also cyclothymia, which is a fancy word for rapid cycling. You'll experience mania and depression quickly. There are also mixed episodes, which is self-explanatory. It's both depression and mania, or hypomania, at once. Like, if one foot is on the gas, and one foot is one the brakes." He leans back again and crosses his legs at the ankles. "Have you felt this way before? Without drugs?"

"Yes," I confirm.

"I need you to see Nurse Rizzo." He stands up. "Right now."

"Right now?" I follow him out the door and through the halls.

"Yes."

We go to the lobby, and I sit down in one of the chairs with a cushion that is only a façade. I press my thumbnail into my other fingertips, trying to quell the anxiety bubbling inside of me like a tar pit. Cameron goes to the front desk for a moment before coming back to me.

"She'll be out soon." And with that, he leaves me alone.

I turn in the chair, pull my legs up to my chest, then bend them to the side. I fidget back and forth before flipping over entirely and sitting on the chair upside down, my head barely missing the tile floor below me. I stay there until I hear Rizzo call my name.

CHAPTER THIRTY-EIGHT

My psychiatrist lowers my dose of Lexapro, saying that I can't be completely taken off just yet. She gives me something called Abilify that's supposed to stabilize me. I am also given a hefty dose of Neurontin to help with the anxiety.

The thing is, I don't want to be stable.

I want to stay this high—this euphoric.

Still, I take the pills. Maybe if I comply and act normal for a moment, they'll let me leave. *Then* I can stop taking the pills.

My moods shift, but not in the way I expect. I still feel elated, high up above the world and the mere mortals who need sleep and food to function. I feel depressed on top of it. While I'm smiling and incapable of sleep, my mind spinning with new thoughts and ideas, I keep thinking about suicide. It invades every blank dark space in my head. It consumes me, dancing with the sunshine that radiates within. I find a sharp piece of metal that was carelessly dropped by a nurse. I had been following her towards one of my appointments and scooped it up. I keep it hidden in my sock and use it to create new slices on my thigh to relieve the pressure building inside me. I want to laugh with joy and spin around, but every time I look in the mirror, I envision slicing my throat open and watching the cascade of blood soak my shirt.

All I want to do is go home.

So, I bite my tongue and tell Cameron and Rizzo that I'm feeling much better while holding back tears. Whether the tears are caused by happiness or sadness, who knows? I sure as fuck don't.

Either way, they buy it. I have to sign a couple papers and wait for my father to pick me up. I wait with my bag of belongings in my lap, staring out the window searching for his car like a puppy. I jump from my seat when I see it and tightly embrace my father when he exits. He holds his arms around me and kisses the top of my head.

"How are you feeling?" There is the growth of an unkempt beard along his chin.

I wrinkle my nose. "I'll be better once you shave your face."

"You need to shave your head, kiddo." He rubs the bit of hair that's grown during my stay.

I am free to go. My lips can't do anything but stretch into a wide smile, splitting my face and hurting my cheeks. Still, I feel that rock in my stomach. The dread, anxiety, and guilt bubbles like a disease. I skipped to the car, joyous that I can finally leave. Dad plays rock music on the way home instead of filling the space with useless noise. Each time a verse that means a lot to him comes on, he'll rewind the song and have me listen to the lyrics. He expresses the importance of the words and the flow of the rhythm that accompanies them.

The surroundings slowly start to become familiar. I notice the rundown houses where I've met Rabbit. I glance upon the skinny, decaying bodies of those with whom I've sat and exchanged murky times. The neighborhood gradually becomes cleaner and more inviting. When we're just a few short minutes from home, my father speaks up.

"The guys are waiting for you at the house," he announces. "They're happy you're doing better. Michelle is more excited than the rest of us, though."

I don't respond. My heart flutters while my stomach fills with stones.

When we park, Michelle bounds to the car like a deer, flinging the door open and pulling me from my seat. Hand wrapped tightly around my wrist, she pulls me forward and I follow without objection. She leads me to the porch and yanks a crystal from her small purse. It has a pink tint to it with a sharpened end. She places it in my hand.

"I found it in Skylar's room." She beams up at me. "But I don't think he's pretty enough to have something like this."

I suppress a laugh, biting my lower lip. "Skylar is plenty pretty." I turn the crystal over in my palm and notice a dip with a metal screen at one end of the flattened surface. The edge of the crystal that isn't sharpened into a point has a hole drilled through the inside of the crystal, stopping at the screen.

Michelle found a pipe.

At least it's clean.

"I think we should give this back to Skylar," I suggest.

She rips it from my hand and holds it to her chest, shaking her head with vigor. "Finders keepers."

"Okay." I give her a hug. "I missed you." I'll tell Skylar later.

"I missed you, too." She hugs me tighter. "Are you better now?"

"I think so."

Xavier and Skylar emerge from the house next, cigarettes between their lips. Skylar's falls from his mouth when he sees me. He pulls me to him, throwing me to Xavier next.

Xavier holds my face in his hands. "You look a lot better."

"Thanks." I push him away. "Casey around?"

Looking at the door, I try to will my eyes to see through the heavy wood. No luck of course.

"She'll be around eventually." Skylar re-lights his cigarette and inhales, the orange tip glowing with his breath.

"Hey, Alana, we need to talk." Xavier guides me off the porch and we walk to the edge of the driveway, away from everyone else. "It's really nice to have you back."

"Yeah." I look at him suspiciously. "Did you bring me to the edge of my property just to tell me that?"

"No." He looks down. "Something else. Noah passed away."

My knees grow weak as the news slams into my already blackened stomach. The monster begins to rear her ugly head. I thought I had killed her, yet here she is, attempting to reclaim her throne so I won't have to process this pain. My eyes begin to well. I tilt my head back and inhale deeply, forcing the tears to stay locked deep inside.

"He gave me his house." Xavier smiles weakly. "Obviously I'd rather have Noah instead of the house, but at least I can get Sky and Michelle away from Dad." He rests both hands on my shoulders. "Move in with us. We'll have the room."

"Yeah, sure." My words tremble. I'll never have the opportunity to apologize to Noah or thank him for helping Xavier save me.

"I'm working on gaining custody of Michelle." He gestures towards his siblings. "If I wait a few more weeks,

Skylar will be eighteen and I won't have to worry about that paperwork and court case."

He's working harder to get his siblings safe. I wonder if they have gone back since my parents gave them a haven. We walk back to the house, and my father hugs me again, knowing the news Xavier just delivered. I hold back my emotions and the tears stay where I've shoved them down, but I can't make my hands stop shaking.

Michelle runs up to me with a few shiny pebbles from the garden and gives them to me. "They're pretty."

"Yes." I nod and sniffle.

"They'll make you happy, Alana." She beams up at me. "You can't be sad, okay?"

I nod, but can't make my lips form words.

I miss Noah.

CHAPTER THIRTY-NINE

The brothers and Michelle leave the house when Emily and Sarah come over and whisk them away. Sarah doesn't make eye contact with me, and I know I'm not invited. I see Xavier scolding her but can't catch the words. It doesn't matter. I need to talk to my parents about moving in with them anyway. I stand in the kitchen with them, chopping up a carrot with a knife. My mind flashes to gruesome images of sliding the blade across my wrists and thighs. I blink hard, trying to push the thought from my head. Still, it lingers like a bad taste on my tongue.

The screaming is getting louder.

"Did Xavier talk to you about me moving in with them?" I ask, staying focused on the vegetables.

"No." My father looks up from the food he is sautéing. "What's going on?"

"Noah gave Xavier his house." I look up for a moment. "Xavier asked me to live with them. They'll have the extra room."

"Are you going to do it?" my mother asks softly. She hasn't really spoken to me since I've been home; her little girl has become an evil ghost, and she has to re-learn how to communicate with me.

"Yes," I state with certainty.

My mind is buzzing, alive with images of self-harm and mutilation. Thoughts of selling whatever drugs are left over accompany them. I can sell a couple things in my room as well. The fewer things I have to pack out of here, the better. Throughout dinner, I don't talk. I have to force the food down. I'm not hungry. I have too much energy for food.

After cleaning up, I head to my room and begin searching through all of the nooks and crannies. There's still a baggie behind the light switch. Also left behind are a few wax papers underneath a floorboard filled with a hit or two of heroin. I pocket them and find a stash of crystal still underneath a brick outside near the porch.

I head out into the city and wander aimlessly in the parts that make my skin crawl. Skinny, homeless men walk around, clutching needles like lifelines. Hordes of people with mean faces and scars hang out near the boarded-up buildings and approach stopped cars. Every now and then, someone gets in—or out. People move erratically at the medians of the city streets. No one dares honk their horn or lift a middle finger for fear of gunfire. People sit on flat cardboard and ratty blankets along the streets. Exchanges are made in broad daylight with little effort to hide the ensuing drug deal. I wait for the magical words to hit my ears.

First, it's "dog food". I walk up to the person, tap their shoulder and lead them off to the inner edge of the sidewalk. I exchange the heroin for cash and go on my way, walking and waiting. I soon hear that someone wants to go skiing, and repeat the process.

Cocaine for cash.

The meth is last and takes a bit longer to get rid of, but I gain the most profit from it. I up-charge, and they don't question the price. $300 richer and drug-free, I head back home. I speed past my parents and lock myself in my room. From there, take pictures of everything that has some sort of value: the television, a handful of new books, an old acoustic guitar, a guitar stand, and some jewelry. I post the photos on an online yard sale and wait impatiently for the fish to bite.

Slowly, over the next few weeks they come over for their new treasures. One by one, they pick up the items and I receive the cash. My parents watch me, but don't say anything. Once I have about $600, I head out to the jeweler that's located in a farmer's market a few blocks down the street.

My hands are shaking, but I haven't been surer about anything before. The air in the market smells like fried food and fresh meats. People are walking along the dirty halls with shuffles and mumbles. I scan the glass-topped counters and try to pinpoint which ring to pick. The elderly man standing by patiently watches me, unsure if he needs to approach. I think my face soon tells him that I require assistance, because he gets up from his stool and walks over to me. His dark hair has speckles of gray in it, and the wrinkles on his face are deep with life.

"My name is Mr. Ross. Need any help?" His eyes crinkle as he holds out his hand.

I shake. "Alana, and yes." I stare back down at a few rings with red and black jewels around rose gold bands. "I need one that is less than $600, but I can't choose. There's so many, and it needs to be perfect."

He beams. "What's the lucky lady's favorite color?"

I smile despite myself, excited that he didn't automatically assume I that I'm getting a ring for my mother—or worse yet, my boyfriend. "Red."

"What about this one?" He pulls one out with a red sapphire sitting on top of a rose gold band.

I look at it carefully, turning the ring over in my palm a few times. The jewel glitters under the bright lights. "Yes."

It only costs me $500—not nearly as bad as I'm expecting.

The jewels are fake, but who really cares?

Ring in my pocket, I dial Casey's number, hands still trembling. I'm not really expecting her to answer; I nearly ruined her life. Eventually, I hear the click on her end, but she doesn't speak.

"Casey?" I question hesitantly.

"Hi, Alana." Her words are soft. "How are you?"

"Better." I sigh. "Much better. Hey, can you meet me under that bridge?"

"When?"

"Right now." My words tumble over one another.

"Be there in ten."

The black pit is fading for now, but the anxiety and adrenaline take hold.

CHAPTER FORTY

We sit at the water's edge, butts on the gravel and dirt as gentle waves lick at our toes. The pregnant silence is filled with the subtle sounds of chirping birds and crickets too far away to locate. The sun is beginning to give the sky a red and pink hue as it slowly sets, making room for the seductive moon. I unlock our fingers and stand up, stripping down to my bra and panties to wade into the cold, murky water. I have the ring safely stowed away in my bra, so I'm not worried about losing it.

"Isn't the water cold?" Casey calls after me.

"Yes!" I tell her with a smile. I splash and laugh. "Come in, though!"

She rolls her eyes, a smirk playing on her face as she too strips down and follows me into the slow-moving river. We are up to our chests, the water just below the gift's careful hiding spot. I walk towards Casey, pushing against the resisting water, and grab her hands. I pull her towards me and hold her close. I can feel her tears as they fall silently.

"I really thought I was going to lose you that time," she

confesses. She looks up and holds my face in her hands. "I love you."

"Casey," I say with my lips pressed together like a fish, "will you marry me?" The words leave me with a wave of relief and anxiety.

She holds my face longer, staring at me with those tear-filled eyes. A sparkle lights them, and her face slowly begins to brighten, lips turning upward. She opens her mouth to speak, but no words come out. Instead, she rapidly nods. I pry her hands away from my face as I take out the ring.

"I don't have a box."

She rolls her eyes. "I don't care."

With the ring placed on her finger, she jumps on me, arms wrapped around my neck. I pull us underwater, allowing the cold to embrace us like we are sick children, intent on freezing the fever from our souls. We stay at the river's edge until the moon finds its rightful place in the sky, speckled by stars guiding lost souls to another world.

I am happy. I can feel it in my chest and stomach. Still, the fiends are howling, itching for a fix. Will this feeling ever go away? Will I ever be free from the entity I named Sunshine?

I glance up at the bridge over our heads, thoughts of jumping circulating in my head. Not to die, but to feel a rush similar to cocaine. I know it won't work; it won't be enough, so I push it from my head.

"Late night dinner?" I offer, standing up and pulling her with me.

"Where?" she asks.

"The only place open right now that I can afford," I state matter-of-factly. Perhaps food and bright lights will help stop my brain from torturing me.

"The diner?"

"Yes."

Hand in hand, we walk in silence. There are two diners in town, but I have only set foot in the other one a few times. However, we frequent this one with large glass windows and old personal jukeboxes at each table often. It's a place to venture after a long night out; a place for quiet celebration and solitude. We each order an omelet and talk of Noah and his passing. Casey is opting out of moving into his house for now. She mentions that she'll move in soon, but now just isn't the time. It feels like a punch to the gut, knowing that she isn't ready to move in with me, but I don't let her see the hurt behind my eyes. Perhaps she's still afraid the monster will once again rear its ugly head.

I don't blame her.

I fear that, too.

As the sun begins to rise, I walk her home. The smile doesn't fade from her face. I decide not to go inside with her. I don't want to wake her parents, and I need to get home and finish packing anyway.

The walk home is drenched in loneliness. The elation that Casey said yes to my proposal dissipates and the knot in my stomach tightens. Intrusive thoughts hammer at my head. I finish packing in a daze. A stupid grin upon my lips and black clouds in my chest, I throw my belongings into boxes and wait for Xavier and his truck.

It's dark out by the time he gets here. The city is silent and the stars are nowhere to be found. Xavier helps me load the stuff up into the bed, not asking me about my strange behavior. I'm thankful for that. I'm not in the mood to share my feelings. We pull ourselves into the cab and sit in silence for a moment, staring at my parents' house.

I can see them any time I want, and I already said my goodbyes earlier.

NIKKI HAASE

"I asked Casey to marry me." I can't keep it inside anymore.

"And...?" Xavier looks at me.

"And what?"

He laughs. "The fuck did she say?"

"Oh, yeah! Yes." I snap and finger-gun-point at him.

He rubs the top of my freshly shaved head and congratulates me.

The rest of the ride is silent. Neither of us knows what to say to the other, and we're both tired. Staying up as the sun falls asleep and waiting impatiently for it to awake is an exhausting task.

214

CHAPTER FORTY-ONE

A horrifying figure fills the deepest edges of my dreams. She's made of decaying flesh that hangs off her bones like rags. Her black eyes are sunken into deep holes in her skull. She laughs manically in a high pitch. I can't escape. Her fingers hook into the corners of my mouth, forcing it open until my cheeks split apart. There are needles in her arms, and there is blood around her nostrils.

These images begin to haunt me every night as I sleep, each one becoming more gruesome and twisted than the last. Part of me is happy that they keep happening. I need to see the beast that lives inside of me, just below the surface. It's my reminder to stay in line.

I'm shaken awake, groaning as I snap out of a nightmare.

"Alana." It's Skylar. His voice is gentle. "Wake up."

"Why?" I challenge, pulling the covers over my head.

"Because I'm bored," he states.

"Not my problem. What time is it?"

"Early." I can hear his shrug.

"That's not a time." I sit up. "Why are you awake anyway?" It's still dark out.

"I'm bored," he repeats in a monotone. "Emily and I were both up, and she wanted something to eat. I made it, she passed out, I ate it, and now I'm bored."

I don't argue. I just pull myself out of bed and grab a pair of sweat pants. Skylar hands me a shirt and turns his head. I don't so much care if Skylar sees anything. We've known each other since we were kids, and we both know there is no romantic connection.

I suppose he's just being polite.

He drags me out of the room and we sit on Noah's old couch. The same one I've passed out on more than once in a drug-induced stupor. We place glasses of water on the same coffee table I had snorted lines of cocaine and meth off of. Skylar doesn't have these memories, so he isn't locked inside his head. He's doing better. I see light in his eyes again. Skylar turns the Playstation on and throws a controller at me. We play a first-person shooter for an hour before Xavier turns up. We re-start the game and give Xavier the last controller, demanding he join us.

We aren't going to let him say no.

He sits down on the floor in front of us, back against the couch, until Sarah calls to him. He sets the controller down and makes us swear that we won't play until he gets back. We wait until he leaves the room to find his character, and Skylar and I annihilate the avatar while giggling uncontrollably like school children.

I keep the smile stuck to my face as the monsters keep reminding me of their presence with groans of protest, demanding I do something to make them shut up.

I will never be free.

Not really.

Setting down my controller, I stand. "I'm gonna go for a walk."

"Really? You're just gonna leave me here, alone." Skylar is being dramatic, his face straight.

"If anything happens, if you're about to die," I lift a finger and take a deep breath before exhaling dramatically, "call Xavier." I smirk and leave the house.

I trudge along the roads, breathing in the misty air as morning begins to take its proper place in the sky. I walk the short distance into the city and aimlessly make my way through the streets, weaving around the crowds and buildings. I ignore the shouts and responses for drugs and duck into a little café. They just opened their doors, and the smell of fresh roasted coffee beans permeates the air, teasing my senses. I stand at the counter and stare at the chalkboard menu. The handwriting is hard to read.

The barista has greasy hair pulled back into a ponytail. There are track marks on her arms, and I can barely see her pupils. "Need anything?"

"Medium coffee," I say softly, the screaming in my head becoming unbearable. "Hazelnut, no cream or sugar."

She turns on her heel and hastily makes the order. "Four dollars."

I hand her the cash and plop myself at a table with only two chairs. Wrapping my hands around the cup, I stare at the liquid inside, sniffing the steam floating from the top. The second seat is soon occupied. I look up, hands still folded around my mug. It's Steven. He is well-dressed again. His tie is straightened and his hair is cut to perfection. His bright blue eyes twinkle when I look at him. He smells like cologne, and there is something off about him.

"Alana, right?"

"Yes. And you're Steven." I smile, trying to be friendly. "What's good?"

He has a scone and a cappuccino. "Work." He shrugs. "The usual. Wanna go do something?"

"I'm engaged." I don't know why I go immediately on defense.

"I'm married." He lifts an eyebrow. "Not like that. I just want to show you something. I'm meeting a bunch of friends somewhere. Just come along."

"Fine," I groan and roll my head back. "Let me finish my coffee."

"No rush."

He eats his scone, and we drink our coffees while talking about life. We discuss getting out of rehab and going back into the arms of our loved ones. He talks about his kid running up to him and climbing onto his arms and legs. He tells me that he and his wife got married at the courthouse, unable to afford anything fancy—although he made her a promise to have something fit for a queen when they renew their vows. I tell him about Michelle's excitement when I got back and inform him of Noah's death. He looks at me funny when I call him "Noah" instead of "Tiger". When I clarify, I watch the light in his eyes shift. We talk over another cup, laughing at memories of rehab and the stupid decisions we've made along the way.

Soon, he leads me out of the café and down the streets. We walk off the usual path and through a broken chain-link fence. I follow him up a hill near an overgrown park. We climb until we reach the top of a lookout and I can see the city lights and the town tucked just beyond. There's a group of people already there, swaying to music and smoking cannabis.

I take the joint that is offered to me and inhale deeply. I let the smoke coat my lungs, but it isn't doing it for me.

Someone offers me a beer, and I chug it down as if I need the alcohol to survive.

I think I do.

The monster is still screaming, foaming at the back of my eyes like a rabid animal.

More than anything, I need it to stop.

Weed can calm the monster into submission, but I want to *eliminate* it. The night progresses rapidly and begins to blur. I don't remember leaving that spot on top of the look-out. I don't know if I formally meet any of the people there. I don't recall passing out in someone's living room, but that's where I wake up. Head fuzzy and pounding, I pick myself up off the floor and stretch. My arms are sore, and my nostrils burn.

How did I get here?

I try to push the thought from my mind.

I can taste the burning aftermath of vomit in the back of my throat and search the house for water. Finding the kitchen, I drink from directly from the spigot. The cold liquid feels like a magical elixir as it fills my empty stomach. I search the apartment for another person, but I am alone.

Where is everyone?

Did I break into someone's house?

I look down at my arm and see one needle mark surrounded by a yellow bruise. I groan, now knowing why my head hurts. I check the trashcan, and sure enough, there is a used rig. There is also a credit card on the kitchen counter and the dusty remnants of cocaine.

I slide down against the light brown kitchen cabinets onto the cold, tile floor. My head finds an uncomfortable spot on my knees and I sigh. I know I felt good last night. I know I had fun. I just can't remember it.

Footsteps stop at the front door just outside. I don't dare

move. I'm shaking, terrified that the monster I have worked so hard to slay has once again taken over. I feel like I'm spinning as I slowly begin to remove myself from my own body. I am slipping into a dream, and I suddenly don't feel real.

I cannot deal with this.

Did Steven betray me?

Where the fuck did he even go?

The footsteps stay outside of the door. Not even a jingle of keys sounds. Voices begin to float through the air. My throat catches on a lump when I match the vocals to their owners: Creature, Rabbit, and Xavier.

42

TWO YEARS LATER

What is being alone like? Not the kind of alone where you sit in your room all night contemplating the ones in your life that cherish your wellbeing. Nor am I talking about the loneliness that creeps up on you when you are physically by yourself. I'm talking about the type where you don't even feel like you belong to yourself anymore. Everyone you have once loved has left you behind in the wake of your own self-destruction.

Now, what is true pain? It's not a scraped knee or broken bone. It sure as hell aren't those trendy cuts scattered across your wrists, shown off for another pathetic woe is me story. True pain tears apart your soul and rips you to shreds until you are lying on the floor, stripped naked and shaking with fear, anger, and self-pity. It leaves you drowning in a pool of your own blood and vomit.

I am the solitary figure in the corner of the old building, save for the few rats scurrying around in the shadows. Under a few candles against the otherwise black room, I stare at Casey's picture. Her hand is raised to the camera, showing off her new ring. Her eyes are closed tight with joy as a large smile plays about her lips with an angelic radiance. A single tear makes its way along my cheek and down my decaying jawline. She had thrown the ring in my face when she discovered my relapse. When I said I wasn't sure I wanted help this time.

Hours before she was about to move in with us, she found my stash beneath the floorboard of my room in Noah's old house. She turned her back and left without a word.

I do not deserve words.

I deserve to be destroyed.

When Casey left, she told Xavier and Skylar what was going on. Xavier already knew that I was struggling again. Creature and Rabbit brought him to me as I sat, shivering, on a stranger's kitchen floor. I still don't know how I got there. Still, Xavier promised to beat me senseless if I came back high and dying. I know he wouldn't dare do such a thing, but I don't think he knows any other way to deal with me anymore. Skylar just stared at me blankly, the life in his eyes gone.

None of it really matters anymore, and I'm not sure why I hold onto the memories of a distant past. The only thing that takes forefront in my mind now are once again the snarls within the confines of my own skull, shattering my inner being with each shaking breath. I slip the picture back underneath the worn pillow and grab the only thing that I know will bring me comfort and silence. Yet it destroys everything I could have been.

Maybe—just maybe—this is all I could be: a failure to rot in the forgotten cracks of a twisted society. I am unseen by man and creature alike.

I lay out the white lines on a handheld mirror and perfect them with the taps of a used razor blade. The side of my leg has fresh slices on it from a desperate attempt to feel something, to release the pressure as if it is a festering cyst. I take the cut straw from the bedside table, warped with water marks and mold, and inhale the drug through my right nostril, plugging my left with my forefinger. Four thick lines within me, I fall back, sighing with relief. I let out a hollow, insane laugh, and it bounces off the walls of the dark place that I have somehow begun to call home. I pull a cigarette from a pack next to the razor blade and light it. The orange tip glows intoxicatingly in the dark, and thin clouds of smoke hover around me like a spaceship.

I'm on top of the world now, toes touching the metaphorical treetops; mankind cannot touch me. I have found a way to stay above the clouds.

I have always known.

Sunshine is alive now more than ever. She controls my every movement, my every thought—my every breath. She is all that remains. Alana is dead.

I am the dark disease that crawls inside of my soul and poisons my blood with tar.

I am the monster.

I guess there's one within each of us. It speaks in tongues and begs us to give way to sin regardless of consequence. The second you give in, thrusting your soul into the dark desires, the monster becomes you. Consumes and destroys you.

Your god will not save you; he probably isn't there anyway.

If you ever do find the courage to face your devil, you're only going to find yourself dwelling with lifeless, battered corpses.

The stupid thing Creature dubbed 'The Drug War' has

shaped me into a hardened version of myself: a gun-toting femme fatale, only high—really, really high.

Though I hardly ever have the weapon loaded—drugs are more important than bullets.

Creature, Rabbit, and I have all moved our way up the ladder in the War. Once Noah overdosed, Creature stepped right into his place. He took over his business and quickly became the man to which low-lives sold their souls. Despite hating everything Creature stands for and how he's almost killed me, I become his right-hand man—woman. I get away with a lot, and people trust me. I am small and look inno-cent, so people don't expect me to be one of the bad guys. We use it to our advantage. Rabbit tags along to a lot of our sales and has a room at Creature's place.

"Rabbit! You idiot!" Creature's voice echoes throughout the old house. "You were supposed to sell that bit, not smoke it!"

Something shatters in the room below as Creature's temper gets the better of him and I jump from the shock of noise. All Rabbit can do is sputter in fear. I check my gun, secure it, and throw my cigarette in the skull-shaped ashtray on the dresser.

"Would you two shut up?" I shout as I enter the room. "Children! Both of you!"

There's a coffee table between the two that meets at their knees. It's bubbled with water marks and burned from forgotten cigarettes and blunts. A small black safe is tucked under the table. Creature stands in front of an oversized recliner with plush cushions and faded stains on the arms. Across from him is a small black, leather couch that Crea-ture and I had found on the side of the road and dragged home. I'd bought a large throw rug at a thrift store to lay under everything in an attempt to bring the room together.

Two large windows bring light into the relatively spotless room. Rabbit and I both clean when we're high on stimulants.

"Rabbit smoked what we need to sell." Creature turns to me, face red. "We're going to be down a couple hundred, so how about you shut up unless you're helping." His once long hair is cut short, nearly buzzed.

"Don't start with me." I glare at him. "I'm not the one who fucked up."

"Yeah, sorry." He takes a deep breath and looks back at Rabbit who stares at his long fingers. "Do you have any personal stash you can throw in for this?" Creature's tone is tinged with panic.

Okay, so maybe Creature isn't at the top—he has to answer to somebody.

"No!" Rabbit is terrified, teeth chattering. "I need what I have!"

Creature leans his head against his hand, shaking. Rabbit can get us killed for this screw-up.

Damn tweakers.

I have learned a few things by stepping up with Rabbit and Creature. The real top dog is some guy named Tito. Of course, that isn't his real name, and I don't need to know what it really is.

If we don't make at least $5000 every two weeks to pay him back for what we get from him, we will die.

Simple.

We take our own personal shares and then sell enough to pay back Tito and turn a profit. Since Creature is the one who works directly with Tito, he handles the finances.

Did we make any money off of this batch?

I know I took a bit more than I usually do.

Our personal stashes grow a little bit each time we restock. The fear that Creature emits begins to overtake me. If we don't get this money, we're dead.

"Give me your wallet." I hold my hand out to Rabbit, waving my fingers and urging him to fork it over.

"No way!"

I roll my eyes, take the pistol from my holster, and whack Rabbit over the side of the head. He holds the wounded area as I reach around and grab the leather pouch from his back pocket.

I hate myself.

I hate everything I have become.

With his wallet in my fist, I walk out of the house and into the cool, misty air. A fog is settling along the city, and colorful, wet leaves cling to the sidewalks and streets. I pull my jacket tighter around me and keep walking.

I know I look sick and tiny in the jacket. It is a small, but it fits me as if I'm a child. My eyes are sunken in and my skin is pale. My arms and legs are painted with blue and purple bruises from the needles' search for decent veins. I have lost my sense of smell from cocaine, and all my muscle definition has deteriorated to nothing but bone.

Once I get to the nearest ATM, I pull out Rabbit's debit card, punch in the code I've seen him press a million times, and withdraw his remaining $300. It's the birthday money his mother gave him in hopes that he will use it to better himself.

Now it's bail money.

I stuff the loot into my bra and turn on my heel, hoping it will be enough to cover the damage Rabbit has done. I walk at a brisk pace back to the house, ignoring the cries for drugs and the creepy catcalls from men on the sidewalk or from their shitty pickup trucks. With the weight of the gun on my hip, I feel a little safer.

Creature takes the cash from me as soon as I enter the living room. He nods as he counts with a satisfied smile. Rabbit looks at me with hurt in his eyes, lower lip trembling at the realization of the betrayal. There is not a thing he can do about it. His so-called friends have robbed him.

He robbed us first.

I thought Rabbit was tough before. He once almost let me die in his kitchen. The first time I saw him cower below Creature, I knew he was just like the rest of us. He had been begging Creature for a rock of crack that we needed to sell. When Creature's lid blew in a red anger at the tweaker's ignorance, I watched Rabbit cry in desperation. He said he would do anything for that hit. Creature ended up selling the rock to some stupid kid on the streets for twenty bucks. Rabbit lost it, screaming, and Creature punched him in the face to shut him up.

It was a good day.

"That money is mine!" Rabbit pleads, trying to stand his ground.

"Nothing is yours," Creature says heartlessly. "Not anymore."

Rabbit opens his mouth to say something but quickly thinks better of it. Creature is right. Everything we possess belongs to either him or Tito. We know that. The only thing we can do is to try and reach that higher plateau of existence until it suffocates us.

We only try to get high and maintain what Noah has left behind, but we'll never be able to fill his shoes.

Noah earned peoples' trust; he built relationships with his clients. He helped them when they asked for it, and he actually cared about the people he sold to. The death of a customer still meant death of a profit, but more importantly, it was the death of a friend. It is—was—why he'd helped Xavier find me the night he dropped me off at rehab.

Creature, Rabbit, and I don't care. We don't care whom we sell to or about their wellbeing. If they show up at our doorstep shaking, bleeding, and on the brink of death, we will still give them their fix—as long as they pay. Death of a customer for us just means that we have to find a new soul to steal so we can pay Tito.

Creature mentions something about taking Rabbit with him to give Tito his money and pick up more. I ignore him. I don't care that they're leaving; I'm just happy to be left alone. I wait until they completely vanish from the view of the window to fully relax. Kicking off my boots, I plop myself down on the oversized plush couch. I open up a small box on the side of the coffee table and take out a fresh syringe and some heroin. I fill the syringe and elegantly stick the needle into the side of my neck. The veins in my arms have collapsed, and I don't want to bother digging around.

Sunshine no longer screams and gnashes within the confines of my head, begging for the next hit, to be on that higher plain of existence. I don't leave that place anymore. I stay one step ahead of my demon, hanging up by her strings and too scared to cut myself free.

CHAPTER FORTY-THREE

The day passes, and soon we have to go back out onto the streets and make our profits. The air outside is damp and chilly as we head down the dirty sidewalk. The sun is bright and high in the sky, but it doesn't seem to provide any heat. It's just annoying. My head is freshly shaved, so I feel the cold quite acutely. Dark aviators protect my eyes and I don a light leather jacket with thick leggings and combat boots.

Despite the cold, the weather is beautiful. Still, I know that within life, there is always death. The sun is lying to me. With everything that is perfect and flawless comes something equally as withered and broken.

Creature and I go out alone while Rabbit stays home.

The two of us walk side by side with perfectly matched gaits, heads held high.

We get along and work together, but Creature is not a friend. Sure, I pretend he is, but I only need him so I can get —and stay—high. The closer I am to the source, the easier I can get my fix. He will always be a tool. He's merely a device I use for my own destruction. I have no friends anymore. I have only accomplices and enemies.

I have no real attachments to Creature or Rabbit, yet somehow my life depends on these two idiots.

The farther we walk, the more familiar the streets become. We walk out of the decrepit city and into my hometown. The darkest depths of my memory climb their way back to the surface and my stomach churns. I take out a baggie of white powder tucked in my sock and inhale the contents through my nostrils to kill the pain.

We find a spot on the sidewalk near an old, abandoned factory building and sit on the cold concrete with our backs against the brick. The town is silent. Not a soul ventures about. Creature offers me a shot of heroin, and though I've just done a line of stimulants, I oblige.

Maybe this time it'll kill me.

Although it hasn't the last four times I mixed the two.

Any piece of me that's still human fades like cigarette smoke on a summer night.

We're waiting for five people; three of them want dope, and the other two just want weed. Why anyone buys cannabis from two shady people high on cocaine and heroin is beyond me. There are far better people they can buy this off of.

Whatever. So long as they pay us.

Time ticks by, and people slowly emerge from the holes in which they hide. All of them rush about their daily routines in practiced steps, brains on autopilot. They simply ignore the dead that sit before them. Creature and I are invisible. I want to keep it that way.

After about an hour, the first three customers stop in front of us, pausing for only a moment, hands in their pockets, hoods up and heads down. Creature and I stand, walking them behind the old brick building.

"Money," Creature says, extending his hand.

I keep a grip on my gun as he counts out the cash that's handed over by the skinniest of the three: a girl who looks about my age with dark round eyes and long black hair.

"Okay, Sunshine." Creature nods and pockets the cash before traipsing off.

I pull the drugs from my boot and bra and hand them their bundles of light brown powder tucked away in wax paper. I instruct them to walk in the opposite direction of where I am going and to stay out of trouble. Then I return to Creature with a smile, excited that the first sale of the day has gone so incredibly smooth. He snakes an arm around my shoulder and kisses my cheek. I push him away.

"We make a good team." He lights two cigarettes and hands one to me. "Sorry I touched you, Sunshine." He's sincere.

"Don't do it again." I inhale the cigarette and watch the smoke glide up into the sky. "We do make a good team."

We don't speak after that, puffing on our cigarettes and watching people pass. My heart catches in my throat when I notice two familiar men on the opposite sidewalk. Xavier looks bigger, and his head is shaved. There's a faint beard on his chin, and his clothing looks more business casual than before. He's donning a button up shirt and a pair of nice jeans. Skylar's hair has grown past his ears and is still messy, falling against his forehead in blond wavy locks.

He notices me, and I see a forced smile on his lips. I raise my hand a little to say hello as silently as possible. He begins to make his way towards me, but Xavier stops him with a firm grasp on his bicep. Xavier whispers something to his younger brother, and they continue on their way.

I shake my head and take a seat next to Creature on the sidewalk, knees to my chest. I miss my friends—my real friends. Every piece of me longs for them to be back into my life. Creature recommends taking another hit and I nod, eager to kill this agony.

Perhaps one more stab will make my stupid misery go away—one more hit to take away the pain.

That's how it is every day now. Another poke of the needle, another handful of minutes digging beneath my skin to find a vein that hasn't already collapsed like a building with a rotting interior and decaying foundation. Of course nothing gets any better—the only things that stop are the screaming, the urge, the clawing need.

For what, inner silence? My own selfish desire to stomp on the toes of death each time I inject brown sap or inhale glass shards of powder?

I ignore the two patrons that come for the weed. I ignore Creature's fake petty loyalty to these people. Hell, I barely even notice the walk back to our house. I don't even bother acknowledging Rabbit, as my boots carry me up the creaky stairs to my room.

I don't want to feel anything anymore. I don't even want to feel high.

All I can think about is the hurt on Skylar's face and the passing glance of disgust and shame on Xavier's.

I grab a baggie of cocaine and a baggie of heroin. Not wanting to go through the hassle of shooting up, I just lay out lines, snorting one after another—alternating between the two drugs. This is supposed to kill me. It is supposed to take me far from this world into a sleep I can't escape.

This will be the sixth time I have attempted this.

Collapsing on the floor, I lie on my back, staring at the ceiling, my hands and feet shaking with energy but incapable of moving. My heart pounds like a steel drum with a bomb strapped to it. It's ready to burst, tear through my ribcage, and destroy the room around me.

I don't move.

I stay there, nose bleeding and wracked with tremors, until Rabbit kicks my door open and drags me downstairs to count our profits. I try to protest, but he isn't having it. Rabbit might lack a set of balls, but he is bigger than me.

All he has to do is pick me up.

Even if I had my gun on me, I still wouldn't shoot him.

CHAPTER FORTY-FOUR

As the days progress, our pockets grow with cash. We have one more deal left to complete and we will have what we need for Tito and then some. No one screws up this time.

By "no one", I mean Rabbit.

Our personal profits are nice and heavy.

The fact that nothing goes awry in our deals gives us a reason to celebrate—even if our celebration is something we take part in everyday: getting high and becoming one with the damned.

Creature prepares dope for himself while Rabbit and I opt out to snort a line of meth. As Rabbit preps the light blue shards for us, he takes me back down the trails of our battered past.

Trails I'd rather leave overgrown.

I play with the ring hanging from a frayed string around my neck as his stories take me deeper into the woods.

"Dude!" Rabbit suddenly exclaims. "Wasn't I the last person you got high with before you went to rehab?" He seems a bit too excited.

I don't want to remember, but I do. I mostly recall Xavier

scaring the literal piss out of Rabbit when he found us and threw the scrawny meth-head into a wall.

I nod in response to satisfy his need for attention.

"Damn, it would have been so much more fun if that guy had never showed up. What was his name? Xander? Javier?"

"Xavier."

"Yeah, that guy was a dick."

My head shoots up and I clutch the edge of my seat, glaring at Rabbit. His pale, bony hands begin to fold inside of themselves.

"He's not a dick," I spit like the words are made of venom. "You almost killed me that night. If he hadn't showed up, I would have died. Talk shit on him again and I will shoot you in the damn kneecap."

"Christ, Sunshine." Rabbit shakes his head. "You wouldn't have died if you could handle your shit. Besides, haven't you tried to kill yourself like, five times now?"

His count is off, and I am on my feet, hand resting on my pistol. I tremble with rage.

My most recent attempt had been last night.

Creature jumps to his feet and positions himself between us, keeping a hand at my chest, but mindful not to touch me. "Sit down," he instructs.

I shake my head.

"Sit the fuck down, Sunshine!"

I drop into the chair and defiantly cross my arms.

"Xavier was your friend, Sunshine." He kneels in front of me. "*Was*. He's not anymore. Do you really think he cares about you now?"

I can't look at him.

"Did you really try to kill yourself?" He isn't concerned. He doesn't have it in him. Does he? "Do you want to talk about it?"

"No," I say with finality. "I wanna do drugs about it."

"Let us know if you need to talk about it, okay?" Rabbit says calmly, and Creature nods.

They don't care.

They can't.

Who would?

Rabbit hands me a compact mirror with two small lines on it and a cut straw. "Peace offering?"

I take it from him. "No hard feelings?"

"None at all."

The lines burn and scratch at the inside of my torn nasal cavity. Rabbit takes his and falls to the floor, arms spread out about as wide as his smile. Creature shoots up the murky liquid that fills his syringe and sprawls beside him. I sit upside down on the couch, head grazing the floor and feet against the back. Creature is silent while Rabbit and I chatter, jumping topics at the speed of light.

Rabbit tells me about Steven and his relapse. He mentions a girl he saw at the coffee shop with pink hair. He tells me about a map he wants to draw of our old town. I give him a story about my time in rehab, telling him about the therapist and my diagnosis. I detail the withdrawal from the mood stabilizers. I mention a dog I saw the other day that looked like a cloud with legs.

There is no rhyme or reason for our conversation, but that's what drugs do. They scatter me into a million pieces, making me incapable of finding myself.

"Why is your name Sunshine?" Rabbit sits up and looks at me.

I flip myself right-side up. "My name is not Sunshine."

"You know what the fuck I mean."

"Because when I first shaved my head, Skylar helped me dye it yellow and Michelle called me Sunshine. It stuck.

Your guys' turns." I want to know. I don't know why I want to know; I just do.

"Not sure." Creature chuckles, moving only his fingers. "Tiger gave it to me because I act strange, I guess?"

Creature's namesake comes from him lacking the emotional capacity of an actual human being. He is cold and unloving. It has nothing to do with him being strange.

"Honestly, I have no idea why I was nicknamed Rabbit." His long fingers sweep through his hair as he rolls his eyes at Creature's answer.

"It's because you're jumpy." Creature cackles.

I giggle because it sounds true.

Creature pulls a wooden box from under the coffee table and takes out a brown, sweet-smelling cigar paper and some marijuana. He rolls up a blunt with shaking fingers while Rabbit and I watch in anticipation. Creature is quick to light it up, then takes a sizable hit and passes it on. The smoke billows around us, dancing and swaying into the ceiling.

"Anyone know how or why Tiger died?" Creature quizzes us before exhaling another cloud.

Rabbit and I shake our heads. We know he died in prison, but that is where our knowledge ends.

"Well, he never really would have gotten busted," Creature says slowly so we can take in his words. "He was too smart for that. He was low on profits for Tito because he cared about his customers too much. Tito tipped off the cops about Tiger's monumental stash, knowing full well that he already had people in jail to take care of Tiger. A week beforehand, Tito had a message sent to his goonies." He passes the blunt to end his story.

It was all planned; Tito murdered Tiger—Noah. Well, Tito's minions murdered Noah.

Noah was a friend, and a good one at that. If he were still

around, none of this mess I've created for myself would be happening. He would have stopped selling to me and helped me get back into rehab before I fell completely off the deep end.

Or maybe I would have gone straight to Creature regardless.

CHAPTER FORTY-FIVE

I find myself alone as usual. On the floor, there's an empty rig at my feet, and I'm sprawled on the cold wood. I have the engagement ring between my teeth as I ride the crash from earlier, taking the easy way down as I float on balloons filled with dope instead of helium. My asylum of stupor and numbness is abruptly halted by a knock on the door.

"Hey, Sunshine." Rabbit slowly opens it a crack. I don't move from my spot, slowly turning my head towards him and blinking. "Can I...uh, talk to you?"

The ring falls from my teeth and dangles once more on that frayed string. I sit up and nod once, inviting him inside. "Close the door."

Once it shuts, he is bouncing on the balls of his feet, looking nervous. His long, pale fingers twiddle together as his eyes fix on their abnormal movements. He looks scared to talk to me. If he is, why is he even bothering? I'm just fine being high by myself.

I wait, watching his eyes dart around the room like a lost child. Why does he hang out with idiots like Creature?

Why do *I* hang out with idiots like Creature?

"So, I've been thinking," he finally speaks. "Creature's kind of a dick."

I laugh and nod. "Great observation."

"And..." he continues, dragging out the word, "I think we'd be better off without him." He takes a breath while mine hitches. "Later though—after the last of these profits are made and everything. Like, we should leave him behind, ya know?" His eyes widen as if he's begging me to tell him that his plan is okay and I'll jump on this wagon with him. "Forget about him. You could get your friends back, that girl...uh, Rain, and your life."

I just stare at him, mouth open in shock as my heart rate slows. That could be the drugs, though. Emotions are weird when you're always high—they don't usually exist.

"I thought I was just business to you." I stand before sitting back down on the bed, head spinning.

"Yeah, well, I don't know what's happened to me." He looks down and is perfectly still for just a moment. "Just think about it, okay?" And with that, he leaves.

I lie back on the bed and let his words circulate through me. My mind centers on seeing Skylar and Xavier again and convincing them that I can get better.

If only I *wanted* to get better.

The drugs keep me high and untouchable; they keep me in the clouds and I don't want to risk coming down. Not that I already haven't. I've still attempted suicide and I have fresh marks on my thighs and just above the crook of my elbow. The ones scattered on the underside of my forearm are beginning to fade, and I only decided to stop self-harming there because people ask too many questions. I slide the ring back between my teeth and stare at the ceiling tiles, wanting nothing more than to cuddle up with Casey on a softer, safer bed. Most of all, I think about the risk of leaving Creature. Will he rat us out to Tito?

Probably.

Will he even care?

Depends if we steal money.

Is it worth it to steal money from Creature and Tito?

Probably, but they will kill us.

I don't want to admit it, but Rabbit is right. The risk is great, but we need to get away from Creature, Tito, and the rest of this life. I sit up, and the world spins for just a second. The front door downstairs opens and shuts and I figure Rabbit has left.

Or Creature is home.

Maybe both?

My mind is spinning as I stumble over to my dresser and take out a small baggie of brown, disgusting powder. I grab a straw and snort the drug from the delicate piece of wax paper. A sigh escapes my lips as the high hits me before heading downstairs. Creature is sitting in the middle of the living room, counting out the newest profits. He's adding up what we still need to sell and what we can keep. I sit beside him and grab a stack of cash, organizing the bills into neat little piles.

"Where'd Rabbit go?" I ask.

"To get alcohol and cigarettes."

We both fall silent as we focus on crunching the numbers. Creature curses a few times in a hushed tone as he re-counts the stack again. Everything has to be perfect.

I stand up. "I'm short."

He points to the safe underneath the coffee table. "6437."

I punch in the code and the safe opens with a satisfying click. Kneeling in front of the table, I take out the scale and the drugs. I weigh them out precisely and separate them in their bags.

"When was the last time you had a hit?" Creature asks me casually.

"Right before I came down here." I put the last of what needs to be divided into its proper place.

"Want more?" He pushes himself off the floor and stretches, hands reaching towards the ceiling.

I look at him and grin. "When don't I?"

Creature laughs and walks out of the room and into the kitchen. He comes back with two rigs and a couple wax papers. He must have had some left over in his stash. He preps the drugs and pulls the coagulated liquid into the syringe. We both watch with bated breath as it moves around in disgusting, yet elegant swirls.

He holds the syringe up to the light and flicks the tip before smirking at me. He looks like a mad doctor in torn up jeans and a graphic tee, needle taunting me from his fingertips.

Or perhaps he resembles an executioner ready to make his first kill of the day.

"I'm not sure now." I rub the back of my neck, mind suddenly turning. "I mean, I've been thinking and maybe I should sober up a little bit." I look at him nervously.

He lifts an eyebrow. "What? Really?"

"I'm not sure," I repeat.

Creature just stares at me for a few long moments, blinking slowly.

"Okay, one more hit." I roll my eyes and crack a half-smile. Who am I kidding? I don't want to be sober. Maybe Rabbit got into my head a little too much.

Creature grabs my arm and pulls me towards him. There's no use fighting—not that I really want to. He taps the crook of my elbow. Creature has a talent for a finding a vein in even the most desolate of arms. He pierces my skin and releases the drug. When he lets go, I stumble backwards and let out a hollow laugh as the high hits me. He gives himself a hit and slumps down on the couch.

"Go take those drugs and make us some money so we don't get killed tonight. The dude's name is Rat, wears a white hat. He's buying all the coke, but keep it separated. The dude's a middle man." He waves me off. "You good to do that?"

"Yeah." I snatch the merchandise. "Wait, that was way too quick. How'd you know that?" We just discovered we are short on cash and I *just* weighed out the drugs.

He holds up his phone. "He texted me."

Here's a quick tip: never deal alone and never deal while fucked up—*especially* if you're alone. This is how you get robbed. When you're doped up, you don't really know what's going on. You think you do, and your mind will convince you that you do, but you don't.

Knowing the risk of messing this up, I still stand on the street alone, back against the same brick building. I prop one boot against the wall behind me and light up a cigarette, cupping a hand over the flame to protect it from the wind. I count the people in white hats to pass the time, analyzing each one to see if they might be the one called 'Rat'.

Time keeps moving, and there are about half a pack's worth of cigarette butts at my feet. A man who stands over six feet tall in a white hat brushes past me. He looks like a skeleton in baggy clothing, and he turns back at me and winks. I keep my cigarette dangling from my mouth and follow him into the alley.

The exchange is quick, and he doesn't speak. He just stares at my chest, practically drooling. My insides are squirming, but I decide not to say anything. I'm not in the mood for some asshole to call me a cunt because I tell him to stop eye-fucking my boobs. He doesn't look at the drugs, so I don't look at the cash. I just shove it into my bra, turn on my heel, and walk off.

His footsteps echo behind me. They continue even as I walk down the street towards the house. I stop and turn around. Rat averts his gaze as if I won't see him if we don't make eye contact. I kneel down and tap the spot at my boot where I keep my gun hidden. I take it out and chamber a bullet, making sure he sees. He groans and curses before turning around and walking the other way.

Rat is a fitting name.

Fucking vermin.

I hurry back with a skip in my step then stand on the porch and stare at the door before entering. Taking the wad of cash from my bra, I quickly count it. My stomach drops, and I can feel fear begin to creep through me. Every little hair stands on my frail, decaying body.

I am short by $500.

The cash is rolled up in such a way that you can't see the deficiency if you don't immediately count it. It's the same trick I have used numerous times on Creature. I guess karma is biting me in the ass. There's no use trying to find Rat—not that I want to see him again.

Tito is going to murder us. I can taste the blood of my future on the back of my tongue like a dirty omen.

I take a deep breath, shake off the fear, and walk inside. Creature is passed out on the floor of the living room with a needle in his arm. I tiptoe around him and unlock the safe under the table, opening the door slowly while keeping an eye on him. I take out what's left—his personal stash—and shove it into my pockets. The safe door shuts with a soft click and I walk over to Creature. I undo the belt from around his bicep, take the needle from his arm, and check his pulse. It's still beating. I gently turn him over so he isn't lying on his back and throw the money on the table.

All I can do is pray that he won't wake up. Not yet.

CHAPTER FORTY-SIX

I walk in circles around my room, contemplating what step to take next. A bag is packed with some clean needles, the bundles of heroin, cocaine, meth, and weed I've stolen, a change of clothes, deodorant, and a toothbrush. I do know one thing: I'm not going to stick around to witness Creature blow up, and I'm not going to let Rabbit take the fall.

Slinging the backpack over my shoulder, I grab Casey's picture, fold it into quarters, and stuff it into my boot. When I leave my room, I turn the knob on the door until the latch is secured back in the lock and cautiously release the knob, one hand pressed against the wood above the doorknob. I don't let go of the latch until the door is completely shut. I can't afford to make a sound.

Rabbit doesn't notice when I silently sneak into his room. He's cutting out lines with a razor blade on his dresser, making sure each one is perfect. Four white shimmery dashes are laid out before him. He smiles with content, excited to let the poison fill his nostrils—for the energy to coarse through his veins and slam into every twitching muscle of his thin body.

"Mind if I have some?" I don't move from my spot by the door.

He jumps up, nearly ruining his artwork, and looks at me with wide eyes. He must be expecting me to just take my share and leave—just as I have done in the past. His fearful expression softens when he sees that I'm not going to move until he gives me the okay. He hands over a straw and urges me forward. I snort two lines and give the straw back to him.

"What do you want?" he asks with a sniffle to get every drop through his nose.

"To leave." I hop from foot to foot. "Right now."

"Why?"

"Well, I'm really short on the last sale of the week, and I have no way to make it up. So, unless I bail, Creature is going to literally kill me. If you don't come with me, he'll probably kill you. Also, Tito will most likely kill all of us."

"How short?" he asks slowly.

"$500." I let out a small breath of air. "You in?"

He stares at me for a long moment in heavy silence, hands shaking before he speaks. "Why are we still here?"

I let him stuff a few things of his into my bag and he takes it from me, tossing it over his shoulder. We walk cautiously through the house as we make our escape. Creature is still out cold, drool hanging from his gaping mouth. The money is on the table, and the used needle gleams viciously next to him in the bright light. Rabbit moves past Creature and scoops up the cash I left there, plus whatever was stacked neatly after being counted without making a sound. Creature barely flinches when Rabbit pulls his wallet from his back pocket. He takes the money tucked in there and returns it to its original place. I watch Rabbit with amazement, envious of his hidden talents.

We don't even look back at the hideous place we call

home. We won't go too far—just far enough to hide from Creature and Tito. We have to stay close enough to find drugs. Even with the threat of being murdered over a measly $500, we still put meth, heroin, and coke on the top of our priority list.

Well, now that Rabbit has stolen the rest of the cash, we are short by almost $4000.

I think.

It could be more. Either way, there will be bounty on our heads.

Outside a rowdy sports bar on the outskirts of town, we settle down in an alley. We both shoot up with the stolen needles and dope and puff on a few cigarettes before passing out on the cold concrete. Rabbit lets me use the bag as a pillow, and I curl up with my biggest hoodie on. Rabbit uses his sweater for cushioning and claims he doesn't need to cover up.

It isn't too long before someone is kicking us awake, telling us that we can't stay there. The guy calls Rabbit a waste, and he calls me a whore. I shake it off, trying not to think too much about it. We gather our stuff, stick it into the bag, and Rabbit hoists it back over his shoulders. We have a limited amount of money and no way to get jobs.

We should have woken up well rested and ran. We should have said goodbye to this place and never looked back. But this is the only town where we can find a quick fix. This is home.

We stay for the poison.

CHAPTER FORTY-SEVEN

It doesn't take long for word to get out that Creature is looking for us—or that Tito is looking for Creature. That doesn't scare us away. I don't think anything will.

Drugs win again.

Daytime passes by relatively quickly, but nights are long and cold. We crash on the couches of rundown tweak houses of those who will take us in. Some find us too risky, wanting nothing to do with the battles that come with being anywhere near Creature or Tito. More than once I consider knocking on Xavier's door, begging for refuge. I know he'll turn me away though. I am a disease that can't be released into someone's home. I may be able to win Michelle over, but I can't expose her to who I have become.

Mostly, Rabbit and I stay hidden in alleyways or on park benches. We pass the time with empty talks of getting clean while we watch our poison boil in spoons and when we cut out lines. We snort, shoot up, or smoke, and soon forget about aimless promises. The brothers would kill me if they saw what I was doing. They had tried to save me and I threw their kindness away.

That night, we lie in the wet, dewy grass as the dark night blankets us. It consumes our senses and snuffs out our souls—although, that might just be the dope. Blood trickles along the inside of my arms from me attacking it with a razor blade in the park bathroom to relieve the building tension the drugs still can't touch.

Rabbit doesn't question it.

I'm happy he doesn't, but can't help but wonder if Skylar would say anything. Would he hug me and tell I'm loved?

Rabbit just babbles on with stories from his past. With my eyes closed, the palms of my hands tickle from damp grass; I'm mostly unaware of any banter running from Rabbit's dry lips.

"Hey, Rabbit." I'm pretty sure I stop him mid-sentence as his mouth slowly closes.

"Yeah?"

"Shoot me," I hold out the arm that isn't bleeding, "please."

We are already above the clouds, so I'm not sure why I want to get higher. I'm constantly chasing something floating above them—something I can't seem to reach. I touch the tops of the white cumulus puffs, but I want to be in space.

Rabbit pierces me with the needle before stabbing himself with a clean one. The drugs run through us like violent ocean waves, crashing abruptly into the concrete dams of our brains. Another silence overtakes us, drifting and swirling with the smoke of our stolen cigarettes. The deathly silence is peaceful and brings warmth to the crisp autumn air.

Subtle footsteps break into our cocoon of solitude. Their footfalls against the concrete echo as they walk around the pavilion a few times. The pattering of steps begins to grow closer, stopping only a foot or two from us.

Fear that Creature or Tito have found us keeps me frozen in place.

I hear a woman scoff in disgust, but she just walks over us. Another one curses and follows her.

Well, it's not our future murderers.

I want nothing more than for one of them to be Casey so that I can beg for forgiveness. I know it's too good to be true.

I wonder if my old family is playing cards or smoking joints until the smoke coats the ceiling with dancing wisps. I wonder if they ever think about me.

I open one eye and look at Rabbit. He isn't moving. I glance over at the pavilion and spot two purses. The person who is guarding them rises to go use the park restroom. I wait until the door closes, get up, and head to the pavilion. I sit down close to the purses and keep an eye out for the women who left them behind. Warily, I open one and quickly dig around. There's a pack of cigarettes, a few tampons, and $100. The other purse has some eyeliner, about eighty bucks, and a couple lighters. I steal these, too. The loot is tucked into my hoodie before I hurry back to Rabbit. I nudge his side with my boot.

"Get up," I demand. "We have to move."

"Why?" Rabbit sits upright and starts gathering our trash. "Where'd you go?" He picks up the bag and follows me away from the park.

"Just...let's go."

Once we're far enough away from the park, I ask Rabbit to stop and open our backpack. I empty the stolen goods, and he grins.

"What did you get?" he asks, peering into the open bag.

He sits down on the sidewalk, face deep into the dark abyss of the backpack.

"Stuff," I say. "Tampons, money, cigs, lighters."

"Why tamp—" He looks up and his eyes widen. "Don't answer that. I'm dumb."

I laugh and take a cigarette. We walk around until we find ourselves at a rundown pub beside yet another alley. They don't say anything to us when we step inside; we only receive smiles. They don't ask us for our IDs, which is good, because I don't have one that isn't expired. We use the stolen cash to buy drinks until we can hardly stand and need to lean on one another to make it back to the park. Rabbit holds me up as I trip over my own feet.

"You can't handle your liquor very well." He sits me down in the grass.

I glare at him. "Can we do more drugs?"

"Yes." He plops down and retrieves a compact mirror from the bag.

I pull an eight ball of coke from my bra and hold it at eye level, nearly drooling.

"Where did you get that?" Rabbit stares at it longingly. "I didn't know we had that much."

"I stole *everything* from Creature." I smirk, a strange sense of distorted pride swelling within me.

Rabbit nods approvingly. I hand the drugs to him and he cuts a few lines before handing me the mirror. "Take all of it."

I snort the four of them and fall back. The scent of kerosene, the instant numbing that travels down my throat and touches the back of my tongue, causes euphoria to rush through me.

Meth is neat.

Heroin has more of a death grip on me.

Cocaine is my mistress—my heaven and my hell.

Rabbit inhales his lines, greedily licks the old credit card he used, and dips two cigarettes into the baggie, sticking a small amount of cocaine to the ends.

"A snowcap for the lady." He hands me a cigarette and bows his head.

We stay up for the rest of the night watching the stars try desperately to poke out from the light-polluted sky. Rabbit holds most of the conversation while my mind races in circles.

What if Creature finds us here?

Does Tito know what we look like?

He knows what Rabbit looks like, and that puts me in danger.

What if I get cleaned up and eat something? Will I look any different?

Do my parents think I'm dead?

I wonder why the township never fixes the pavilion.

Why is nightfall so quiet?

I can't make my brain stop, so I shoot up to fall asleep.

Or die.

We'll see what the morning brings.

CHAPTER FORTY-EIGHT

Maybe we should have avoided the park. Maybe we should have just skipped town right away—taken our final hits before bolting. We could have done something that would prevent us from our current predicament: my head pounds as Rabbit and I are pinned against a tree with a gun pointed at us. The weapon waves carelessly as it passes between the center of our eyes.

"Do you know how much you're worth?" a guy with baggy jeans and a stained t-shirt says. "Creature will be ecstatic when he finds out who I got!"

Rabbit and I had been sleeping on the edge of the park, right by the tree line of the thinning forest. We figured if we were far enough away from everyone, we wouldn't be recognized by the wrong people. We were incorrect. This guy had kicked us awake and demanded that we walk into the woods. When I had questioned him, he took his gun out and told us he wouldn't ask again. He waited until we were far enough away that we couldn't see the park before he told us to stand against a tree.

"Who are you?" Rabbit asks, lifting an eyebrow.

"Shut up!" the guy shouts. He flips his red hair away from his ear and pulls out his phone, holding the gun with the other hand. "Stop talking so I can call Creature and let him know where we are."

Creature has spread the word that he's looking for us. I'm sure he promised something astronomical for any worthwhile information: a generous amount of money and a Mount Everest-sized pile of drugs. Both of these will get the local dealers and addicts looking for us as if our blood is made of gold. I look at Rabbit, knees wobbling. I'm terrified. If this guy doesn't kill us, Creature will.

And if Creature doesn't, he'll pass us Tito.

Rabbit's head is down as he takes deep breaths, hands raised. He's muttering in a panic, begging this guy to not hand us over to our murderers.

"Shut up or the whore gets it!" He points the gun at me with the phone at his side. He still hasn't called anyone.

"Do it!" I shout. I don't want to be alive anyway, so why am I scared? "Come on, you coward! Sell me with a fucking bullet in my skull! Go on!"

I'm ready to let it tear apart my skin and embed itself in my brain. I close my eyes tight when he racks the slide, and I wait for the split-second of warm blood before death.

But that release never comes.

Frozen in fear, the few seconds Rabbit and I stand there seem like hours. The gun does go off, but it's above our heads. The bullet's crack still echoes and makes my ears ring. It takes me a while to open my eyes. The redheaded moron lies before us, blood trickling from a small cut at the back of his head.

"Well, don't you look like shit?" Skylar throws a block of wood off to the side.

Tears well in my eyes when I see our rescuer. I don't

bother asking how he found us, it's not important. I'm sure Skylar hates me. I'm positive he wouldn't mind seeing me dead, yet here he is, knocking out an armed man. I open my mouth to speak, but the words won't leave my tongue.

"I really did miss you, Alana." He pulls me into a hug, and I sniffle back the tears that threaten to spill.

Rabbit has fallen to the ground, slowly descending to the grass with his back against the tree. His head is in his hands as he shakes.

He needs a fix.

Fuck, *I* need a fix.

"How about you come with me to Noah's old place," Skylar says. "You know, the place you used to call home? Xavier's out of town and him and Sarah are no more, so they won't be able to kick you out." He holds my hand in his. "Come home, Alana."

"About time he kicked her to the curb," I scoff.

Skylar shakes his head, but I can see the smirk on his lips. He grabs Rabbit by the arm and yanks him to his feet. "You can come, too."

"Who's Noah?" Rabbit questions, brushing himself off and staring at Skylar. "Who are *you*?"

"Noah was Tiger," I state blankly, sure I've told him this already. "And he's Skylar, Xavier's younger brother."

"Hi." Skylar raises a hand. "I'm Skylar, Xavier's younger brother."

"Got it." Rabbit nods. "Thanks for saving us."

"Um...Sky?" I'm hesitant as the words try to find themselves. "Thanks. I really miss you guys and I want to come back, and I know it's not—"

"Would you shut up?" He rolls his eyes and begins to lead the way. "One thing at a time. Let's just go home and you two can take showers, because you both stink."

We walk through the town with Skylar guiding the way. Rabbit keeps the backpack slung over his shoulder, heavy with drugs, paraphernalia, and few other items. He gives me a few uncertain glances, and I keep returning them with reassuring smiles.

How reassuring can a smile be if it's coming from someone who looks like a skeleton?

There are thousands of butterflies trying to break through my stomach, and I'm sure I'm in a dream. I keep digging my nails into my palms to tell myself that I'm awake. The pain reminds me of my torn apart arm, and I become grateful that Skylar hasn't said anything.

Has he even noticed?

Rabbit nudges me. "You sure about this?" he whispers.

"More than I've been about anything else."

There is no other way.

We will be safe there.

Maybe.

CHAPTER FORTY-NINE

Rabbit passes out on the couch after we take our showers. I forgot what steaming hot water feels like on my skin—we'd been washing up in gas station sinks. While Rabbit sleeps, Skylar and I watch cartoons in silence. Skylar sits on the floor with his back against the couch, and I lie on the carpet, head resting on a pillow from Xavier's room.

Finally, he breaks. "Alana, you look terrible. What the hell happened?"

I'm not sure what I'm supposed to say, so I keep my mouth shut. I can't even bear to glance at him, my expression still blank. We both know what happened: once again, I messed up. I hurt everyone around me along the way.

I am a selfish, monstrous bastard.

No one matters and nothing real exists to me—just drugs.

That's a lie.

My family matters; my friends matter. My brain just doesn't allow them to be front and center all the time. Skylar offers me some food, and I shake my head.

"Come on, you need to eat," he urges.

"No, I don't." My words are hollow. I turn over and look up at the ceiling, blinking back tears. The drugs make sure I don't feel hunger—not really.

Skylar has changed slightly since I last saw him. In a good way. It makes my heart lighter to see his growth. His head is shaved, which is a departure from his long blond locks, and he's wearing a new tattoo on the back of his neck: a small lion's head with Dante's name written elegantly in the detailed lines of the mane. Skylar has filled his small frame with muscle and he's beginning to look more like his brother, Xavier. He joins me on the floor, hands folded at his chest as he also stares at the ceiling.

"So, are you going to go back to rehab?" I can feel his eyes on me as he turns his head.

"Didn't work last time."

He goes quiet again for an extended moment. "Well, I'm not going to let you back on the streets. My best friend is not going to die on me." I hear him choke on his sorrow as he attempts to regain himself. "Xavier can decide what to do with that guy." He points at my traveling companion.

"Rabbit," I mutter. "We call him Rabbit."

Skylar doesn't say another word. He pulls himself from the floor and leaves the room. A few moments later, the melodic plucking of an acoustic guitar fills the air. I close my eyes and let out a deep breath. I'm starting to feel sick, and my skin is crawling. A dark, empty pit grows in my stomach and I scratch at my sleeves, the cuts on my arms beginning to itch and sting.

I want my next hit.

I need to be numb. I need this screaming to stop.

I lust for the poison, but instead I curl up and keep my eyes closed, refusing to move. I count my breaths and press softly on my inner forearm, letting the adrenaline fueled by the pain course through me as if it is close enough to what I crave. I have to fight this. Yeah, I want the drugs, and I can feel the nagging pull from deep within my bones. However, I also long for the life I once had, alongside the ones I actually care about and love.

I'm just terrified of facing Xavier.

Rabbit probably won't stay; he'll split the moment he wakes up. That's fine by me. I'm not his babysitter, and he can take care of himself. To be completely honest, I won't be surprised if he runs off and turns me over to Tito.

Oh well.

Burying my face in the pillow, I let the first deep slumber I've had in months overtake me.

CHAPTER FIFTY

I know I passed out on the floor. I know I had my head stuffed in that pillow that smells like Xavier, knees curled up to my chest.

So, how did I end up in Skylar's old room?

The floor is made of dark wood accented with deep maroon walls and white trim. A single throw rug lies under a poorly constructed pinewood table. A cheap thrift store chandelier hangs from the center of the room and casts vague light into a few of the shadowed corners. Posters, old jacket patches of punk bands, and stickers cover every inch of the ceiling.

My body is sore and aching, a pool of sweat soaks the bed, and I have to fight the urge to puke on the floor.

I really need a fix.

I need a line of white powder to burn my nostrils and numb my throat. I need the pick-me-up so I can stand without feeling like death. I need a swirling mix of brown dope so I can flirt with death himself while feeling more alive than ever.

But I can't find the will to move. The emptiness inside

me somehow weighs a thousand tons, turning my muscles into mush and my soul into tar. I lie here, listening to the chatter that takes place on the floor below me. No matter how much I concentrate, I can't seem to match the disembodied voices to faces that I recognize in my mind. Several times, I question my sanity, wondering if I'm imagining them.

Is this just some sort of disgruntled hallucination caused by an overdose?

I begin to feel my dark, poisoned soul leave me. I look at my hands in disbelief. I know I am alive, but I don't feel like it. I know I'm awake, but I'm not fully convinced.

"Okay, Alana," I whisper to myself. "Get up."

I sit up slowly and swing my legs off the bed. The sudden movement makes my stomach lurch, and its contents have no chance of staying inside. I vomit on the floor, some of it getting on my legs and feet. Head in my hands, I groan.

I am pathetic.

I have reached the stage of a rotting, living corpse once again. Only this time, I really don't want to go through with it.

I want another hit.

Sneaking out of the room, I head to the bathroom to drink cold water from the faucet and grab a towel. After I clean up my mess, I lie back down on the bed, giving up on rising. My eyes close and I drift into a half-sleep. The kind where you're not entirely falling into a slumber, but it's close enough. I swear I hear the door open, but I don't move. I just lie with my back to it, curled up in a ball under the blanket.

"You sure you want to stay in here?" I hear Skylar ask.

I don't know if it's directed at me so I don't answer. There is no response, just the click of the door shutting. I'm no longer alone—I can feel someone watching me. Yet I remain still. The bed caves near my feet.

Her floral perfume fills my nose as Casey moves her fingers along the back of my head. I haven't shaved in a few days, so there's a soft layer of fuzz on my skull. I don't open my eyes or turn to face her. I can't. I'm terrified of seeing even the slightest hint of hurt.

"Alana, why the hell do I still love you so much?"

Finally looking at her, I turn and sit up. I want to smile, but I can't muster the strength to fight past this crippling depression. All I can manage is a weak curl of the lips. To be this close to her again—and not in a coffin—is something I never thought I would experience. Casey's eyes are filled with pain.

I am the cause.

The ring now hangs from her neck; she must have taken it while I was passed out. It's rightfully hers anyway.

"I'm not sure why you still love me either," I say softly, staring at the blanket. "How?"

"Remember how I said I'd be with you: bumps, spins, crashes, and all?" she gently asks.

"Yeah. You said you didn't want me to drown."

"I'm not going to let you drown, Alana." She kisses my lips and gets up. "But if Xavier decides to kick your ass when he sees you, I'm not going to stop him. Oh, and we took the backpack."

With that warning, she walks out.

The reminder of having to eventually face Xavier sends chills through me, but it's not like I can avoid it. He does live here. Besides, I need him back in my life. If anyone can straighten me out, it's him. He'll beat Sunshine out of me if he has to. That just might be what I need: for someone to hand me my own worthless ass.

I curl back up on the bed, hiding under the covers and shaking with sickness. There's a faint crinkling in my pockets as I move around. I sit up and stare at the door for a moment, making sure it isn't about to open. Digging around my small, nearly worthless pockets, I pull out a few baggies of white powder and some wax papers filled with brown poison.

Why didn't I check for them before?

How the hell did I forget I had them on me?

I'm a terrible drug addict.

I watch the entryway with paranoia as I snort two wax papers' worth of heroin. The cocaine is tucked safely in my bra and I lie back down. It isn't as good as shooting up, but it'll do for now. The tiny wax squares scatter across the floor, and I have a satisfied grin on my face. The shaking stops, the screaming in my head vanishes, and I no longer feel empty.

All is quiet again.

CHAPTER FIFTY-ONE

My sleep is deep and filled with vague dreams. Sadly, they aren't made of candy-coated lies of a better tomorrow. Faceless ghouls guide me along a path I have treaded more than once. Near complete darkness consumes my thoughts. The comforting dreams of death—and the silence it can bring with it—hold me with strange warmth. Perhaps fear should creep through me at this invasive thought. It should jolt me out of bed in terror. However, the thought of dying brings comfort.

They would be better off without me.

I know they would.

Their worry will fade, and I will be left to drift into the nothingness that comes with the afterlife.

No more screaming, no more need to fill every last fiber of myself with drugs until I am on top of the world again. It would be just pure, peaceful silence.

The dreams of death don't last, as nothing good lasts forever: beautiful glass shatters, and roses wilt and die.

I open my eyes, still groggy with exhaustion. Xavier has me against the wall. The look on his face could scare the devil back into his hiding hole. He yells at me, but the words sound like a mumbled mess as I struggle to regain consciousness. I want to be angry with him for being woken up in such a violent manner. I would never expect Xavier to lay a hand on me, especially when I'm merely skin and bones—just a few pounds away from floating on the wind like a battered feather.

All I can do is let the tears fall from the corners of my hardly opened eyes. I am so happy to see him again, to be in the same room with him again. Even though he's yelling at me and pinning me against the wall with his forearm on my chest, I feel safe. A few minutes pass before he finally lets me go. Xavier turns away from me and towards the door, fury in his trembling muscles, and he mutters something under his breath.

He probably wants to hit me.

I don't blame him; *I* want to hit me.

He spins back around. "Alana!"

My heart stops as fear fills me. "Yes, Xavier?" The words tumble from my mouth.

"You are a vile, low-life, scumbag, ignorant, selfish piece of shit." He levels his eyes with mine and points his finger at me, the tip nearly touching my nose. He isn't wrong. "I despise everything you've become. You killed yourself, and you dragged us down with you! For what? A single fucking hit!" He picks up the wax papers. "You come back into my house, greeted by nothing but pure hospitality from Skylar, and this is how you repay us? Fuck you, Alana."

"It's not—"

"Don't lie to me!" he shouts, face red. "I'm not an idiot. I've played this game before."

"Are you going to kick me out?" I slump onto the bed in

shame, head hanging. I'm afraid of his answer. "Did you kick Rabbit out?"

"You mean Justin? I dropped him off at the methadone clinic." He sits beside me and sighs. "I'm not going to kick you out. I want to, and I talked to your parents about it. They think you'd be better off if I kept an eye on you. Besides, Skylar wants you here, and so does Casey and Michelle. You wanna know the truth, Alana?"

"Do I have a choice?"

"No." He slowly shakes his head. "We miss you. You're still family to us, and you're not going back out there. But we're doing this on *my* terms this time." He points to himself. "This room is all you'll see for the next ten days. You'll be going to see Doctor Rizzo and Doctor Cameron when you're finally clean to set your head a bit straighter."

I laugh. "That will never happen."

"Shut the hell up." He hugs me. "I love you, Alana, but you need to prove to me that I'm not doing this for nothing."

He stands up and walks out of the room, locking the door behind him. I wait until the heavy footsteps reach the end of the stairway before I tuck myself deep under the blankets, eyes welling with tears once more.

There is one thing I know for sure: this is going to be hell.

CHAPTER FIFTY-TWO

The sickness drags on, taking its deathly toll on my body—or what's left of it.

Commence puking and cease living.

Or is it commence living?

At this point, I don't care. I just want it to be over.

I want to crawl back into the tattered bed I have built in the bottom of the hole I dug for myself so many years ago. I find comfort in that darkness. It is as close to what the doctors call 'hypomania' as I can get, and I don't want to come down.

The door is locked from the outside, and jumping out of the window won't work. The fall will break my legs and then Xavier will find me on their lawn like a shattered gnome.

Michelle is the one who escorts me to the bathroom whenever I need it. I guess they know that I won't run off on her—I can't disappoint her. She is too young, and she doesn't understand my condition. We told her I'm sick and that's it. She holds my hand as we walk across the hall and she tells me about her day while I shower, brush my teeth, or use the toilet. I encourage her to draw more and to keep fiddling with the ukulele that she'd been given years ago.

Xavier brings me food. I see him the most. He comes in even if his hands are empty. Most of the time, he'll just sit at the far end of the room on a metal folding chair, a psychology book or something from his college classes gripped tightly in his fingers. He peeks over the edges of his text to watch me shiver my addiction away. When he does have food, he never sits down and eats with me. He never brings me a few beers to pass around or shares what is going on in the world.

He hates me, and he isolates me.

But his method is working.

Every now and again, he'll bring in a joint and smoke with me. It eases my nausea and gives me an appetite.

Other days, he scoots the chair closer and sets his books down on the floor. He'll give me words of encouragement lined with distaste, as if this concoction will somehow lift my rotting spirits and make me whole again. I usually just turn my back to him, curling up in a ball.

When Xavier isn't around, Skylar slips notes under the door. They usually tell me to keep my head up and that he has something green and sticky waiting for me once I complete this dreaded task. He tells me it is better than whatever Xavier is giving me—although it's likely the same.

Soon, I am able to get up without vomiting or shaking. I can eat at a normal pace and don't have to nibble. I only feel slightly normal when Xavier brings in a bit of cannabis to smoke to calm the tortures of withdrawal. As usual, Xavier comes into my locked room. Only this time he doesn't pull out that stupid metal chair, and his arms are free of any books. He sits on the edge of the bed and stares at me, eyes drilling into my head.

"What do you want?" I ask him, raising a single eyebrow.

"You ready to leave this room?"

"No." I stare at him with a blank expression, my lips a thin line. "I love it in here."

A smile breaks across his face and he chuckles, shaking his head. "I can't afford for you to see Cameron or Rizzo right now though."

"Oh, and I was really looking forward to therapy." The sarcasm escapes my tongue like a thick liquid.

He laughs and pulls me to my feet, wrapping me in a hug. "I'm proud of you."

"Thanks." The word is weak, and I embrace him tightly, the widest smile I can possibly possess stretching from ear to ear.

Xavier walks me out the door, and I follow his shadow, finally leaving the damned space. I run down the stairs and hug Skylar tightly before grabbing Casey and twirling her around in circles.

I don't feel healed. Not really.

I still feel sick. I can still hear the faint scratching of the emptiness inside me. The pull of gross euphoria that attempts to rip my soul from my skin.

CHAPTER FIFTY-THREE

The first thing I do with my freedom is leave the house. I need to see the sky. I need to bask in the light of the moon. Xavier hands me his cell phone before I head out and tells me to call someone if I need anything.

I walk the hollow streets of the city alone. With the night cast across the sidewalks and buildings, no one walks in rushed strides to go nowhere. The tight groups of giggling people have broken apart, tucked away safely in their beds. Only a few scattered addicts, itching their necks and faces and sniffling, a couple whores, and a handful of dealers wander the city at this hour.

I am the outcast, yet I belong.

Once an addict, always an addict.

Sunshine screams within the confines of my skull, pulling the strings of my psyche until I find refuge in an alley. I take a deep breath, and my knees shake as I lean against the wall. Hands planted on my thighs, I try to focus as my world wickedly spins. My adrenaline soars, and my hands vibrate. My brain tells me to run and get out of here, but I can't move.

This can't be happening!

I am defeating my monsters.

I am stronger than this!

Or am I? Will this insane inner battle ever stop?

It can.

Just one more hit.

One more hit turns into three filled syringes, a pipe of crystals, and an eight ball waiting to journey its way up your nose. Then, I'll be back at square one—fighting death and avoiding life.

Most people just crumble and die out. They become another street statistic; another news report to worry about for a day or two before moving on.

Nobody actually cares.

I hear an irksome little tune from my back pocket, and my eyes narrow in annoyance.

I guess some people care.

I push the green button on the screen. "What?"

"Well, hello to you too, my friend." Skylar chuckles. "Where are you? Come home and help me smoke this pipe."

"I'm just out. I needed fresh air. I'll be home eventually." The sun is beginning to make its way above the tops of the buildings, breaking through the overcast sky. "I'm fine though. Just need some time alone."

"You spent ten days alone."

"Yeah, I know. I'll be home eventually," I repeat before hanging up the phone and slipping it back into my pocket.

I pull the hood of my sweater up over my head, shove my hands into the soft center pouch, and walk with my eyes on the concrete below me. I don't stop to take in the sunrise as it shines light along the edges of the buildings. I don't lift my head when a man catcalls me and then shouts 'bitch' when I ignore him. I have places to be, and I don't have time to stop and look at the watercolors of the sky or pay attention to the desperate lowlife with a masculinity complex.

I arrive at the rehab center quicker than I expect—not that I'm really consciously heading to this place. I stare at the doors to the main entrance for quite a long time. When I was last here, I was so high I couldn't walk. I ponder walking away and going back to the house, letting my troubles drift above me in thin layers of smoke. I don't really want to go back into the clinic, and I'm not sure why I'm back.

Even if I want to go inside, I'll be kicked out rather quickly. Even if I did have insurance, I can't afford the treatment. I can't even afford to step into the lobby, let alone talk to someone and get back on my meds. So, I continue to stare at the doors in a dazed stupor.

It's too early for any of the patients to be awake, and none of the therapists have arrived yet. An orderly is probably snoozing away on the couch in the lobby, dreading the wake-up call.

Why am I even here?

I turn my back to the building and sit on a curb, flicking rocks across the street while watching cars pass. I glance at the building when I know everyone will be waking up, and I'm shocked at the familiar faces I'm able to get glimpses of through the window. They belong to people I met with Creature and Rabbit. I wonder if Tito found Creature.

Are Rabbit and I still being hunted?

Is Rabbit inside those walls?

Maybe Tito will forget about us.

That's unlikely.

He won't forget; money is involved.

The fear shakes my body. Am I being watched? Did someone identify me already and report my location to the men who want me dead? Like an animal, I am being hunted —and it's my own damn fault.

A few cars line the small parking lot next to the clinic. Each spot has a sign that designates it to a worker. I don't bother looking up to see who's pulling in. My mind is too busy playing out the countless ways I can be found and tortured. Cameron takes a seat next to me, but I only glance at him from the corner of my eye.

"So, you're back?" His voice is deep and soothing.

"Not really," I reply, still looking down. "I don't know why I'm here honestly."

"Well, Alana, you must be here for a reason. What's up? Talk to me. Free of charge."

His eyes bore into the side of my head, trying to pull the pain from me without words. I finally turn and look at him, staring with tears welling in my eyes. I wipe a sleeve across them and take a deep breath.

"You know it's okay to cry," he states, frowning.

"Shut up." I try to hold in a laugh. "Cameron, how do I get the screaming to stop? How do I make this craving go away? How do I make my brain stop swinging wildly from lows and highs? How do I make it *stop*?" I twist the ends of my sleeves in my hands with the nervousness that flows through.

"You don't." He is calm. "Not really. You learn better coping skills to ease it into submission. You re-train your brain. You *talk* to someone instead of suffering alone. As for the mood swings, that's easy. Go back on your meds and contact your doctor when they stop working." He stands up and offers a hand.

"I can't afford meds." I take it and stand up with him. "I don't have insurance."

Great advice, Doc. Tell me to see a doctor I can't afford and just re-train my brain.

So, I have to live with the devil I've dubbed Sunshine until I die.

Which won't be too long if Tito finds me.

"Is Justin Kelly here?" I ask.

"Yes. Do you want to see him?"

"Maybe later, yeah."

"I'll put you in." He begins to walk away. "Take care of yourself, Alana. If you need anything, you know how to reach me."

CHAPTER FIFTY-FOUR

Skylar and I are lying side by side on the floor with our eyes closed, smoking cigarettes as the lingering skunk smell of marijuana drifts around us. Our lips are pulled back into dumbass grins. Skylar sits up and begins rolling another joint on the coffee table. Xavier says we can smoke in the living room as long as Michelle is at school. The moment she steps foot into the house, we are confined to our rooms or we have to wait until she's asleep. I lift myself and take a dramatic step towards Skylar before plopping down beside him and watching him work his magic with the green buds and thin paper. He lights it up and we smoke in more silence, drenching ourselves in it.

There is nothing to say between us—nothing that hasn't already been said.

Are you better?

I missed you.

What happened?

I'm not better and I did miss them, but I gave up. I guess that's what happened.

Skylar stands and looks at me for a long moment before

speaking. "Xavier wants to know if you want Justin to live here—you know, after rehab."

"Rabbit is terrified of Xavier." My mouth gapes open, and I tilt my head to the side.

"So are you," he points out matter-of-factly.

"Fair point." I snigger. I don't really fear Xavier—I respect him. My smile soon fades. "That's actually a bad idea. I'd be too close to a former contact. I can't have that."

He nods to show his understanding. "I'll let him know."

We don't stay in our cannabis-filled paradise for long. Tomorrow promises to be a long day, and I need to be sober. After all, I have to face my parents eventually.

But that isn't until tomorrow. I can breathe for a few more hours. Skylar and I head into the kitchen to cook dinner before Xavier and Casey get home from school. We've only started boiling a large pot of water before Michelle comes into the room. She holds her backpack in one hand and lets out a large yawn before dropping the bag on the floor. Skylar holds up three fingers and stares at his sister. Her eyes narrow, and Skylar drops a finger. Groaning, Michelle picks up her belongings and carries them to her room before returning.

"Can I help?" she asks.

Skylar picks her up. "You can make the whole thing."

"I can't cook!" she protests.

"Neither can your brother," I tell her, "but that's never stopped him."

Skylar shoots me a look but doesn't say anything. We take Michelle out to the living room to watch cartoons until the water is bubbling and rolling like an angry beast. I pull a chair over to the stove, have her stand on it, and give her the box of spaghetti noodles, instructing her to drop them into the water.

"Okay, now what?" She looks up at us.

Skylar opens a jar of pasta sauce and hands it to her. He steps away for a moment and comes back with a smaller pot and places it on the burner beside the spaghetti. He turns on the burner and looks at her.

"Do not touch the buttons. Understand?" His voice is stern. He sounds like Xavier.

She nods and holds up the jar.

"Say it," Skylar demands.

"I understand." She looks at him, and he pats her head.

"Dump it into the little pot and put the lid on," I tell her.

Michelle plops it in and watches it splatter a little. Skylar helps her off the chair and carries her to the microwave. "Set it for eight minutes."

Once she sets the timer, we go back to watching cartoons. This is a normal life. This is what I should be doing. I should be craving *this* peaceful feeling of teaching a child basic skills, hanging out with my best friend, and waiting for my girlfriend.

But I keep craving cocaine.

And heroin.

And meth.

I keep wanting the high that makes me feel like a goddess.

I will never be satisfied with a life like this.

Will I?

Still, I push the clawing feeling aside. Skylar pan-fries sausage to add to the sauce, and I keep Michelle occupied by helping her stick some pyramid studs on one of her jackets.

"Dante would like it," she tells me while piercing one through the collar.

"Yeah," I agree, "he would."

The cooking is done and the table is set before Xavier and Casey get home. They talk about their days at class while Skylar and I listen. Michelle chimes in every now and then to tells us about school as well.

It is peaceful.

It is normal.

It doesn't feel right—not anymore.

CHAPTER FIFTY-FIVE

Morning comes quickly—or at least it feels like it does. My sleep is invaded with twisted faces masking themselves as the ones I love. They are phantoms swirling in the background of my new life—screaming and vomiting at my feet, begging me to give up.

A ray of sunlight pours into the room through the window. I hear the metal rings sliding against the curtain rod as the veil that keeps the light contained is moved back, allowing it to cascade into my dark space. It permeates my nightmares and grounds me in reality. I throw the blankets over my face as the warm glow hugs itself around me.

"It's time to get up," Casey says softly. She's standing next to the window.

I groan in protest.

"Alana, it's two in the afternoon."

Another groan escapes my throat.

Casey rips the covers off of me and jumps onto the bed. She smells like strawberries and her smile lights up the room, putting the sun to shame. She kisses the spot between my eyes, the top of my freshly shaved head, and then my lips.

Why had I ever betrayed such a beautiful woman?

She shakes my shoulders and begins chanting, "Wake up!"

I sit up and wrap my arms around her before planting my lips to her collarbone. She pulls herself up and waits patiently with her arms crossed as I take a dramatically long time to get out of bed. I overdo the stretching and yawning as if I'm a broken toy being reassembled, needing every joint and sinew to pop back into place. I shove my leggings on with slow, careful tugs before following Casey downstairs and into the living room.

Only Skylar and Emily are home. I haven't seen Emily since I relapsed. Her red hair is bundled on top of her head in two cute little space buns, her face framed with short, blunt bangs. She wears dark red lipstick, and her winged eyeliner is so sharp it could kill a man. She smiles at me and turns back to Skylar.

Their heads are bowed over a game of cards strewn across the coffee table, expressions stern without a betraying glance or smirk. It looks like an intense, nose-deep game of poker. The pile of change on the table between them seems to confirm my suspicions.

"Go fish." Emily smirks, breaking their silence.

Never mind. It's not poker.

"Where's X?" I ask, sitting down next to Skylar on the floor and examining his cards.

"School." He shields his hand a moment before letting me see again. "Why?"

"Curious." I turn to Casey. "Why aren't you in school?"

"I skipped."

Skylar looks at his cards before peering suspiciously over them at his girlfriend. He looks to me.

"I think she's conspiring against me." Skylar raises an eyebrow. "What do you think?" He holds the cards up to my face, making them touch the tip of my nose.

"Dude, it's *Go Fish*." I laugh.

"No! It's more than that!" He slams his cards on the table and raises a fist. "It's liberty, justice, and freedom, dammit!"

I look at him with narrowed eyes and a tilted head. Casey laughs before walking out of the room.

"It's *Go Fish*," I repeat.

"No one asked you, Alana." Skylar picks his cards back up.

I watch them play their intense game of *Go Fish* that will apparently determine our freedom, and I feel like I'm standing outside of myself again. I can feel my soul slowly abandoning my body, and I can't seem to reach out far enough to bring it back. My limbs are made of helium, and I am trapped inside of a dream.

Because none of this can be real.

Suddenly, I'm acutely aware of my breathing and the beating of my heart. I dig my nails into the tips of my fingers to try and ground myself, but I keep becoming removed from my physical body. Casey comes back into the room and hands me my jacket and a set of car keys. I stand up, kiss her cheek, and I put the jacket on before setting the keys on the table.

"I'll walk," I tell her.

There is a look of mistrust in her eyes that sparks like coal fire. Who can blame her? I have destroyed our trust—shattered it on the ground around us.

"Okay." She sighs, grabs my cheeks, and plants her lips

on mine. "Be safe and behave. I want you alive and well when you see your parents again."

I swallow hard, my spirit drifting higher away from me. Will it become trapped in the house, incapable of following me outside, or will it stay tied to me, attached to my skin by a thin strand of thread?

CHAPTER FIFTY-SIX

Tears well in my eyes as I walk, filling me with guilt as my mind plays scenes of the worried face of my mother. A lump forms in the back of my throat as I think about the disappointment that will radiate from my father as he blames himself for my faults. Even when I'm not around, I cause them pain. I tilt my head back and force the tears away. I have mascara on, and the last thing I want is black pigment to streak down my cheeks like dark rivers when I see them again.

I am a disgrace.

I walk along the streets with my head down, hidden beneath my hood. Cars zip past on their way to work or home. Groups of teenagers travel the sidewalks, laughing and smiling. I hardly notice the chaos around me; I'm too lost in my head—or better yet, I'm too busy trying to keep my soul tethered to my physical body. I turn down an alley that'll shortcut me to my house. It is desolate and eerie. The isolation suffocates me with worry.

Yes, I want to be grounded, but not like this.

Creature and Tito are still looking for me.

My heart begins to pound and my vision blurs.

Once Rabbit gets out of rehab, it won't surprise me if he goes running to tell them about me. Even if he doesn't, it's not like I can hide forever. We all live in the same town.

Creature won't hurt anyone he doesn't have to; he will leave everyone but me alone. Tito, however, won't care who he has to hurt to get to me. I don't want to tell anyone about my situation—mostly because I don't feel like talking to the police. So, I'm putting everyone's lives at risk without their knowledge because I owe a damn drug dealer money. And there is nothing I can do about it. I have crossed enemy lines, and the entire squadron is out to find and kill me.

I stop to lean against a brick wall, hands on my knees as I force myself to breathe deeply. I have to wait for my head to stop screaming, for my heart to stop trying to escape my chest. I am flushed with warmth, and the want to rip myself from my own skin. I sit on the cold asphalt until I stop shaking; it's only then that I start walking again. I'm not inside of my body anymore. I am soaring just above it, watching myself walk to my parents' house.

My dark force is beginning to flick the back of my brain. It's subtle, but persistent. It is begging me to turn around, find a dealer, and take a line of sweet escape. I ignore her, but it's hard to ignore something that encases every part of me.

Sunshine is alive, and she is hungry.

I keep going, focused on the concrete beneath my boots, and pushing Sunshine as far away from me as I can.

I pull my hood down and stare for a few seconds at what had once been home. The house still looks a little unkempt —in a neat, quaint sort of way. The bushes are trimmed, but could use a bit of a touch up. Strands of weeds poke up around the garden. The porch needs a fresh coat of paint, and the mail hasn't been taken in yet. I grab the stack from the metal box fixed to the side of the house and step inside. I don't bother knocking.

"Mom?" I choke out into the hallway. I can hear the television playing in the other room. "Dad?" I kick the door gently and it shuts behind me. "Guys?" I call out again, anxiety suddenly filling me at the realization that I am going to see them—I am going to see their pain.

I make it halfway through the hall before my mom runs towards me. I stop dead in my tracks when I witness the relieved, yet worried smile stretching across her tear-stricken face. She looks older, the lines in her face heavier from stress. Her hair is thinning, and she is a little smaller. She wraps her arms around me and invades the top of my head with scattered kisses. My mom holds me back at arm's length and examines me for a moment.

"Oh, Alana!" she cries and embraces me again.

I have been dead to them.

Hell, I have been dead to *me*.

My arms hang limp for a moment before I finally hug her back. "Hi, Mom," I mutter.

She leads me urgently into the living room by the hand. My mom stands me in front of my father, who is sitting on the couch. He instantly shoots to his feet and picks me up, spinning me around while holding me tight. There's a bit of gray in his short, dark hair and there's a shadow on his chin and jaw. Dark bags hang below his eyes.

Has he slept? It doesn't look like he has. He also looks like he's lost weight and I can't help but blame myself.

It is my fault after all.

Once he lets go, we sit down. A deathly silence hangs over us, the television set the only noise to fill the gaps. The air is tense with what to say, how to act, what to do. It isn't like there's a *How-to Deal with Your Druggie Daughter Who Ran Away and Was Found Nearly Dead, Only to Run Away Again* handbook.

"Alana?" My dad speaks through the thick awkwardness. "How could you be so stupid?"

I am taken aback, but I respect his courage to be upfront. He isn't wrong. I *am* stupid. All I can do is lower my head and shrug. There isn't an answer. Not a good one.

"We thought you died," he says softly. "We were so scared we had lost you."

"You did." My words escape me in slow, measured steps. "For that time, you did."

My mom stands up and leaves the living room. I hear her in the kitchen, pulling things out of the fridge and chopping something on a butcher's block. My dad just holds me, telling me how much he's missed me and how much he loves me.

How?

How can someone love something so diseased? How can anyone care about something so broken and tainted?

Mom returns with three bowls of salad, each one dressed with a little bit of vinegar and oil.

We talk amongst each other for hours after we scarf down the food. We jump topics, chat about the news, the guys, school, college, Michelle, anything to not linger too much on the cause of all this pain.

Soon, last hugs are shared, along with promises for a speedy return and a long sobriety.

At the very least, a *longer* one.

CHAPTER FIFTY-SEVEN

The hellion in my head is becoming unbearable, but it's getting a little lighter. It's beginning to keep me awake again, my mind spinning with a thousand tasks I want to complete. I have to force myself to stay in bed and not move at four in the morning as I fight to convince myself that I don't need to drink and organize the bookshelf by color.

We all sit around in the kitchen, absentmindedly nibbling at food and trying to fill the voids in our stomachs that dinner can't seem to reach. Casey is drawing something for school, Xavier is deep in a schoolbook again, and Michelle is doing simple math homework. I finish my banana and stand up—it's the only thing I've eaten, but it feels like enough.

"I'm going out," I declare. I need to try to clear my head, and this isn't working.

"Do you want company?" Casey asks.

"No, I'm okay. Thanks though." I smile weakly at her.

I pull on a hoodie and shove a pair of heeled booties on my feet before heading out the door.

I'm on a mission: I have to talk to Rabbit.

The walk to the clinic is beautiful in a dark and dreary sort of way. The sun is setting under the horizon, and the last of its light casts eerie shadows over the buildings and rain-soaked streets. Familiar faces roam the sidewalks now like the undead.

I once walked with those zombies. I was once one of them, and I don't want to be noticed now. I quicken my steps until I reach the clinic. Hopefully they'll let me in and talk to Rabbit—if he even wants to talk to me.

I can't decide whether Rabbit has become a friend. We've gone through a lot together—we helped each other survive. Yet, I'm not sure I can trust him.

Head held high and shoulders rolled back, I enter, my square heels clinking on the tile. The receptionist is deep in a thoughtful phone conversation, calling the person on the other end things like 'honey' and 'dear'. I plop down on the wooden bench pushed against a large window in front of the desk. My feet rapidly tap the floor and I twist my fingers against one another.

"Alana?" a soft voice calls from somewhere down the hall.

My head pops up and I scan the room and see a nurse with freckles and red hair piled up on top of her. "Oh!" I rise to my feet. "Hey, Aztec."

"Don't tell me you're here for another run." Her face looks distraught.

"No." I shake my head. "I'm just here to talk to Rabbit— um...Justin."

Don't worry, Doc, I can handle Sunshine on my own right now.

"Oh, well in that case, do you want me to show you to his

room? They just ended group therapy. The guy pretty much keeps to himself. Really jumpy."

"Yeah, he's always been like that," I reaffirm.

We talk about how I'm doing as we make our way down the halls of dorms until we get to the correct room.

"Justin, Alana is here to see you."

I don't wait for an okay sign or for the door to open before I step past Aztec. The door closes behind me with a slight kick from my foot, and it nearly slams on the nurse's face. I grab a chair and push it in front of the entrance. This isn't a conversation that can wait, and it isn't one that needs an audience.

"Rabbit." I nod and take a seat.

He's sitting on his bed, his back against the wall and throwing a balled-up piece of paper into the air before catching it with a bored expression. He places it on the small bedside table when I sit. Rabbit looks healthier already. His eyes aren't dull and he seems to have finally gained some weight. His hair isn't greasy and he smells like soap.

"Sunshine."

It's all the same. No real names. No personal information. Perhaps the habit will never be broken. I suppose we will forever remain Sunshine and Rabbit.

Perhaps we're not friends.

We never *were* friends.

This is business—life or death.

We exchange formalities, passing friendly banter between one another as if our words are made of hot coals. I ask him how he's doing and if he plans on staying clean. Most people I've met through this place will perk up as they announce that a month or so of therapy has helped re-wire their brain a little bit—it helps them see the right path, even if it doesn't always work in the long run.

Not Rabbit though. He hates rehab, but he hates being sober more. He doesn't want to be forced to feel those emotions that he's worked hard to suppress over so many years. He plans on going right back to his old ways once he's finished. All of this is a joke to him—twisted way to pass a little time and lie low.

"Have you talked to Creature at all?" I'm hesitant to ask, but it's why I came.

"Nah," he tells me.

"Are you going to?"

"I hope I don't have to." He pauses. "But if he shows up and it's me or you, Sunshine...well...it's nothing personal."

"Yeah, sure." It feels personal.

I turn and leave, closing the door with force behind me. My heels clack on the floor as I walk out, not acknowledging anyone as I exit the clinic. I've seen this conversation turning out the way it did, and I'm an idiot for thinking Rabbit would have my back. We escaped death together— we stared down the barrel of the same gun. I can only hope that Creature will leave us alone. Though we still have Tito to worry about, and I've never actually seen his face.

Hood up over my head, I throw my hands into the large pouch pocket as the sky groans and opens up above me. Buckets of rain are thrown from the clouds onto the already soaked ground.

The rain doesn't bother me too much. I welcome it. My head is spinning, and I can't get a grip on what is real. One side of me wants to disappear into the darkness. Another begs for me to run away—run and never look back. I can find more drugs and fill my system with poison that brings me to my knees and elixirs that allow me to soar higher than any bird. My hellhounds are slowly ripping me to shreds, piece by piece.

Both sides of me have one common factor: they want drugs.

And I want them *now*.

CHAPTER FIFTY-EIGHT

The next day rolls around, and Sunshine is still present and strong, weaving her screams between the inner workings of my subconscious like a cross-stitch pattern. She pounds wildly in my chest cavity, biting into the soft cartilage around my heart; she grips my stomach with a tight fist. She keeps me awake, telling me to do anything but sleep. I hold my composure around Xavier—I'm far too scared to fumble so carelessly out of my 'I'm sober now' act.

I still am, but I feel so close to the edge.

Without drugs, there is nothing to silence the lust, the urge, the want. There is nothing to help mask the fear that keeps swimming through my head like a loose shark.

I'm almost willing to destroy everything I have done in order to be alive again.

Perhaps my demons are still in complete control, waiting patiently to fully take the reins once more.

So what am I supposed to do? I feel my psyche pulling itself apart, ripping me in half—I want to kill myself, yet I want to live on top of the world. I guess I can't do much of anything. Once an addict, always an addict, right? Well, at least that's what they told me in rehab. What kind of phrase is that anyway?

I'm just supposed to throw my hands up in surrender and let Sunshine take the wheel of my fate?

Bullshit.

I think that the barracudas that swim within me, tearing me to shreds on some days, yearning for the razor and keeping me up with racing thoughts, will subside once I got sober.

I'm wrong.

Rabbit will be free in a week or so.

I'm pretty sure it's a week.

My brain is scattered from not sleeping. It's probably been three days since I got more than four hours of sleep. But, I'm pretty sure it's a week before he gets out.

A fear I'm unfamiliar with is beginning to grow and fester in the pit of my stomach. My anxiety is skyrocketing and I vibrate with energy. I feel sick with dread of ever being found—of being ratted out.

Rabbit isn't going to keep his mouth shut. I can taste it like venom on my tongue. His cowardly ways are going to get me killed. Staring at the ceiling, letting the thoughts race around, I find myself missing Noah, tears sparkling the corners of my eyes. If he were still alive, perhaps I wouldn't be so afraid.

I probably wouldn't even be in this mess.

Rolling over, in bed I nuzzle closer to Casey, burying my face in her long hair, trying to clear my head. Still fidgeting, I roll back over and watch the ceiling, taking deep breaths to keep everything at a low, and tolerable rattle.

I can hear the others carrying on and giggling downstairs. We are the only ones still locked away in our room with the curtains over the window to keep the light out.

Casey had stayed up with me until six in the morning, and I am forcing myself to stay in bed a little longer in the hopes that I can trick my body into thinking I've actually rested.

A loud ring from my phone jolts me from my stupor. Casey groans and pulls the covers over her head. I answer on the third ring.

"What?" I mutter with distaste.

"Sunshine?"

"Who is this?" I sit up, concerned, the pit of fear in my stomach growing darker.

"It's Rabbit!" He sounds ecstatic. "They let me out early! Apparently, my progress was incredible or some bullshit. They fall for anything!" He laughs.

He isn't wrong. I'd convinced them I was doing better although I stayed awake for three days. They thought I was fine when I began to lose the connection between my soul and my physical body. The doctors told me I was just healing when I planned on doing a hundred things in a single day. They're easily convinced if you just say the right words.

"Anyway." His voice snaps me back. "I scored some crystal and blow and wanted you to come celebrate with me!"

I fall silent while, my alter ego Sunshine jumps with joy and begs me to say yes.

"Sunshine?" he presses. "Come on."

"No." I speak with decisiveness as my brain screams at me, protesting my answer. "And Rabbit, don't call me again." I hang up, throw the phone across the room, and lie back down. I kiss Casey on the top of her head and wrap my arms around her.

I have to stay sober.

CHAPTER FIFTY-NINE

Not only can I not sleep, but eating is becoming a challenge again. I keep telling myself that if I can't control my thoughts, my emotions, or my surroundings, I can always control what I put in my body. Regardless, in this dark, low mood, everything tastes like charcoal coating my tongue. Drinking only black coffee, my mind races with images of Rabbit, wide-eyed and shaking, talking to Creature with blood around his nostrils. This dark illness inside of me is growing stronger, turning me inside out, and I am weak. I do my best to hold it together for everyone, but I can't help suspect that they know—that they can see this shadowed entity controlling my every move.

I don't want to hurt them again, but I'm not sure how much more of this I can take though.

In an attempt to clear my head faster, I self-harmed a few hours after talking to Rabbit. My blood rushed with adrenaline at the pain, but it didn't work. I still feel awful, and now my hip burns if I move the wrong way.

Everything within me is growing weak under the want—the *need*—for a hit. How can I be sober this long and still crave something so destructive? My mood is sinking again, and I'm unable to handle the push and pull of the mania and the depression combatting for a front row seat in my brain. On the floor, I am drowning in my own self-despair, incapable of getting up.

The house is empty, and I'm alone with my thoughts and a razor blade. I twirl it in my hands, pricking my fingertips with the sharp corner of it. I want to feel something other than this urge to destroy myself. My stomach growls.

"Shut up," I mumble. "I'm not feeding you right now."

An hour passes by, and I haven't moved from the floor. The front entrance creaks open, and I quickly hide the razor blade and wipe the droplets of blood from my fingertips on the inside of my shirt. Skylar walks into the room and he frowns at me before lying on the floor beside me, his arms fold across his stomach. He is silent for a few moments, but I catch him looking at me every now and then from the corners of my eyes.

"You should eat something." His tone is flat, almost demanding.

"No." I have no intention of eating today—perhaps tonight, but not now.

"Alana." He sits up. "Thanks."

"For what?" I sit up too and look at him.

"A few years ago, you were the only one who could calm me from my panic attacks. You were the one who stood by us when Dad beat us half to death. Hell, you even fought him off a few times. You were the one that held us together when Dante killed himself." He sighs. "I just thought you should know. You were there for us, and we need you and—"

"Sky, stop. That's what friends do." I stare at him intensely. "Why are you rambling?"

"Emily." His head hangs.

"What about her?" I haven't seen her in a while. Not that I've been paying much attention.

"Xavier saw her with another guy, kissing him and being flirty. I just told her to get her stuff and get out." He shrugs as if it isn't a big deal.

"You gonna be okay?" I ask.

Skylar is composed. I wonder if he's been through so much trauma and pain that something like a breakup is almost nothing to him—almost as if he is now immune to it.

"Yeah, I'll be okay. I just don't think I'm gonna date for a while." His eyes tell me otherwise. "Anyway, eat something."

"Really, I'm not hungry," I lie, my stomach betraying me.

"You need food!" He stands up and brings me with him.

"I don't want any damn food!" I rip away from his grip and lie down on the couch, curling my knees to my chest.

He sits at my feet. "We're worried about you." His voice is quiet. "You've stopped eating again. You're quiet for a few days and bouncing off the walls the next. Casey says you're not sleeping either."

"I'm just stressed. I've changed, Sky. I'm not who I use to be." I turn around and face the back of the couch.

"What aren't you telling me?"

"I don't want to talk about it yet."

He rises to his feet. "I love you, Alana, and I'm here when you're ready, okay?" Skylar walks away and I drift into a long nap.

CHAPTER SIXTY

There's a pressure on my legs and I groan awake. The blanket is pinned around my head.

"Anyone know where Alana is?" I hear Xavier laugh.

I haven't seen Xavier in a few days; he buried himself in his books.

"Get your fat ass off of me!" I rip through the blankets he has pressed around me.

"Oh, there you are." He smiles at me and gets off of my legs, pushing them out of his way. He holds a plate with a burger and some sweet potato fries in one hand. Xavier sticks it on my lap and it's still hot. "Eat."

"No."

"Eat," he repeats, his voice low and demanding.

"Xavier," I murmur, "I don't want to."

"I'm not asking you. I'm telling you to eat." He speaks to me as if I'm a defiant kid. "I'm going to stay here with you until you eat at least half of that burger. That's all I ask—half of it. I'll eat the rest." He holds his pinky out. "Deal?"

"You're an ass." I link my pinky with his and take a reluctant nibble of a fry. It tastes like cement, but I swallow it anyway.

I can't argue with Xavier like I can Skylar. Xavier had gone out of his way to find me and throw me into rehab when I was near death. He didn't back down when I struggled with getting sober, and he picked me up, kicking and screaming, to make sure I climbed out of the grave I'd dug. They've all been there for me, but Xavier has kept me alive.

The two brothers watch me carefully over their own burgers as I struggle to consume a couple more fries. What the hell is wrong with me? I'm sober! How are my phantoms still so loud? Why are my moods shifting so dramatically? They swing around like a reckless child with a bat. Why do I keep thinking about self-harm and suicide? The only emotion I have that makes sense is fear—fear that Rabbit will tell Creature and Tito where I am; cracking under the promise of a hit.

I want to tell Skylar and Xavier what is going on in my mind, the non-stop struggle to keep my head above water, but would they even know how to help though? I don't deserve it. I'm being pathetic. They have already done more than enough and I should be able to handle this on my own.

Right?

"I'll take that." Xavier reaches over and steals my burger, chewing a huge bite.

"Was that so bad?" Skylar asks.

"Meh." I at least ate the fries. "Where's Casey?" I want her here. I *need* her here.

"She's with her parents for the week," Xavier tells me. "I think her uncle is in town or something. I don't remember. She said she'd be back this coming weekend."

"Oh." My shoulders slump.

"Alana," Skylar says softly, "are you okay?"

I want to grab him by the shoulders and shake him.

No!

I'm not okay!

I'm terrified to leave the house. I'm terrified to live a normal life for fear that it'll be pulled out from under me. I don't know what is happening in my head. Well, I do, but if I acknowledge what the doctors told me, it means that I'm weak and incapable. I just want drugs to calm the surges. I have come so far and promised I'll stay clean, but I am close to breaking.

I have to keep fighting.

"Yeah, I'm fine," I answer.

CHAPTER SIXTY-ONE

A week passes, and I am finally beginning to feel better.

Better than better, actually. I'm beginning to read excessively, holding the book at the spine while I walk around the house and twirl Michelle in circles with my free hand. She wears a new purple tutu and dances every second possible.

I re-organize the bookshelf in the bedroom, matching up the colors of the spines and making sure it creates a rainbow from top to bottom. Then I move the furniture around in the room and want to paint the walls a new color.

Xavier helps me move the fridge at midnight, and Casey caves in to helping me organize the tea bags into labeled mason jars when I can't stay still at four in the morning.

Skylar, however, has caught me throwing away food and spices, my hands shaking with energy. He makes me sit down on the couch and smoke a fat blunt with him. It is the first time I sleep in two days.

He asks me again if I'm was okay.

I tell him I am fantastic. And I am.

I learn to bake new cupcakes and pies, mastering designs on top of the cupcakes and the lattice of the pies.

I am energy and energy is me.

On one of the days that I'm reading and baking, Skylar and Xavier take Michelle to see their deranged mother in the hospital—she has been driven to insanity by the hands of her abusive husband. I'd nearly forgotten about her. I never really see her though. She mostly hides in her room, clutching onto hope that her husband will show up dead.

Casey stays in the kitchen with me, painting on canvas, her hands colorful with her art. Every so often, I'll put the baking supplies down to bend over and plant a kiss on her forehead, cheek, or lips. My soul has swelled with love for her.

The ring is back on her finger, and I couldn't be happier.

After the baking is done, Casey decides to settle down for an afternoon nap on the couch. I can't stay holed up in the house by myself, so I head out the door. It is the perfect day for a walk, so why not? Perhaps I can release some of this vibrating energy into the sun above, become one with nature as I walk the concrete sidewalks. I don't have a set destination.

Do I need one?

There is a skip to my stride, and I'm unaware of my surroundings, only feeling the warmth of the afternoon sun on my skin.

I know the crash isn't far away. I have to enjoy the feeling of euphoria and bliss while I can though.

I want to chase it. I know cocaine can keep me this high; it can keep me up above the clouds. I have to stay strong—and sober.

A few familiar faces pass but I'm careful not to make eye contact. I have to bite the inside of my cheek to keep myself from talking to them, pulling them into a whirlwind of pressured speech, with words that force their way from my mouth like a tsunami. I can't help the smile that splits across my face though. One of the guys I see throws me off—he looks like Rat. He's the man who called for the bounty on my head, yet somehow also aided in my recovery.

Is he my enemy or my savior?

The thought of Tito and Creature causes my stomach to fill with rocks of anxiety. The urge claws at my insides. I can never kill my inner addict. Sunshine will always taunt me. I am her after all, right? I stop for a second and pull a pack of cigarettes from my back pocket. I tuck my head down and cup my hand over the end of it before lighting it up.

I should be paying attention to my surroundings.

I should keep moving.

I'm not welcome on these streets anymore.

"Sunshine!" I know that voice.

The color drains from my skin, and I'm suddenly sick and empty. I can feel my soul pull from my body and drift above me until I am no longer real. I am being held to my physical self by a string once more.

I am found.

My heeled boots hit the concrete as fast as I can muster. Creature catches up with me though and slams the back of my head with what feels like the butt of a pistol.

My world goes black.

CHAPTER SIXTY-TWO

I know where I am before I come to. The smell of this old house that I have once mistakenly called home would always bring about a strange, sickening comfort. I'm restrained to a wooden chair, my wrists and ankles zip-tied down. The face that stares back at me when I open my eyes is unfamiliar though.

He has light brown hair and stubble under his chin. His brown eyes are so dark they're almost black, and he reeks of expensive cologne. He's wearing a suit with polished shoes, a straight tie is hanging around his neck. He looks surprisingly well-kept for someone in such an evil place.

"Sunshine," he says calmly, "allow me to introduce myself." He places a hand on his chest. "My name is Tito."

I gulp hard. He keeps his head in front of mine, following it as I move my eyes so that I can't see past him. I fidget against the restraints of the chair and feel the barrel of a gun press against the back of my head.

"Don't move," Creature commands.

I hold still.

"Now, Sunshine, I have a favor to ask you." Tito's voice is

soft and terrifying. His smile is taunting and yet comforting, and it makes my insides curl with disgust and confusion. "I need you stay very still. Do you understand?"

I'm too afraid to nod or speak. Not that I have time to before I feel a needle prick the side of my neck, releasing an almost forgotten drug into my bloodstream.

I want to fight and scream, but I can only smile as my muscles relax and my head grows fuzzy. It's finally silent in my mind. No more buzzing, no more vibrating energy, no more dark clouds suffocating me. I am still hanging onto myself by a thread, but at least the feelings circulating wildly within me are gone long enough for me to breathe.

Tito chuckles. "Better?"

I don't speak; I just roll my eyes back and sigh. I am high. So damn high. I wonder how much Creature put in the syringe to get me feeling this good. It can't be much. I nearly have to remind myself this isn't about old friends having another hit together. This is sinister, and I'll be lucky to leave this room alive. I'm high, but I'm terrified.

Creature moves from behind me and sits on the floor at my side. Tito stays where he is, keeping his face in front of my view, inches from my nose now. His breath smells like mint and rosemary, and he has a bit of dried blood on the inside of his left nostril. His fingers stroke the barrel of a pistol resting on his thighs. Creature cuts one of the zip ties from my wrist and yanks my arm towards him. He grips tightly around my small wrist, and I can feel the bruises begin to form under my skin. I try to struggle against him, but he just pulls harder until I stop. He ties a belt around my bicep and begins to tap the inside of my elbow.

"You owe me money," Tito talks while Creature works and I struggle to keep from nodding off. "Five-thousand dollars"

"No," I remark, immediately wanting to stuff the words back into my mouth. "It's four-thousand dollars." I can't stop them from tumbling out of my lips.

"Interest," he explains simply.

"I don't have the money." I stare at the gun that lies in his lap. "Is it really worth this?"

"You've had all this time to collect, Sunshine." Tito leans closer, ignoring my question. "You didn't think we'd stop looking for you, did you?"

"Listen, shit for brains, I don't have your damn money!" I nearly spit in his face.

Creature holds up a syringe, the metal glistening in the pale lighting. He looks at Tito for confirmation, and Tito shakes his head, raising a hand up. He asks me for his money again, and again I tell him no. Even if I did have it, how am I supposed to get it if I'm tied up as a prisoner? It's not like I am going to randomly carry around a few grand in my pocket. Tito looks at Creature and nods once.

With the cue, Creature jams the needle into my arm and releases the drugs. It hits strong. On top of the hit he just gave me, this is too much at once, and I retch, vomiting on my legs and Tito's shoes. He doesn't seem to care really. I'm sure he's had much worse happen to him. Creature immediately grabs another zip tie and straps my arm back to the chair. My muscles shake, but I feel a surge of peace. Despite the sickness that travels through me, my mind races with the want for more.

Not just heroin.

Anything I can get my hands on: cocaine, meth, crack. It doesn't matter.

This brown, deadly liquid is great and all, but it isn't what I really want.

This is a strange punishment, although, I'm sure if I'm

given just one more hit, I'll fall victim to a deadly overdose. This is already too much. I can feel my heart pounding, my head shrinking, my stomach turning.

"My money." Tito sounds like he's talking to a child.

"Is not something I have," I tell him with a brave smirk.

"Sunshine." He finally stands up, taking his gun and holding it in his right hand. "Your friend was just as irritatingly difficult to work with." I still can't see past him. "He said he wouldn't tell us where you were or that you even helped in this whole ordeal, but we knew. He didn't have the money either, but we made sure he knew that that wasn't acceptable."

Tito finally steps away.

Rabbit is hunched over, lifeless and strapped to a chair, just a few feet in front of me. A broken needle is snapped off in the crook of his arm, and there is vomit on his shirt. It's the bullet wound in his forehead that makes me sick. Blood mixes with the puke on his clothes. His face is dirty with it, and crimson pools at his feet. A large splatter of it is splayed with brain matter, and is sticking to the wall behind him.

I can't scream.

I can't run.

All I can do is whimper, tears rolling down my cheeks; a heavy weight of emptiness fills every last inch of me.

"Creature, go upstairs and gather more syringes." Tito is beside me, a soft hand on my shoulder. "I am so terribly sorry about your friend, Sunshine. You understand though."

Tito keeps talking to me, but I'm not able to make out the words. His speech tumbles into a messy mass in my ringing ears. All I can do is stare, mouth agape, at the hole between Rabbit's eyes. In an odd moment, the drugs seem to subside suddenly. The room looks clearer.

I hear Tito mumble something about Creature taking

too long and he sets off upstairs to find him. I wait until I hear the last footfall on the top of the steps and the sound of a closing thud. Looking frantically around the room, I try to find something that will help me. Leaning to the side, the small rickety wooden chair smashes under my weight— well, at least it breaks the arm of the chair so that I can free one of my hands. I shimmy my way over to Rabbit and search his pockets, biting my lip so that I don't break down.

I need to work fast—Tito and Creature aren't far off. I find a pocketknife and free my other arm and my legs. I don't turn to see if the two men are close by. Instead, I drop the knife, grab my phone from the coffee table, and bolt out the door, running as fast as my legs can carry me.

CHAPTER SIXTY-THREE

A bullet grazes my shoulder, and I keep running. Another nips at my thigh like a piranha. The blood is warm, and the wounds make my muscles throb with pain. Still, I don't slow down. Their voices shout my nickname and it is the fuel that keeps me going. I dart into a tight alley and shimmy my body through a compact open window that leads into a musty basement with no light. I hide, biting my sleeve as tears roll down my cheeks. Struggling to pull my phone from my bra, I listen closely for the two to make their way closer to me. I hold my stomach, trying to keep more vomit, and fear, from spilling over and giving me away. I can hear them faintly at the edge of the alley, but I don't dare peek up to see exactly where they are. My fingers shake as I dial the three digits and hold the phone up to my ear.

"Nine one one, what's your emergency?"

"Two men are trying to kill me. I'm hiding in the old abandoned Quaker building on the edge of Broad Street," I choke out, my is mouth dry. "One's in a suit and the other guy is in jeans and a collared shirt. One's named Tito and the other one goes by Creature." I try to give as much detail as possible in the smallest voice I can manage.

"Where in the building are you?" the operator asks kindly.

"I can't tell you."

"We'll send someone out immediately. Just hang tight, okay?"

"Yeah." I end the call and stay under the window. Sinking down, I bring my knees to my chest. My face becomes buried in it and I bite onto my sleeve again.

I'm in pain; my shoulder and thigh are bleeding with the raw wounds. My body is tired from running and the onslaught of drugs. I want to curl up and fall asleep until this is all over, but I have to stay awake.

Creature and Tito know I'm hiding somewhere in this area; the alley leads to a dead end. They keep walking up and down the skinny path, shouting my name and telling me everything will be okay if I just come out.

They only want to talk.

With bullets and the money I owe them.

I just wait, silently sobbing and bleeding. Fear clenches in my stomach while I hold back any noise. It feels like I stay hidden in that basement for hours.

When I hear sirens pull up and block the alley my chest becomes lighter. I stand up and step away from the wall to see the red, white, and blue lights flashing wildly like beacons of hope. I never thought the sight of cops would make me feel so relieved. I generally avoid the police as much as I can.

As most addicts do.

"Hands up!" I hear one shout. "Drop the weapon!"

The pistol clatters onto the concrete and I look up at the small window. There is no way I'll be able to climb out of it;

I can't lift my arm over my head to jump up and grab the ledge. With my injured limb held loosely at my side, I hobble way through the decrepit building. It's dark, and damp, and smells like dust and rotting wood. Abandoned chairs and pieces of old factory equipment haunt the empty space. I navigate around blindly until I find the door that leads out to the front of the street. The sidewalks are crowded, and the sky is pink, night falling fast around us. Staying hidden in the doorway, I pull my phone out again. I punch in Xavier's number and wait for someone to pick up.

"I'm at the old Quaker building," I speak before anyone can talk. "Please, just come here." I hang up before he's able to respond.

I stumble towards the commotion and lock eyes with Tito and Creature, watching them as they're searched. There are four cop cars there, blocking the only way out of the alley—except the front door to the building I hid in.

"You fucking bitch!" Creature shouts, lunging towards me. "I'll fucking kill you, Sunshine!" The officer slams him harder into the car and says something to him in a fierce tone.

The cop who is holding Tito cuffs him and throws him into the back of the patrol car before he makes his way to me. He embraces me in his arms, whispering that I am safe now and he won't let harm come to me. I let out a quick cry into his shoulder and he holds me tighter, repeating again that I am safe now. I push him off of me and wipe the tears away.

"Are you okay, miss?" he asks before he sees the blood. He presses a button on the radio on his shoulder and calls for an ambulance. "I'm Officer Holton," he introduces himself before leading me to his car.

I shake my head when he opens the passenger door for

me to take a seat. I don't want to be anywhere near Tito, who's smirking wickedly at me. I walk away and sit on the curb. The officer joins, handing me a bottle of water. I take a grateful gulp. Officer Holton moves towards me, a gauze pad in one hand. I shrug off my jacket off and let him patch me up. I hold my leg straight out so he can stick a bit of cotton padding over my leggings.

"What's your name?" he asks, wrapping tape around his first-aid handiwork on my leg.

"Alana," I tell him. "I'm the one who called. Those are the guys that I was talking about to the operator." I notice my voice is shaking and take a deep breath to try and calm it. "Tito runs the biggest ring in town. Creature is his right-hand man."

"Are those their real names?" he questions, his voice calm. He has short dark hair and hazel eyes. One arm is covered in bright tattoos.

I shrug and take another sip of water.

"An ambulance is coming," he says softly, as if the tone of his voice will pacify all that happened. "Do you have anyone you want to call?"

"I already did." My hands are still convulsing—my body feels light as it soars higher. I'm still in the clouds, and yet I'm grounded, afraid, and alive. "Please call off the ambulance. I can't afford it. My friends will take me."

He nods, presses a button down on his radio, and speaks to someone on the receiving end. "I'm staying here until they show up, okay?"

"Officer Holton," I look up at him, "they murdered someone. The body is at an old house about four blocks from here. It has a red door. Number forty-three on Elm Street."

He remains steady. "Do you know the victim's name?"

"Yes. His name was Justin Kelly." I stare at the pavement. "No one else is in there. I'm sure of it." And I am. People don't dare dwell in the same place as Creature does. Not without express permission.

He stands up and walks to his buddies, relaying the information to the officers that remain. They duck back into their cars and speed off, sirens blaring.

Holton stays with me while his friends drive away to find Justin. Then, Xavier's car pulls up. He steps out of the driver's seat and runs towards me. Xavier lifts me to my feet and hugs me tightly, nearly crushing me. I sink into his arms, suddenly sobbing, though no sound comes out.

If I could just be a little higher, I could ignore this feeling that runs so deep through me. I was almost killed. I'd been found. I saw Rabbit with a bullet wound in his head. He kept his mouth shut. He lied to them about me and he'd been killed for it. In the end, Rabbit saved my life.

Officer Holton stands up. "If you need anything, give us a call, okay?" he is speaking to Xavier.

"Yes, sir." He doesn't let go of me.

Not until the others show up to take their turns. Casey holds me and begins showers me with kisses, her own tears running down her face. Xavier sniffles away some of his own, but he turns before I can really get a good look. Casey presses me close to her, cuddling my head into her chest.

"What happened?" Xavier asks as we walk to his car. "Were you shot?"

"Just grazed," I moan. "I don't feel it. Creature shot me up. I'm so damn high, X."

Xavier rolls his eyes and kisses the top of my head. "I'm just glad you're alive."

Skylar is sitting in the front passenger seat. He gives me

a fist bump and tells me I look awful, but he's happy I'm still with them. I laugh and it feels forced.

I don't start with Creature and Tito. I tell them about what the doctors at the clinic had told me so long ago about my bipolar diagnosis. I tell them how I dumped the pills down the toilet and about my stay with Creature and Rabbit. How, the mood swings were only kept in their place through self-medication. I tell Xavier about the money I owed to the biggest drug dealer around and how Rabbit and I ran off together, hiding from the men who wanted us dead. I apologize to Casey for lying to her about so many things. I apologize to Xavier for putting everyone in danger. I tell them I want to see my therapist again and I ask Xavier to take me to the clinic immediately so I can get back on my meds.

Xavier catches my eye in the rearview as he makes a turn that will take us to the ER instead of the clinic. "We'll go there next," he verifies. "Seriously, Alana, you were *shot*. Why didn't you take an ambulance? We could have met you there."

I grin. "You're cheaper."

"We love you, Alana," Skylar states, turning back to face me. "Let's get you straight again."

"How about no?" Casey lifts an eyebrow and kisses me.

Skylar and Xavier laugh, and in that moment I know I will be okay.

Not perfect.

I will never be cured.

I know I will still struggle, fighting dark souls that wail at me to take in sweet substances that tear apart my entire being. I know I will have to continue to keep my soul from drifting away from my physical body at times. I can feel it in my chest that I will still see the evil thing in the mirror that begs me to split my skin open. But I can fight this though.

I will be okay.

I will survive.

And I will continue to do just that.

Probably.

END

ABOUT THE AUTHOR

Nikki Haase is the author of Broken Melody and the Experiment X series. Born in Honolulu, she currently resides in Pennsylvania with her super supportive boyfriend, Mike, and their tiny hyper-active dog, Kira. Nikki has an Associates Degree in English Literature from Bucks County Community College and is earning her Bachelor's in Creative Writing at Southern New Hampshire University. In her spare time she enjoys reading, writing, playing with aforementioned hyper-active dog, and dyeing her hair bright colors.

You can see more of her work on:
www.nikkihaasewriter.com
Follow her on Instagram: @nikkihaaseauthor
Follow her on Facebook: @NikkiHaaseAuthorPage
And, don't forget to leave a review!

ACKNOWLEDGMENTS

First acknowledgement goes to the patience of my readers. I appreciate each and every one of you!

I'd like to thank Dani for going through Broken Melody to help me pick out a few things and slowly bring it to life.

Thank you, Mike, my boyfriend, for being supportive and understanding when I get 'lost' in the story.

Huge thanks to my family for also being super supportive! (Love you guys!)

Last, but not least, thank you Nikki Rae from Metamorphosis Editing Services for polishing this story so that it could shine.

IF YOU OR SOMEONE YOU KNOW IS STRUGGLING, PLEASE REACH OUT AND GET HELP

Phone Lines:

    National Suicide Hotline: 1-800-273-8255

    Crisis Text Line: Text 'HOME' to 741741

    Narcon: 1-888-520-5711

    National Drug Helpline: 1-844-289-0879

    SAMHSA: 1-800-662-4357

Online Counseling (check with your insurance provider for coverage):

    www.betterhelp.com

    www.talkspace.com

    www.7cupsoftea.com (Free options available)